# AN UNFAITHFUL HUSBAND, AN AGGRIEVED WIFE, AND A CUNNING PLAN FOR REVENGE THAT'S TOO CLEVER BY HALF. WHAT COULD POSSIBLY GO WRONG?

Becky Miller is stunned to discover that her husband, Walter, is having an affair with a scatterbrained cocktail waitress. In retaliation, she devises a clever plan that will place her philandering husband squarely in the sights of both the police and the IRS before she divorces him and leaves him to the tender mercies of his dopey girlfriend. But as she sets her scheme into motion, things go tragically wrong and Becky winds up a victim of her own carefully-orchestrated plan. Shortly thereafter, a female torso floats to the surface of a Phoenix canal and the case is assigned to homicide detective Sean Richardson and his partner, Maggie McClinton. DNA tests confirm that the victim is Becky Miller. But what seems at first to be a fairly straight-forward investigation turns out to be much more complicated, and as their case becomes increasingly convoluted, Sean and Maggie must sort through the havoc that Becky Miller has left in her wake and somehow find the solution to an especially gruesome crime before anyone else pays the ultimate price for a scheme that's gotten way out of hand.

FATAL BLOW is a meticulous and engrossing procedural – from the perspective of both the dogged detective and the surprising, enterprising criminal."—*Lou Berney, Edgar Award winning author of The Long and Faraway Gone*

"Beautifully written and tautly plotted–one of the best procedurals I've read in years." — *Christine Carbo, Award-winning author of The Wild Inside*

i

# FATAL BLOW

## James L. Thane

**Moonshine Cove Publishing, LLC**
Abbeville, South Carolina U.S.A.

Copyright © 2018 by James L. Thane

ISBN: 978-1-945181-46-7
Library of Congress PCN: 2017959523

Cover design by Moonshine Cove Staff; cover photographs supplied by the author.

# About the Author

James L. Thane was born and raised in western Montana. He holds B.A. and M.A. degrees from the University of Montana and a Ph.D. in History from the University of Iowa. His  principal area of specialization was the history of the American West. He has worked as a janitor, a dry cleaner, an auto parts salesman, a sawyer, an ambulance driver, and a college professor.

Always an avid reader, Thane was introduced to the world of crime fiction at a tender age by his father and mother who were fans of Erle Stanley Gardner and Agatha Christie, respectively. He began his own writing career by contributing articles on intramural basketball games to his high school newspaper.

While working as an historian, Thane wrote one non-fiction book and a number of magazine and journal articles. He also wrote and produced two television series for PBS affiliate, WQPT. His first two novels, *No Place to Die* and *Until Death*, are both set in Phoenix and feature homicide detective Sean Richardson.

In his off-duty hours, Jim enjoys reading, music, and movies. He also likes hiking, golf, and tennis, though he is, sadly, much better at hiking than he is at golf and tennis. He divides his time between Scottsdale, Arizona and Lakeside, Montana. He is active on Goodreads.

You may also find him on Facebook and at:

www.jameslthane.com.

This book is dedicated to the memory of my sister,

Sally Thane Christensen

# Acknowledgments

As is always the case, I'm grateful to a number of people who have helped along the way. Retired Phoenix homicide detective Tim Moore, who is himself a very good writer, generously toured me through every nook and cranny of the Phoenix P.D. headquarters building and graciously answered all of my questions, even the stupid ones. Bob Barrett of the Central Arizona Project provided valuable information about how the CAP canal actually works and explained what would most likely happen if someone were inconsiderate enough to dump a body into it. He was also polite enough to believe me when I assured him that I was asking only for literary reasons. Any mistakes I might have made or liberties I might have taken with the information they provided certainly rest with me and not with them.

At Moonshine Cove, thanks to Gene Robinson who was willing to go to bat for this book.

Like every other writer, I'm enormously grateful to the booksellers who have supported my earlier novels. In particular, I'd like to single out Patrick Millikin of the Poisoned Pen Bookstore in Scottsdale, Arizona—a great bookseller and a very good friend to me and to scores of other crime fiction authors.

I'm indebted to the members of the Hardboiled Discussion Group at the Poisoned Pen and those of the Crime Fiction Book Club at the Changing Hands Bookstore in Tempe for their friendship, for the always interesting discussions, and for steering me toward so many great books that I would never have found on my own, even if the Changing Hands group did once make me read a book about sausage dogs.

I'd also like to thank those readers who have posted reviews of my earlier books to sites like Amazon, Goodreads and others.

On-line reviews, even if they only amount to a couple of sentences or so, are becoming increasingly important to a book's chances of success, and I'm grateful to those who took the time to do so.

My wife, Victoria, continues to keep me grounded and somehow still turns every day into an exciting new adventure. My cat, Zane Grey, remains of minimal assistance, but the people on Facebook seem to like him quite a lot.

Finally, I'm indebted to the many bartenders who have sustained me through this difficult endeavor, most especially Dan, Ioana, Kara, Matt, Ricki, Eddie, Rochelle, Jillian, Margaret, Mari, Vinnie, Scott, Cathy, Sara, Leanne, Todd, Christina, Jen, Kim, Kimberly and Paul. Here's to you all.

Other Works by James L. Thane

The Sean Richardson Trilogy

*No Place to Die*

*Until Death*

*Fatal Blow*

# FATAL
# BLOW

*James L. Thane*

1

Becky Miller assumed she was in no way responsible for the fact that her husband had chosen to nuke their marriage vows by jumping into the sack with a cocktail waitress who was dumber than a box of rocks.

It was true, of course, that Becky had cut him off almost completely from the marital privileges he assumed to be rightfully his. But as she saw it, Walter had no one but himself to blame for that either. Through the fifteen years they'd been together, Becky worked hard and sacrificed a great deal to maintain the body that had driven her husband to distraction in the early days of their courtship and marriage. Walter, on the other hand, rarely ever met a drink, a dessert, or an appetizer that didn't seem to have his name on it.

Like clockwork, twice a year, on January second and on July twenty-fourth (his birthday being the twenty-third), Walter vowed to start a new diet and get back to the gym. And like clockwork, twice a year, by January ninth and July thirtieth, his new regimen lay in tatters.

It was as though he'd exhausted his lifetime's allotment of self-discipline, fighting to stay in shape so that he could play point guard for Arizona State. Walter had started for the Sun Devils in his junior and senior years and Becky still remembered the rush she felt the first time she ever saw him naked. She was twenty-two that night; Walter was twenty-three. He had the body of a god, she'd thought. But fifteen years and eighty-five pounds later, Walter could have served as the stunt double for the Pillsbury Dough Boy, and Becky could barely stand to look at him naked, let alone think about making love with him.

When Walter whined because they never had sex any more, Becky was brutally frank about the matter. She promised that she'd start having sex with him again when he made a genuine and sustained effort to get back into shape, and that she'd do so enthusiastically once he actually got there. But until then she told him not even to think about it.

Becky's ultimatum did not stop her husband from complaining about the situation or from occasionally begging her to relent. But neither did it inspire him to push his flabby ass away from the dinner table and back to the gym. And then one night in March, it occurred to Becky that Walter had finally stopped bitching about the subject altogether.

She assumed that he'd probably gotten tired of being repeatedly rejected. Or perhaps his deteriorating physical condition finally left him with no libido to worry about. Whatever the case, Becky stopped thinking about the issue until a Thursday night late in April, when she walked into Walter's study and noticed that he'd gone down to the kitchen without logging out of his e-mail account.

2

In the middle of summer, the northern Sonoran Desert is no place for the faint of heart. It's bad enough that, even without any human assistance, the mid-day temperatures often rise to well over a hundred degrees for days on end. But turn loose into that fragile environment the developers, politicians, and climate-change deniers who determined that it would be a brilliant idea to pave over a significant portion of the desert, and what you get is the huge urban heat island that is metropolitan Phoenix, where the summer temperatures simply fly off the chart.

At times like this, Phoenicians are fond of reminding each other that at least we don't have to shovel the heat, but the thought did nothing to improve my mood as I sat sweltering in my office in the Homicide Unit on a Monday, with the temperature outside already at 109 degrees. It was still short of one o'clock in the afternoon. Even worse, it was still only early June. God only knows what the rest of the afternoon might bring, let alone the rest of the friggin' summer.

I was trying to imagine why anyone with an ounce of brains would choose to live in a climate like this when the sergeant stuck his head around the open door. Wasting no time on pleasantries, he said, "Two kids just reported a floater in the CAP canal off of Bell and 62$^{nd}$. Patrol confirms the report and says it's a female torso with no head or arms. It belongs to you and McClinton."

I hauled myself out of the chair, took a quick look at the report, and stepped across the narrow hallway to my partner's office where I found her on her cell phone. She looked up to see me and said into the phone, "Sean's here, Mom. I gotta go." She listened for another moment, then said, "I will. Love you too."

She dropped the phone into her purse, turned back in my direction and I said, "We're rolling."

\*\*\*

The scene was located behind the campus of a large church complex that was located just south of the CAP canal in northeastern Phoenix. We got there a little after one o'clock and I braked to a stop in the parking lot behind the church, ten yards short of the chain link fence that separated the parking lot from the canal.

Several squads and an ambulance had preceded us, and the patrolmen were attempting to contain the neighbors who were beginning to assemble and who were straining to get a view of the activity. A couple of television news vans had also beaten us to the scene, and the patrolmen were holding them back as well. A news helicopter circled overhead, doubtless broadcasting the circus live to the greater metro area, just in time for lunch.

A few hardy weeds had grown up along the bottom of the fence, and a fair amount of litter had blown up against it. Beyond the fence, the desert was graded to a flat tan surface, devoid of any vegetation, stretching perhaps fifteen yards to rim of the canal itself. The channel was about eighty feet wide at this point, running from west to east behind the church and the homes that were built along the south side of the waterway. Beyond the fence that protected the far side of the canal, the land sloped up, creating a natural barrier dotted with desert scrub plants for as far as the eye could see in either direction. To the east, the McDowell Mountains rose into an azure sky, and in the center of the emerald-green water, the body, or what was left of it, floated lazily in a slow circle as it drifted down the canal.

As Maggie and I got out of the car, a Crime Scene Response Team van pulled to a stop beside us, followed by a pair of department divers. While the techs and the divers prepared for their respective tasks, Maggie and I walked over to one of the squads where a young female patrol officer was trying, without much success, to comfort a woman and two small children.

I guessed the woman to be somewhere in her late twenties. Wearing dark green shorts and an Arizona Cardinals tee shirt, she was a tad overweight with stringy blonde hair and a very light complexion that had no business whatsoever being exposed to the blazing mid-day sun. The two children clinging to the woman and crying were also dressed in shorts and tee shirts. The boy looked to be about six; his sister was perhaps a year or so younger. They too had very pale skin, and I wondered if the family had recently moved to Phoenix from someplace like Illinois or Minnesota where they didn't get three hundred and twenty-five days of sunshine every year.

The children stopped crying for a moment and watched apprehensively as Maggie and I approached. I acknowledged the patrolman, who introduced the woman as Janelle Grisham. I turned to her and said, "Ms. Grisham, I'm Detective Sean Richardson of the Phoenix PD. This is my partner, Detective Maggie McClinton."

Grisham nodded and forced a slight smile. Gripping each child by a shoulder, she said, "These are my children, Erin and Jason."

Maggie and I scrunched down to the level of the children and she said, "Erin and Jason. Those are very nice names. I'm Maggie and this is Sean."

The little girl buried her face in her mother's leg while her brother tentatively put out his hand. I shook it gently and said, "It's nice to meet you, Jason."

"It's nice to meet you too, sir," he answered, and then offered his hand to Maggie. They shook hands, then Maggie and I rose back to our feet and Maggie said, "Can you tell us what happened here, Ms. Grisham?"

The woman shook her head. "Only what I told them when I called. The kids were out playing before lunch. They came running back into the house and said that there was a dead person floating in the canal. I walked back up here with them, thinking that they were kidding or probably mistaken. When I saw that they weren't, I lost my breakfast. We ran back home and I called 911. Then we came back down here and waited for the police to come."

The woman had nothing more to offer and so we sent her and her children back home. Meanwhile, a CAP employee appeared with the key to a gate just upstream from where the body was floating. Now dressed in their wetsuits, the two divers followed him through the gate and used a rope to lower themselves down into the water. They swam out to the center of the canal and tied another rope around the torso, then they gently towed the body to the edge of the canal. Maggie and I stepped through the gate, walked a hundred yards downstream and waited for them.

While we waited, we were joined by the county medical examiner, Matt Kramer. Kramer was in his middle forties and as fastidious in his dress as he was in the conduct of his office. In spite of the early afternoon heat, he was wearing a well-tailored light tan suit over gleaming cordovan shoes, a blue dress shirt, and a tie with a muted check pattern. We were the only two men at the scene and probably the only two within a twenty-block radius who were wearing suits and ties, and standing there in the mid-day sun, I wondered if that was more a commentary on declining social standards or on our own lack of common sense.

The divers reached the edge of the canal, lifted the torso out of the water, and passed it into the hands of the ambulance attendants who laid it gently on a plastic sheet. The woman's head and arms had been crudely severed from her body, and the torso was badly scraped and bruised. Some of the damage might have been inflicted before the torso went into the water, but I assumed that much of it had occurred as the body rolled and tumbled along the bottom and sides of the concrete canal. Given the condition of the body, it was impossible to make a very specific guess about the victim's age, but the length of her legs and torso suggested that she had been a bit taller than average. A silver ring on the second toe of her left foot glinted in the bright sun.

Matt officially pronounced the woman dead, not that there was that much doubt, and the ambulance attendants then zippered the remains into a body bag and carried it back up to their vehicle for the trip to the morgue. I looked to Matt and said, "How long before you can give us a time of death and a probable cause?"

He shook his head. "I don't know, Sean. I'll get her on the table later this afternoon and by this time tomorrow I can probably give you some preliminary answers. Once she went into the water, it would have taken at least a couple of days for enough gasses to collect in the abdomen and in the body tissues to bring her to the surface again. So I think you can safely say that she's been dead for at least that long.

"As for the cause of death, I think we can be fairly sure that she didn't accidentally tumble into the canal and drown. But with only a portion of the body to work with, I may have some trouble determining how she did die. It'd sure as hell help if you could find the missing pieces."

I looked back up the length of the canal and nodded my understanding. "We'll get teams out right away working back up both sides of the canal and dragging the water. It's hard to imagine that anyone was able to get the body over this fence, so we need to figure out where they got her through it. Once we find the spot, maybe somebody from the CAP can estimate how long it would have taken a body to move from the entry point down to here."

Kramer raised his eyes to the top of the fence which was about six feet high and topped by three taut strands of serious barbed wire. "That sounds logical enough." He sighed. "Let me know if and when you find anything. In the meantime, I guess we'd all better get to work."

***

I called the sergeant, who promised to coordinate with CAP officials in organizing the effort to drag the canal and search the area above the point where the torso was found. We were hoping, of course, to discover the missing pieces of the victim as well as the spot where she'd been put into the canal. The only problem was that the canal originated in Lake Havasu City, some three hundred miles north and west of the point where the body was recovered.

The canal, which the Central Arizona Project had completed in 1993, was built for the purpose of diverting water from the Colorado River to the thirsty citizens of the Phoenix metro area, to surrounding farmers, and to a number of Indian communities. I assumed that the torso could not have passed through any of the pumping plants along the route of the canal, which meant that it must have been put into the water no more than thirty or thirty-five miles from the spot where I was now standing. Still, even that would be an awful lot of ground to cover.

Maggie listened quietly to my end of my conversation with the sergeant. Once I disconnected, she shook her head. "Jesus, that's a job I wouldn't want to have on a day as hot as this, walking back up this damned concrete ditch looking for the rest of that poor woman."

Nodding, I said, "Yeah, well, I know that we've got to go through the motions of searching, but I doubt very much that anybody's ever going to find the missing pieces. If the killer was just going to leave them around for us to discover that easily, why would he have bothered to cut them off in the first place?"

"Yeah, shit, you're probably right. I'll bet that by now they're buried deep out in the desert or some other friggin' place where nobody'll ever find them."

*** 

While the divers and the Crime Scene Response Team waited for reinforcements to arrive so that they could begin the search of the canal, Maggie and I drove back downtown to the Police Headquarters building on West Washington Street. We climbed the stairs to the Homicide Unit where Maggie dropped her purse on her desk and draped the blazer she'd been wearing over the back of her chair. Then we walked on down to the sergeant's office.

The Sergeant, Russ Martin, had been leading the Homicide Unit for nearly seven years. Thin and fit in his late fifties, he was as good a boss as we could have asked for. He gave his detectives the freedom and support that was necessary to get the job done, and, when necessary, tried his best to protect us from the fulminations of the department brass above. He looked up from the report he was reading and waved us into chairs in front of his desk. Gesturing in my direction with his reading glasses he said, "So, what've we got?"

He listened as Maggie and I described the scene in greater detail than I'd given him on the phone. Then he leaned forward in his chair and said, "Okay, while the search teams are looking for the rest of the victim, you two start with the missing persons reports. If you don't find her there, we'll have to hope that the media coverage will prompt someone to call us with the name of a woman who hasn't come home or who's failed to show up for work without explanation over the last few days. Then, once we've got an ID, we can begin trying to figure out how in the hell she died and who dumped her into the canal."

***

Back in my office, Maggie and I began digging through MISPERS reports, looking for a woman who might match the torso the Grisham children had discovered. We were searching for a Caucasian woman, probably in her late twenties to mid-forties, with no visible tattoos. Our main hope of an early identification was the toe ring that the victim was wearing.

During the previous week, three white women in the age range we'd targeted were reported missing, but none of the reports indicated that the women listed wore a toe ring. One of the three reports noted that the missing woman had a large butterfly tattoo at the small of her back, and thus we eliminated her from consideration.

While Maggie sat by my desk, I called the father who reported one of the other two women missing. His twenty-three-year-old daughter disappeared a week and a half earlier, but he never knew her to wear a toe ring. I waited while he conferred with his wife. He then returned to the phone and told me that his wife concurred; their daughter had little interest in jewelry and didn't have a ring on any of her toes.

I thanked the man for his help and assured him that someone in the department would contact him the instant we might have any news about his daughter. Then I disconnected and called the husband of the other possibility, a Mr. Walter Miller. At eight minutes after three the previous Thursday morning, Miller called to report that his wife, Becky, failed to return home from a meeting of her book club.

The report further indicated that on Saturday morning, Becky Miller's Audi was found in the parking lot of a Basha's supermarket on North Scottsdale Road. The store manager called the police because the car had been sitting in the same the parking space for three days.

Unfortunately, the parking lot was not under video surveillance and thus detectives were unable to determine exactly how long the car had been in the lot or who might have left it there. Even more unfortunately, someone had wiped down the steering wheel and the area around the driver's seat of the Audi, eliminating any fingerprints that the forensics team might otherwise have been able to develop from those surfaces.

According to the report, Ms. Miller was thirty-eight years old, and at five feet, seven inches tall, and a hundred and twenty-eight pounds, she'd be a very close match in height and weight to the torso we'd pulled from the canal.

Miller's husband apparently owned several sports bars scattered around the metro area, and on my second phone call, I found him in his office in the northeast corner of the city, not far from the spot where our victim had been discovered. I identified myself and he said in an anxious voice, "Do you have some news about Becky?"

"I'm not sure, Mr. Miller. But I do have the report you filed, and I was following up. There's a section of the report that asks for a description of any jewelry that Mrs. Miller might have had on the night you reported her missing. It indicates that she was wearing a diamond wedding set on her left hand. Do you know what other jewelry, if any, she might have been wearing that night?"

"Well, certainly she would have been wearing *some* other pieces," Miller replied. "The problem is that my wife has a fairly large collection of jewelry and I don't know what else she might have had on. She always wears her wedding and engagement rings of course, but other than that, she could have had on a variety of things. I would assume that she was wearing at least one or two bracelets and probably a necklace as well."

I asked if his wife often wore rings in addition to the wedding set.

"Oh yes; she has a number of other rings."

"Does she ever wear a toe ring?"

The anxious tone suddenly returned to Miller's voice. "Yes, she does sometimes wear a toe ring. Why do you ask?"

Deflecting his question, I said, "Can you describe the ring, Mr. Miller, and can you tell me where she wears it?"

He hesitated for a moment, then said, "It's a simple silver band. She always wears it on the second toe of her left foot."

I closed my eyes and hesitated for a couple of seconds. Then I said, "Okay, Mr. Miller. I've added all of that to the report. Are you going to be in your office for a while? I'd like to come out and talk to you in person and get some additional information."

"What's happened?" he demanded apprehensively. "What do you have to tell me that you can't tell me over the phone?"

"To be completely candid, Mr. Miller, I'm not sure that I have anything at all to tell you. But my partner and I would like to follow up on your report. If it's convenient, we can be there in about thirty minutes."

Over the phone, I could hear Miller swallow hard. "Okay," he said. "I'll be waiting."

3

Walter Miller's office was about twenty-five miles north and east of the Headquarters building. I opted to drive and pointed my department-issued Chevy in the direction of the Piestewa Freeway, which would take us most of the distance. I accelerated up the ramp, merged into traffic, and settled into the HOV lane where traffic was moving along at a brisk seventy-five miles per hour, in spite of the fact that the afternoon rush hour was now approaching critical mass.

The posted limit was sixty-five, but most Phoenicians assumed that this was simply an advisory and it was not at all uncommon to be driving ten miles over the limit only to find yourself being passed by drivers going fifteen miles an hour faster than that. Every once in a great while, the Highway Patrol actually stopped someone and wrote them a ticket, but this seemed to make little or no impression on most other drivers who simply continued on their merry way.

We were just passing the exit for Bell Road when Maggie's cell phone began buzzing. She dug it out of her purse and connected to the call. A moment later, she turned away from me. In a soft voice, she said into the phone, "I'm fine. And you?"

She listened for a minute or so, offering the occasional "uhuh," and then said, "I'm sorry, but I don't think that'll work for me. My partner and I are on our way to a crime scene right now and I'll probably be tied up well into the evening."

Again she paused to listen, then said, "That might work but I can't say for sure yet. Can I call you tomorrow? ... Okay, I've really got to go now, but I'll call you then and let you know. ... Yeah, bye."

She returned the phone to her purse and sat, starring out the window to her right. I gave her a second, then said, "Our case isn't interfering with your social plans, is it?"

"Maybe a little, which is a good thing. Otherwise, I'd have had to invent something."

"Patrick's trying to speed things up again and you're still trying to keep them slowed down?"

"No, that wasn't Patrick."

"Oh."

She waited a bit, then shook her head and said, "Shit."

"Shit, what?"

"My friend Vicky and I went to hear this band at the Rhythm Room on Friday night. During one of the breaks I got to talking with the bass player, whose name is Lester. He bought me a drink after the last set, and I wound up giving him my number.... Stupid!"

"I take it that you're having second thoughts?"

"Yeah. He's a very sexy guy and he plays a mean bass. And after a couple of drinks, giving him my number seemed like an excellent idea. But now, cold sober, it just seems retarded. I need to get clear of Patrick and then take a long vacation from men before I start thinking about somebody new."

"Where are things with Patrick?"

"On the slow road to nowhere.... Jesus, Sean, I told you it could never work. His being a minister was never going to allow us to take our time and have any sort of relationship that did not involve getting married sooner rather than later. And with his two little girls in the mix...."

"He's still holding out hope, even though you're taking a break from each other?"

"Yeah. I'm sure he's hoping that, after not seeing each other for a while, I'll be missing him and be anxious to get back together. But that isn't gonna happen. The truth is, I *am* missing him, and I miss the girls too. But it's also pretty clear by now that, no matter what he says, he really does resent it when the job gets in the way of the relationship. And I know from my experience with Timothy that it's only going to get worse as time goes on. No matter how I feel about him and Yolanda and Claire, it's time for me to cut my losses before breaking it off gets even more painful for all of us."

"Shit," she said again.

***

Thirty minutes after leaving the department we pulled into a strip mall where Walter Miller kept his office in the back of what was, apparently, his original sports bar. I parked in front of a UPS store next door, and we walked into the bar to discover that Happy Hour was well under way. About thirty customers sat at the bar and in the booths that lined the walls of the place. A few people were shooting pool, and around the bar, television sets were tuned to various baseball games and other sporting events, as well as another in the never-ending editions of Sports Center.

I flagged down the bartender, an attractive young brunette, and told her that Miller was expecting us. She directed us down a hall toward the back of the bar, and we found Miller at a desk in his office, staring at something on his computer screen. Like the bar area in front, the small office was decorated in a sports motif. A variety of team pennants and posters hung from the walls, and on a credenza to the left of the desk a flat-panel television set was tuned to a baseball game with the sound muted.

Miller appeared to be in his late thirties and, although it was hard to judge his height since he was sitting down, he looked like he might run an inch or two taller than my six-one. I guessed that he was a good hundred pounds heavier than my one seventy, and he looked to be carrying most of the weight in his face and around his middle. His thinning dark hair was combed straight back from a high forehead, and he was dressed casually in a pair of khaki pants and a lime-green golf shirt. I tapped on the door and he looked up, startled. "Detective Richardson?" he asked.

"Yes, and this is Detective Maggie McClinton."

Miller invited us in and Maggie and I went through the motions of showing him our shields and IDs. He offered us a couple of chairs in front of the desk, then sat down heavily in the chair behind it, picked up a remote control, and turned off the television set. Looking at me directly, he said, "Why did you want to know about Becky's toe ring?"

24

"We'll get to that in a minute, sir. "But if you don't mind, we'd first like to run through the information you gave the officer the night that you reported Mrs. Miller missing."

Miller's expression suggested that, in fact, he did mind. But he shrugged and said, "Okay."

Looking at the file, I said, "You reported your wife missing early last Thursday morning when she failed to return home from a meeting of her book club?"

"That's right. The club meets on the first Wednesday of every month. Becky is usually home by ten thirty — never later than eleven. And if she isn't going to be home on time, she always calls me. But last Wednesday night, she didn't come home and she didn't call.

"By eleven, I was starting to get worried, I thought that maybe she'd been in an accident, or perhaps she'd had a flat tire or something like that, you know? I tried calling her cell several times, but I always wound up getting her voicemail. I left messages, asking her to call me, but she didn't.

"By midnight, I was a nervous wreck. I called a couple of the other women in the book club. They told me that the meeting had ended at the usual time and that Becky said she was heading straight home. I called a couple of her other friends, but they hadn't heard from her, and when Becky still wasn't home by three in the morning, I called the police to report her missing. I've been going out of my freaking mind for the last five days, especially after her car was found like that."

Nodding, I said, "And I take it, of course, that you've remained in touch with Mrs. Miller's friends and that they've still heard nothing from her."

"Yes, I have, and no, they haven't. They're all worried sick too. We all know that Becky would've never just taken off on her own without saying anything to anyone. Obviously, something very bad must've happened to her."

"When was the last time you saw your wife, Mr. Miller?" Maggie asked.

"At dinner, Wednesday night. We ate at home around six thirty. Becky left about seven thirty to go to her meeting and I came back here to do some paperwork. I went home around ten and turned on the news, expecting her to walk through the door at any minute. But, she didn't."

Miller's voice broke and he looked away briefly. Then he looked back to a framed photo on the corner of the desk. "Is this Mrs. Miller?" I asked.

He merely nodded and picked up the photo. He looked at it for a long moment, tears pooling in his eyes, and then handed the picture to me. It was a head and shoulders studio portrait of an extremely attractive blonde with large dark eyes, prominent cheekbones, and long wavy hair. "How long ago was the picture taken?" I asked softly.

Miller sniffled. "Two years."

"And this is still the way she looks?" Maggie asked. "She hasn't changed the color or the length of her hair, for example, or started wearing glasses?"

"No," Miller answered. "Or yes, I mean. This is still the way she looks. She hasn't changed anything."

"How long have you been married?"

His voice broke again. "Fourteen years next week."

"Mr. Miller," I said, "We're sorry to have to ask these kinds of questions, but were there any problems in your marriage? Is there any reason why Mrs. Miller might have decided to leave of her own volition and without saying anything to anyone?"

He shook his head. "No. Absolutely not, Detective. Like any other couple, we have the occasional argument, but we've never had a fight of any consequence. And even if we had, Becky's not the sort of woman who'd simply up and take off without explaining why, leaving everyone who cares about her worried sick."

We let him collect himself for a moment and then Maggie asked, "What other family does your wife have, sir?"

Again, he shook his head. "None. She was an only child, and her parents are both gone now. Becky and I were not able to have children of our own. We talked about adopting, but we never got beyond the point of thinking about it. She has an aunt and an uncle somewhere in the Midwest, but she hasn't seen or heard from either one of them in years, except for the occasional Christmas card. As a practical matter, I'm the only family she has."

I glanced back to the report in my lap. "Just to double check, Mr. Miller, the missing person's report indicates that your wife has no tattoos, scars, or birthmarks of any kind?"

Miller brought his hands together on the desk in front of him and simply shook his head, as if trying to ward off the bad news that he was certain he was about to hear.

I waited a moment, then said as gently as I could, "Okay, Mr. Miller. I'm very sorry to have to tell you this, and I don't want to alarm you unnecessarily, but the reason Detective McClinton and I are here is because a body was found this afternoon. Or, more accurately, a portion of a body was found."

Miller's eyes widened and a look of sheer terror flashed across his face. "You're telling me that it's Becky?"

I shook my head. "We don't know that, sir. It's only a possibility, and we don't know how strong the possibility is. There is no easy way to say this, but the body we found is missing its head and arms. The victim is a white female who might be anywhere in age from her late teens to her early fifties. She did not have any tattoos or other distinguishing marks, but she was wearing a silver ring on the second toe of her left foot."

Miller turned away, dropped his head into his hands and began sobbing. "Oh, Jesus," he cried. "Oh, sweet Jesus. It can't be her."

After a minute or so, he dug a handkerchief out of his pocket and wiped his eyes. In a soft voice, Maggie said, "We very much hope that it isn't your wife, Mr. Miller, and at this point it's only a possibility. The victim we found may be someone else."

Miller blew his nose and turned to Maggie. "When can I see her?"

"You can't, sir," she replied gently. "And there's no need. What we'd like to do at this point is accompany you to your home and collect Mrs. Miller's toothbrush and hairbrush. Our lab will use them to run a DNA test which we can then compare to the DNA of our victim. That will tell us whether it's your wife or not. We'd also like you to give us a list of your wife's friends so that we can talk to some of them."

Miller slowly nodded, looking as though somebody had just sucker punched him hard in the gut. After a long minute, he braced his hands on the desk, pushed himself to his feet, and said, "Follow me."

***

Out in the parking lot, Miller shoehorned himself into a Lexus sedan and we followed him a couple of miles south down Scottsdale Road. From there he turned west, led us into an upscale neighborhood, and parked in the driveway of a tan stucco house. The house itself was large and tastefully decorated. A wall of glass at the back of the home opened out into a fenced-in back yard with a pool, spa, and an outdoor kitchen. Miller led us upstairs and through the master bedroom into a large bathroom. "This is Becky's bathroom and closet," he said, pointing to the walk-in closet off the bathroom. "Mine are down the hall."

On the vanity next to the sink was a toothbrush holder with a single red toothbrush sticking out of it. I dropped the toothbrush into an evidence bag, then sealed and dated the bag. A hairbrush was lying on the vanity, and in the hairbrush, I could see several strands of long, blonde hair. Miller watched as I carefully sealed the hairbrush in a second evidence bag. Looking at the bag, rather than at me, he said, "How soon will you know?"

"Not for several days. I'm very sorry, sir. I know that the wait will be extremely difficult for you, but unfortunately, there's no way to accelerate the process. The lab will begin the tests immediately, of course, but it takes several days for them to be completed."

Miller nodded. "You'll let me know immediately, either way?"

"Absolutely, sir."

We waited while Miller put together a list of his wife's friends along with their addresses and phone numbers. He handed me the list and walked us back down to the front door where Maggie and I once again expressed our sorrow for his situation. Then we headed back to the station so that the crime lab techs could begin the grim process of determining if our victim was, in fact, Miller's wife.

4

Over the next couple of hours, Maggie and I outlined a general plan of attacking the case. As necessary, we would draw on help from the other members of our squad, but as a practical matter, the investigation would be our responsibility. We were not yet sure, of course, that our victim *was* the Miller woman, but the circumstantial evidence pointed heavily in that direction and so we'd operate on the basis of that assumption unless and until it proved to be wrong.

I finally gave it up and left the office a little after nine. Lunch and dinner had both been preempted by the onset of the investigation and my stomach was beginning to protest. At this time of night, I wasn't about to go home and cook dinner for myself, so I slipped my car into gear and headed north to Tutti Santi.

The restaurant was doing a brisk business for nine-thirty on a Thursday night, especially in the middle of summer when the snowbirds had fled the Valley along with everybody else who had any common sense and the means to get away. I took my usual seat at the bar and Stephanie dropped a cocktail napkin in front of me. Without even having to ask, she pulled a bottle of Jameson from the shelf, poured a generous serving neat into a rocks glass and set it on the napkin, along with a water back.

I asked about her evening, which she said had been fine so far. She asked about my day, and I assured her that she really didn't want to know. "You're on a new case?"

"Yeah, and it's pretty ugly."

"You're right, then. I *don't* want to hear it. But if you really wanna talk about ugly," she said, gesturing at the television set above the bar, "just look at what the D-Backs are doing tonight."

We spent a couple of minutes talking about the Diamondbacks' lack of pitching and the miserable season that was resulting, then I ordered some Fettuccini Carbonara and settled in with my whiskey. Departmental regulations prohibited drinking while driving a city vehicle or while on call, but I was going to need a good night's sleep and thus figured that this particular regulation, like any number of others, was better observed in the breach.

Stephanie moved down the bar to pour a drink for a guy I didn't recognize and who was trying to make a big impression by dropping a hundred-dollar bill on the bar to pay for a three-dollar beer. Thirty pounds overweight and somewhere in his late forties, he was dressed and groomed in a pitiful and totally unsuccessful effort to look like he was still in his early thirties. Across the bar and keeping her distance, Stephanie was thirty-two, tall with glossy dark hair that fell to the middle of her back and a body that would kickstart the heart and most other vital organs of any normal, heterosexual male. I knew it wasn't going to end well, but you couldn't blame the guy for trying.

An hour later, The Dodgers had finished putting a giant can of whoop-ass on the D-Backs. I'd finished the pasta and was nursing a second glass of whiskey when the guy down the bar finally gave up the battle and beat a sullen retreat after Stephanie refused three times to give him her phone number. He sulked out the door, leaving me alone at the bar. Around me the staff was cleaning, setting up tables, and otherwise preparing to close for the night. Stephanie finished wiping down the bar and said, "Do you want a little splash?"

"No thanks, I'm good Steph. I'm ready to settle up."

She ran my credit card and I signed the slip. She collected the check folder, leaned across the bar, and said in a low voice, "Are you feeling a little randy, or would you rather just go on home tonight?"

I smiled. "Maybe more than a little randy, actually."

"Good. I'll be another twenty minutes or so, then you can follow me home."

Forty minutes later, I trailed her up the stairs to her second-floor apartment and waited while she unlocked the door. Once inside, she dropped her purse on the floor, turned and gave me a long, deep kiss. I pressed her back up against the door, moving my hands along the length of her body. Finally, I broke the kiss. Still pressing her against the door, I said, "I didn't think I was going to have a chance tonight, what with your new boyfriend there."

She laughed and shook her head. "That stupid bastard? When he finally realized that I wasn't getting wet just looking at him and that I really wasn't going to give him my number, he left me a buck and a half against a twenty-dollar tab."

"My lucky night, I guess."

"Mine too," she said, as I bent to kiss her again and slipped my hand under her shirt.

\*\*\*

It was a transitional thing for both of us. At least that's what we'd been telling ourselves for the last few weeks that we'd been sleeping together. Until four months earlier, Stephanie lived in Ohio, married to a jealous, domineering jerk with a vicious mean streak. She'd finally broken free, divorced the S.O.B. and moved to Arizona. Understandably, she was now determined to maintain her independence and live as she saw fit, without answering to anyone else, especially not to the most casual of boyfriends.

Which was more than fine with me.

I'd now been widowed for a little over a year. For eighteen months before that, my wife, Julie, was hospitalized in a persistent vegetative state, after being hit by a drunk driver. Technically brain dead, she was kept alive only by a machine that pumped water and nutrients through a feeding tube into her body.

Julie had signed a living will, stating very clearly that in circumstances such as that, she did not want her life to be prolonged by artificial means. In her medical power of attorney, she entrusted me with the responsibility of ensuring that her wishes were honored, but her mother adamantly insisted that the feeding tube should not be removed and utilized every legal trick in the book to prevent me and the doctors from honoring Julie's wishes. It was the most agonizing and heart-breaking eighteen months of my life, and the legal battle continued to rage until, mercifully, Julie contracted pneumonia and finally slipped away from me.

Her loss haunted me still. Well-meaning friends insisted that it was "time to get on with my life," and I knew that would be Julie's advice as well. But that was far easier said than done. I still had no interest in any sort of permanent relationship with another woman. And the last thing I wanted to do was to give any woman the impression that I might possibly be a candidate for such an arrangement.

I was still feeling my way along emotionally when I first met Stephanie and by that time it was well over two years since I'd had any sort of physical relationship with a woman. We circled each other warily for six weeks or so, talking across the bar and gradually getting to know each other until we finally realized that we were both basically on the same page. And then one night she asked me for the first time if I'd like to follow her home.

We now spent a night or two a week and the occasional weekend together, but neither of us had any interest in moving in together and neither of us expected it to last forever. We agreed to see each other exclusively for as long as it lasted and other than that, our only commitment was to respect and value each other and to enjoy the time we had together. And for us, for now, that was enough.

5

Becky Miller did not share a bathroom or a closet with her husband. Nor did she share his computer.

Becky's computer was on her desk in the sitting room off of the master bedroom, and she used it to send and receive e-mail, to track the family's household finances, and to download music for her iPod. Walter's computer was in his study down the hall and Becky generally steered clear of the room. The study was Walter's personal space and Becky respected his privacy, as he, in turn, respected hers.

Once a week, Lisa, the cleaning lady, ventured in and spent thirty minutes or so vacuuming and dusting the study. But Becky was not the sort of wife who prowled through her husband's papers or who surreptitiously went through his pockets or his wallet to see what he might be up to or what he might be guilty of. She assumed that, like any other normal adult, there were some things that Walter chose not to share with his spouse. But she also assumed that these were probably things of no great consequence, much on the order of the things that she elected not to share with him.

A little after nine o'clock on a Thursday night late in April, Becky was sitting at her desk paying bills when she ran out of stamps. Mentally kicking herself for not picking up more stamps, she walked down the hall to ask Walter to give her a couple. As she came out of the bedroom, she saw the top of his head disappear down the stairs in the direction of the kitchen.

Normally, she would have waited for him to come back up and then asked him for the stamps. But she was tired and in a hurry to finish up the bills so that she could crawl into bed with the new Megan Abbott novel she was anxious to start. She knew that Walter kept a roll of stamps in the top left-hand drawer of his desk, and so rather than wait for the time it would take him to put together a snack, eat it and return, she decided to simply help herself.

Becky walked around the desk, opened the drawer, and peeled three stamps off of the roll. Then she closed the drawer and in turning to leave, saw that a Yahoo! mail account was open on Walter's computer. She really wasn't spying, but she couldn't help noticing that there was an error message on the screen that warned, in bold red letters, "There was a problem:"

In plain black type, the message went on to explain that, "Either there is a syntax error in one of your address fields, or you have used a nickname which is not in your Address Book. Please enter a valid e-mail address (e.g., in the format person@yahoo.com) or use a nickname from your Yahoo! Address Book. Your message has **not** been sent."

Her curiosity naturally aroused, Becky noticed that the message was addressed to "cathystanton2." In the "Subject" line were the words, "I had such a GREAT time!!"

Looking more closely, Becky realized that her husband was attempting to send a reply to a message that "cathystanton2" sent to him. In doing so, he inadvertently deleted the remainder of her e-mail address.

From down in the kitchen, she could hear the sounds of Walter laying out the foodstuffs necessary for the creation of the roast beef sandwich that he made as a snack nearly every evening. She put down the stamps, sat down in the desk chair, and quickly read the two messages, which made perfectly clear the reason why Walter no longer hounded her about sex.

Calmly controlling her emotions, Becky gripped the computer's mouse and clicked on the "Back" button, which took her to the original message from "cathystanton2@hotmail.com." She clicked the "Back" button a second time, which returned her to the e-mail program's Inbox. There she saw a long list of messages from "cathystanton2." Each of the messages, save for the most recent, was marked with an arrow pointing left, indicating that Walter had responded to the message.

Downstairs, Walter was now putting things away, having apparently finished constructing his sandwich. Becky calculated that it would take him about three minutes to wolf down the sandwich and get back up to the study. At random, she selected one of the messages from "cathystanton2" and opened it. When the screen refreshed, she quickly forwarded the message to her own e-mail account. She did the same with three other messages, and then returned to the Inbox.

From the kitchen, she could hear Walter putting the plate he had used into the dishwasher. In the Inbox, the four messages she forwarded to herself were now all marked with right-pointing arrows. Becky checked the box next to each of the four messages and then clicked the "Delete" button. The messages disappeared from the screen and Becky exited the e-mail program to Walter's home page. Then she picked up the three stamps and hurried down the hall to the bedroom just as Walter came back up the stairs.

6

On Tuesday morning, Maggie and I divided the list of Becky Miller's friends, assuming that we could cover the ground faster if we interviewed the women separately. The first name on my half of the list was Jennifer Burke, a member of Miller's book club. As Maggie left to begin working on her own portion of the list, I grabbed the phone and dialed Burke's number.

The phone on the receiving end rang twice and was then answered by a woman with an attractive, throaty voice that sounded like it belonged to someone in her late thirties or early forties. I identified myself, explained why I was calling, and asked if it would be convenient for me to come over and see her.

In a tone that was now decidedly more somber, Burke said, "Well, Detective, like half the other divorcees in the valley, I sell real estate. I'm working at home this morning, but I do have appointments this afternoon. How soon could you come by?"

I double-checked the address, then said, "I could be there in about thirty minutes, if that's okay."

"Thirty minutes would be fine. I'll see you then."

\*\*\*

Burke's home was a second-floor condominium in a gated community that bordered the Kierland Golf Club in north Phoenix. I got there just after ten, phoned Burke from the gate, and she buzzed me through. I parked in a visitor's space across from her building. A woman I presumed to be Burke was standing in front of the building, waiting for me.

She was an attractive brunette, a trim five-three or four, with dark eyes and a very good figure. Her hair was layered and cut short, exposing her neck. Apparently already dressed for work, she was wearing a black skirt, shoes with a medium heel, and a raspberry-colored blouse. A small diamond hung from a gold necklace that dropped into the front of the blouse, but she wore no other jewelry. I couldn't be sure if her makeup was expertly applied or if she simply wasn't wearing any, but seeing her in person, I narrowed my estimate of her age to middle thirties. I introduced myself, gave her my card, and she led me through the front door and up the stairs.

The top of the stairs opened into a large living room with sliding glass doors that led out to a balcony overlooking the golf course. The place was open and airy, with a small dining room and what looked like a very efficient kitchen equipped with high-end appliances. A hall off the living room led, I assumed, to the bedrooms and bathrooms.

Burke and/or her decorator had painted and furnished the unit in warm earth tones. An oversized couch faced a fireplace flanked by custom-built bookcases that ran from floor to ceiling. The bookcases held a high-end sound system and a number of CDs; otherwise the shelves were nearly full of books, mostly in hardcover editions. At a right angle to the couch, what looked like a very comfortable leather club chair with a matching ottoman faced the sliding glass doors. A reading lamp and a couple of books sat on a table next to the chair, and there was no television set anywhere in sight. I stood at the top of the stairs for a moment, admiring the room. "Very nice, Ms. Burke."

She thanked me, her pride in her home obvious in her voice. I walked across the living room and looked out at the view. Below me, a golfer was setting up to what looked like a wedge shot of about eighty-five yards to a green protected by bunkers on the right and a small pond on the left. Burke walked over to join me and said, "Are you a golfer, Detective Richardson?"

"More or less," I replied. "I play, but I don't have time to play or to practice often enough to be any good at it. Do you play?"

"Occasionally. I'm not very adept at it either, but it's a good excuse to be outdoors on a nice day. Walking the course and carrying my clubs, I can at least have the satisfaction of getting the exercise, even if I don't score very well."

I nodded my agreement. "Yeah, that always been my rationale too."

We watched as the guy below us plugged his ball into the pond and slammed his club into the ground. Burke smiled and gave a gentle laugh. "Probably a good thing the slider is closed so we can't hear what that guy's yelling about now."

"No doubt," I said, returning her smile.

Burke turned away from the window and her smile faded. Looking up at me, she said, "Well, I know you didn't come here this morning to admire the view of the golf course, Detective."

I nodded and she gestured toward the couch. "Please sit down. I have coffee made. Would you like a cup?"

"If it's already made. Thank you."

"Cream or sugar?"

"No, thank you. Just black is fine, please."

I sat down on the couch and she returned a minute later with two mugs of steaming coffee. She handed me one, then sat in the club chair, tucked her skirt under her legs, and looked at me expectantly. I took a sip of the coffee, set the mug on the table in front of me, and said, "I understand that you're a member of Ms. Miller's book club."

"Yes. Actually, Becky and I started the group together. There are eight of us now and we manage to get five or six women to most of the meetings, which is just about the right number for a healthy discussion."

I looked in the direction of the bookcases opposite me. "What sorts of things do you read?"

Burke took a sip of her coffee and set the mug down on a coaster on the table next to her. "Our tastes are pretty eclectic. We read both fiction and non-fiction, classics and current books. We try to alternate, reading something fairly serious one month and then something a bit lighter the next. We generally try to stay away from trashy romance novels and from bubble-headed 'chick-lit' books. This month we read Anne Klauson's new book, and next month it's *The Cut* by George Pelecanos."

"Well, for what it's worth, I'd say you have excellent taste. I've read most of Pelecanos's books and liked them a lot."

"Me too," she said with a sad smile, "although Becky is actually the principal crime fiction fan in our group. She picked the Pelecanos novel."

"You said that you and Mrs. Miller started the book club together. I gather that you're close friends?"

Burke nodded. "We've known each other for about five years. Actually, Walter and my ex-husband knew each other casually and introduced us at a gallery opening one night. Becky and I hit it off immediately. After that, we would occasionally go out together as a foursome, but more often than not, Becky and I would get together for lunch or to go to a gallery or a movie or just to have a girls' night out. We discovered early on that we were both avid readers, and so we'd often talk about the books we were reading. The book club grew out of those conversations."

"Where did the book club meet last week?"

"Here. Initially we rotated the meetings among the homes of all the women who belonged, but after a while we fell into the practice of meeting only at the homes of those of us who are single. That way we didn't have to put up with the distraction of somebody's husband or boyfriend or children wandering into the middle of the discussion."

I nodded. "Mr. Miller told my partner and me that the meeting last week ended about ten thirty?"

She pushed a stray hair back into place. "A little earlier, maybe. After we finished the discussion, Becky and another woman stayed and helped me clean up. I suppose we finished up with that about ten thirty, and then Becky and Sarah left."

"What did Ms. Miller say when she left — did she tell you what her plans were at that point?"

Burke dropped her head, closed her eyes for a moment, and pinched the bridge of her nose with her right hand. When she looked up at me again, tears glistened in her eyes. In a breaking voice, she said, "She told me she was tired and that she was going straight home to bed. We had talked about doing the Scottsdale Art Walk the next night, and she promised to call me Thursday morning so that we could finalize our plans.

"I walked her down to the door and gave her a quick hug. She went over to her car and we waved at each other as she was driving away. Then a couple of hours later, Walter called to say that she hadn't come home and I haven't seen or heard from her since."

With that she began sobbing in earnest. I offered her my handkerchief and sat quietly while she worked through the tears. After a couple of minutes, she dried her eyes and blew her nose. "I'm sorry," she said in an anguished voice. "I'm just so scared for her, and I miss her so much already. I can't stand to think that the body that was found yesterday might be her."

I shook my head. "There's absolutely no need to apologize, Ms. Burke. I understand how you must feel. And while I don't want to hold out any false hope, we're not totally certain that the body we found yesterday is Ms. Miller. There's still a chance that it could be someone else."

Looking at me with pained eyes, she said, "I feel horrible wishing this tragedy on someone else. But Becky is my closest friend. Losing her would be almost too much to bear. But then I worry that, if it isn't her, could something even worse have happened to her? Could something even worse still be happening to her at this very moment? And the thought of that is unbearable as well."

"I understand, and I'm very sorry. I know how difficult this must be for the people who care about her."

Burke nodded, blinking back more tears, and I said, "Assuming for the moment that the body we found is not Ms. Miller, can you think of any reason why she might have decided to disappear of her own accord?"

Twisting the handkerchief in her hands, Burke shook her head. "No, I can't. Becky was my closest confidant, and I hers. I was probably more open than she in discussing the things that were going on in my life, but we had no secrets of any consequence. We talked about virtually everything."

"You hadn't noticed any change in her lately? She didn't appear to be unusually moody or quiet, for example?"

"A little, maybe, but not to any serious degree. When something began weighing on Becky, she'd sometimes brood on it for a while, turning it over in her own mind before discussing it with me. I knew her well enough not to push her — to let her get to whatever it was in her own time. But I didn't really have the sense that she'd been building to anything like that lately."

"How was her relationship with her husband?"

Burke picked up her coffee mug and took a small sip. Then she carefully set the mug back down on the coaster and folded her hands together in her lap. Finally, she looked up to meet my eyes and gave a small shrug. "Okay, I guess."

She paused for a moment, looking back down at her hands. "I'm probably not the best person in the world to be asking about marital relationships right at the moment, Detective. I'm only a few months past a very bitter divorce and so my views on these matters are probably a bit harsh."

"Still, you *are* Ms. Miller's best friend ..."

She looked up and gave me a sad smile. "I appreciate the fact that you're using the present tense, Detective, and yes, I *am* her best friend.... So, what can I say? Becky and Walter have been married for fourteen years, you know what I mean?"

I shrugged. "Perhaps, but why don't you spell it out for me?"

In a distinctly harder and more cynical voice, she said, "May I ask if you're married, Detective?"

I shook my head. "No, Ms. Burke, I'm not. I was married for seven years, but I was widowed a little over a year ago."

Her face colored and she brought a hand up to her mouth. "I'm sorry. I had no business asking a personal question like that."

I waved off her apology. "There's no need to be sorry."

"Yes, there is. I had no call to be flippant. Please forgive me."

"Really, it's all right."

We sat quietly for half a minute or so, then she said in a soft voice, "What I meant to suggest was that Becky's marriage to Walter had lost its spark a long time ago, at least as far as Becky was concerned. They'd built a fairly prosperous and comfortable life together, and to all external appearances, they had a successful marriage.

"But Walter's a jock. He likes beer and ball games and hanging with the boys, and he has very little interest in books, art, or other cultural pursuits. From what Becky says, when they were first together, he made a sincere effort to expand his horizons in that regard because these were things that she liked to do. In return, she tried to take a genuine interest in sports, letting him teach her the nuances of the games so that she could watch more intelligently.

"I gather that, as is often true with a lot of couples, during their early years together, they were so attracted to each other physically that they were happy to make those kinds of accommodations for each other. But inevitably, as the passion cooled so did their efforts to find common ground in these other areas. Increasingly, they went their separate ways. Walter spent more time out with the boys. Becky spent more time with her female friends, and they gradually settled into a marriage of convenience. Neither of them was especially happy, but neither of them was sufficiently unhappy to want to end the marriage."

"So essentially, the problems in her marriage were not that serious, and there was no other reason why Mrs. Miller would have decided to leave of her own accord. And if there had been, you would have known about it?"

Burke nodded. "But I hope to god I'm wrong about that, Detective Richardson, because the alternative is simply too awful to contemplate."

## 7

For three days after discovering her husband's infidelity, Becky Miller wrestled with the issue, thinking about how she should react to the knowledge and trying to determine if, when, and how she should broach the subject with Walter.

The four messages she had quickly forwarded to her own computer were all fairly recent. They offered no real clue as to how long Walter had been involved in his relationship with "cathystanton2," or about how serious the relationship might be. Was this a casual fling, or was it something more?

After stewing about the matter, Becky decided that she needed to amass more information before deciding on a course of action. Accordingly, four days after she'd first seen the e-mail messages, she pecked Walter on the cheek as he left for work. Then she went up to her computer, logged onto the Internet, and spent a couple of hours googling computer spyware programs.

After studying the features of several keyboard tracking programs, she downloaded a copy of PC NoSecrets. She billed the charge to a credit card that she used for household expenses, knowing that Walter would never see the statement.

Following the instructions on the company's website, she copied the installation program to a CD and then logged off the Internet. She walked down the hall, flipped on the lights in Walter's study and booted his computer. When the homepage appeared, she slipped the CD into the drive and installed PC NoSecrets. She created a password and a hotkey sequence that would allow her to access the program. Then she set the program to run in stealth mode.

If the company's website were to be believed — and Becky fervently hoped that it could be — the software would now record all of the activity on Walter's computer. The software would be impossible to detect and would leave no trace of the fact that it had been installed on the machine.

***

At nine o'clock the next morning, Walter left for work. Becky sat at the kitchen table for thirty minutes or so, drinking a cup of coffee and reading the *New York Times*. Then she went upstairs to Walter's study and turned on his computer. Once the machine had booted, she used the hotkey sequence she selected to launch the PC NoSecrets program. A dialog box appeared, asking for her password.

In the box, she typed "walterisabastard," and clicked "OK." The screen refreshed, bringing up the PC NoSecrets Viewer, and Becky selected the "Keystrokes" tab. Again the screen refreshed, indicating that on the previous evening, Walter had opened Microsoft Excel, and Internet Explorer. Becky selected Internet Explorer and then opened the "View Keystrokes" window. In it she saw that at eight twelve on the previous evening, Walter opened a Yahoo! e-mail account, signing in as "WJM12," and using the password, "ASUpointguard."

Knowing that she'd be more comfortable working at her own desk, Becky turned off Walter's computer, went downstairs, and poured herself a second cup of coffee. Back up in the sitting room, she turned on her computer, logged on to the Internet and went to Yahoo.com. There she clicked on the mail icon and when the screen refreshed, she typed Walter's screen name and password into the appropriate boxes.

The inbox appeared, and again Becky saw the long list of e-mails from "cathystanton2." The messages were listed in reverse order with the most recent message at the top of the list. The latest e-mail was sent the previous day, and the arrow next to the message indicated that Walter had already responded to it.

Without opening last night's exchange, Becky scrolled down through the list of messages. She guessed that there were nearly a hundred of them, dating back to the middle of November.

She clicked on the first message, which "cathystanton2" sent on November eleventh. It was a brief note in which the woman told Walter that she enjoyed meeting him and thanked him for giving her a ride home. "It was my first date with the guy," she said, "and he

45

turned out to be a real jerk. Thanks so much for coming to my rescue." The message ended with a smiley-faced emoticon and was signed, "Cathy Stanton."

Becky clicked on the second message up the list and found both her husband's reply to Stanton's original e-mail and a second message from Stanton back to him. In his reply, Walter indicated that he enjoyed meeting Stanton as well, and that she seemed like a very attractive and interesting woman. He was glad he was able to help her out of a "difficult situation."

In her message, Stanton thanked Walter again. She included her cell phone number and her address, in case he had forgotten them, and asked if she could express her gratitude more appropriately by buying him a drink sometime. Walter readily agreed to the proposition, and the two scheduled a date for the afternoon of November fifteenth.

Stanton, who claimed to be a thirty-two-year-old divorcee, was a cocktail waitress in an upscale lounge not far from one of Walter's sports bars. She apparently worked Tuesday through Saturday nights, and as November faded into December, she and Walter progressed from having drinks together a couple of times to eating lunch together twice in one week. Following the second of these luncheon dates, Stanton wrote Walter a message leaving no doubt about the fact that lunch was not the only thing on the menu that afternoon.

During the month of December, Walter and Cathy Stanton "lunched" together a couple of times a week, usually in the middle of the afternoon, before Stanton had to go to work and while Walter could claim to be out of the office attending to business at one or another of his establishments. The correspondence made it clear that Walter told Stanton that his wife was no longer having sex with him. Stanton insisted that she found that impossible to believe. How could any woman not be sexually attracted to someone as virile as he? Stanton suggested that Becky's loss was her gain, and that she couldn't be happier about it.

Stanton's messages were replete with misspelled words and grammatical errors; she could barely write an intelligible sentence, let alone an intelligent one. Becky quickly concluded that the woman was dumb as a stump and that there was a very good reason why she was still a cocktail waitress at the age of thirty-two.

But Becky also quickly concluded that although Stanton might be lacking in brainpower, she was apparently more than making up for it with other of her vital organs. Perhaps it was simply an indication of how sex-starved Walter had been, but he was clearly intoxicated with the woman. He told Stanton repeatedly that she was beautiful, and in one message insisted that she was "fantastic in every department — and I do mean in EVERY department!!!"

By early February, Stanton was pressing Walter for a stronger commitment. Reading between the lines, Becky realized that the two lovers had begun discussing the possibility that Walter might leave her for Stanton. At that point, Becky had no idea whether Walter was seriously considering the idea or if he was simply stringing Stanton along. But she suspected that there was at least a part of Walter (and she was pretty sure she knew exactly which part) that was intrigued by the prospect.

Becky also knew, though, that Walter was not a complete idiot, and that unless his raging hormones had caused his brain to go into total meltdown, he would never seriously think about leaving her. Even if he wasn't getting laid at home anymore, Walter still had any number of good reasons for staying there, and clearly, he understood this.

In response to Stanton's messages, Walter reminded her that separating from Becky would be a complicated undertaking with profound financial ramifications. He tried to soothe Stanton by assuring her that he loved her and that he wanted to spend as much time with her as he possibly could. He regretted very much that, for the foreseeable future though, they would have to be content with the relationship that they had.

Stanton, though, was clearly not content and as February progressed, she became increasingly unhappy about the situation. She suggested that Walter was stringing her along and that he only wanted her for sex. She complained about the fact that they could hardly ever see each other outside of her apartment. It hurt her, she insisted, that he could not acknowledge her publicly. Walter responded that there was nothing that would thrill him more, but his situation was what it was, and there wasn't much that he could do about it at this point.

Reading his reply, Becky nodded silently. *Not at this point, indeed. And not any time soon either, Sweetheart.*

8

On Tuesday, the day after the torso was removed from the canal, a search team discovered a hole in the chain link fence that guarded the waterway. Someone had cut the fence, creating a passageway through it, near the point where the canal intersected Happy Valley Road in north-central Phoenix, slightly less than ten miles north and west of the spot where the body was recovered. Someone — presumably the same person who cut the fence — had then used several pieces of thin silver wire to bind the fence back together again so that the damage was barely noticeable except upon very close examination.

Tracks in the gravel suggested that a single individual had dragged a large object from the hole in the fence to the concrete bank of the canal, and then, presumably, dumped the object into the water.

Matt Kramer estimated that the victim had been dead for approximately five days before her body was found and that the torso had probably been in the water for about two-thirds of that time. CAP officials said that several of the gates that rise up from the bottom of the canal to control the flow of water had been raised during this period. They speculated that the body had tumbled along the bottom of the canal and was then trapped for some length of time against one of the gates, which would account for at least some of the damage done to the torso. But Matt's examination revealed no injuries to the body, save for its dismemberment and for the bruises and scrapes that were almost certainly inflicted by the canal. And, absent the other body parts, he was unable to establish a cause of death.

The examination of the torso revealed no evidence of recent sexual activity, but given the length of time the body was in the water, as well as the fact that the victim's head was missing, the M.E. could not conclusively rule out the possibility that the woman might have been the victim of a sex crime. Regrettably, the search teams failed to find any of the missing body parts or any other physical evidence that might advance our investigation.

Through the rest of the week, while we waited for the results of the DNA tests, Maggie and I interviewed a number of Becky Miller's friends, scheduling the sessions in and around the work we were doing on our other open cases. Unfortunately, though, the women were unable to tell us anything that we didn't already know. All of them insisted that Miller appeared to be in good spirits in the weeks before her disappearance. None of them knew of any problems that she might be having, and no one could suggest a reason why she might have decided to disappear of her own volition.

Finally, on Monday morning, a week after the body was pulled from the canal, the lab confirmed that DNA samples taken from the torso matched those from the toothbrush and hairbrush that we had taken from Miller's bathroom. At that point, our victim was no longer unidentified, and Becky Miller was no longer in the department's Missing Persons file.

***

Maggie and I could now officially put a name to our victim, but we still had no way of knowing whether Miller was killed by someone that she knew or by a stranger she encountered on her way home from the meeting of her book club.

Her car appeared to be in perfect working order when found in the supermarket parking lot. It was nearly full of gas; the spare tire was in its proper place in the trunk, fully inflated and seemingly undisturbed, and there was no damage to the body of the vehicle, all of which suggested that Miller had not experienced car trouble of some sort that might have caused her to abandon the vehicle and seek help. Nor did it appear that anyone forced the Audi off the road and kidnapped Miller from it.

Neither the car keys nor the victim's purse were found in the car, and besides the fact that someone carefully wiped down the area around the driver's seat, the only interesting thing about the car was the fact that the seat was set well back from the steering wheel, suggesting that the last person to drive the vehicle was fairly tall.

Phone records indicated that the last call from Miller's cell phone was made at seven forty-four the evening that she disappeared, apparently while she was en route to Jennifer Burke's condo. She thus apparently felt no need, or perhaps did not have the chance, to call for assistance when she crossed paths with the person who murdered her. Efforts to track the phone's current location were unsuccessful.

At least for the time being then, we had no evidence to suggest that Miller had been killed by a stranger and no leads to pursue in that direction. We mapped out the most direct route leading from Burke's home to Miller's and had the lab print out eight-by-ten photos of Miller and of her Audi. At around ten thirty p.m., Maggie and I and the other members of our squad would drive the route, visiting all the businesses and other public places along the route and showing the pictures to see if someone might remember having seen Miller or her car on the night she disappeared.

We assumed that we would have to go through the process two or maybe three times before we would be able to catch most of the people who might have been working along the route that Thursday night. We also knew that our chances of finding anyone who might have seen Miller or her car were exceedingly slim, especially since we were not at all certain that the route we had mapped out was the one the victim actually took. Still, we couldn't ignore the possibility that someone might have seen something that would advance the investigation. We would also try to locate any video surveillance cameras along the route that might have recorded Miller or her car passing.

Beyond that, we would release the photos of Miller and her car to the media and make a public appeal for information relating to Miller's whereabouts the night she disappeared. We understood that this would inevitably produce scores of useless tips that we would have to pursue to no avail. But again, we couldn't ignore the possibility, however remote, that the appeal might produce some valuable information.

Otherwise, we were left to begin digging deeper into Miller's personal life in an effort to determine if someone acquainted with the victim might have had a reason to want her dead. The first and most obvious task in that regard was to determine who, if anyone, might have benefited in some way from Miller's death, and to that end, Maggie and I scheduled another interview with the victim's widowed husband.

We met him at his home at three o'clock on Monday afternoon. Miller opened the door wearing jeans and a wrinkled tee shirt. His eyes were red and raw; he hadn't shaved in at least a couple of days, and he looked like he hadn't slept in a month. He led us into the living room, and we offered our condolences.

Miller shook his head and tears pooled in his eyes. "Jesus Christ," he said softly. "This is so unbearably hard. I'd been expecting the news for the last week, but still, when you called me this morning, it was like somebody ripped my guts out."

"We understand, sir," Maggie said. "And again, we're very sorry. We also apologize for intruding on you at a time like this. But naturally, now that we've identified the victim, we're anxious to begin moving as quickly as possible to determine who might have committed this crime."

Miller wiped his eyes with the back of his hands. "I understand, Detective, and of course, that's what I want you to do." He gestured toward the couch and said, "Please sit down."

Maggie and I took the couch while Miller sank into a large upholstered chair opposite us. He looked at me expectantly, and I said, "Mr. Miller, can you think of anyone who might have had some reason to want to harm your wife?"

"No, of course not," he said, seemingly surprised. "Becky had no enemies at all. There was no one who even mildly disliked her. Obviously, the killer had to've been a stranger."

"Well, sir," I said, "certainly we are exploring that possibility. However, your wife's car was found undamaged and in good working order. There was no sign of any sort of violence in the car, and Mrs. Miller's purse was not found in the vehicle. She didn't call you or anyone else that night to say that she was having some sort of difficulty. Given all of that, it's at least possible that after leaving her meeting, Mrs. Miller met someone with whom she was acquainted, that she went willingly with that person, and that for some reason, that person killed her."

"But that's impossible. Some animal must've forced his way into the car somehow and made Becky go with him."

"Certainly, something like that may have happened," Maggie said. "And, as Detective Richardson says, we are pursuing that possibility. But we do have to look at other possibilities as well."

Miller shook his head and I said, "Did you ever drive your wife's car, sir?"

He gave me a puzzled look. "A few times, maybe, but hardly ever. Why do you ask?"

"When you and Mrs. Miller went somewhere together, did you usually take her car or yours?"

"Mine, almost always. But again, why do you ask?"

I gave a small wave of my hand as if to suggest that the issue was of no great consequence. "These are just routine questions, Mr. Miller. Naturally, our technicians are making a thorough examination of your wife's car, collecting fingerprints, fibers, and whatever other physical evidence they can find. We'd like you to come in to the department sometime during the next couple of days and let our technicians take your fingerprints and a DNA sample for purposes of elimination. That way we can focus on trying to identify the other fingerprints and forensic evidence that the techs find in the vehicle in an effort to determine who else might have been in the car in addition to Mrs. Miller."

Miller simply nodded.

"Changing the subject, sir," Maggie said, "can you tell us how Mrs. Miller generally spent her time? I gather that she was not working outside of the home?"

"No, not at the moment. She had a degree in elementary education and for the first ten years after we were married, she was a teacher. She taught fifth grade for the first three years and then the sixth grade after that. But, contrary to what so many people seem to think, it's a brutal job and it takes an enormous amount of time even under the best of circumstances. And fifth and sixth graders can be especially difficult. They're just at that age, you know. Some of them are real little shits, and it only takes a couple of them to ruin an entire class.

"After doing that for ten years, Becky was simply burned out. For some time, she'd been talking about leaving teaching and doing something else, and then her mother died and left Becky some money. Also by then, my business was doing well enough that Becky really didn't have to work anymore if she didn't want to. So she quit teaching. She took a year off completely and after that she did some volunteer work. She also got a part-time job working a couple of days a week in a bookstore. She didn't make any money at it of course, but then she didn't need to. It was just something she enjoyed doing."

"And when she wasn't volunteering or working at the bookstore?" I asked.

Miller shrugged. "Well, she spent a lot of time on the house, cleaning and decorating. She loved to read and could easily lose an afternoon in a good book. She often went shopping or to a movie or something with one of her girlfriends."

Maggie made a note and looked up at him. "Did your wife keep a diary, Mr. Miller?"

He shook his head. "No, at least not that I was ever aware of."

"Did she use a computer?" I asked.

"Yes. We each have our own computers. Hers is on her desk up in the bedroom."

*\*\**

I asked Miller if he could show us his wife's desk and computer, and he led us up the stairs and into the large master bedroom. The desk was in a small sitting room off of the bedroom, on the opposite side of the room from the bathroom and closet. A laptop computer sat on the top of the desk, along with a couple of books, a small Waterford clock, and a photo of the Millers smiling into the camera on a white sand beach that looked like it might have been somewhere in the Caribbean.

While Miller watched, Maggie and I went through the desk, but we found only stationary, routine office supplies, and a carefully organized drawer of hanging files. Most of the file folders held financial records — tax returns, household expenses and the like — and we saw nothing of any immediate interest. I closed the desk drawer, and turned to Miller. "If you don't mind, sir, we'd like to take your wife's computer with us. We'll want to have our techs examine the machine and see if we might find anything there that would offer a clue as to what might have happened to her."

Miller was clearly unhappy about the prospect. "But surely, that's a waste of time. What could you possibly hope to find on Becky's computer that would be of any help?"

"Unfortunately, sir," Maggie said in a conciliatory tone, "you never really know until you look. In all likelihood, we won't find anything useful at all, but we do have to cover all the bases."

Miller shook his head. In a heated voice, he said, "You're barking up the wrong tree, Detective. As I tried to tell you before, there's no way that Becky knew the person who did this to her. You need to be trying to find out what in the hell happened to her on her way home from her meeting that night. There's some sick fuck out there who somehow got her out of her car and killed her, and you sure as hell aren't going to find the bastard in her computer."

"That may well be," I said. "But as Detective McClinton says, we have to consider every angle. And please understand that we're not ruling out the possibility that Mrs. Miller was killed by a stranger. We're just trying to be as thorough as possible."

Miller insisted again that we would find nothing pertinent on his wife's computer but finally agreed that we could take it if we thought it was necessary. He watched as I unplugged the computer and wrapped up the power cord. I wrote a receipt for the machine, handed the receipt to him and said, "Just a couple more questions this morning, Mr. Miller, and then we'll get out of your way. Did Mrs. Miller have a life insurance policy?"

He waited a long moment, his eyes boring into mine, and then answered in a slow, deliberate voice. "No, Detective Richardson, she did not. We have a mortgage insurance policy that's designed to pay off the loan on the house in the event that either of us died while we still had a mortgage. We took that out years ago when Becky was still teaching and when we needed both of our incomes to make the house payment. I have two policies on my own life that would have gone to her if I would've died first. Becky was covered under my health insurance policy at work, but there is no death benefit associated with the policy."

"I'm sorry for having to ask, sir. I understand that these are unpleasant questions, and we certainly don't mean to imply anything by asking them. But these are the types of routine questions that we have to ask in any investigation like this."

Miller merely nodded.

Maggie gave him a moment, then said, "You told us the other day, sir, that Mrs. Miller had no family other than you. I assume, then, that you are the principal beneficiary under her will?"

He gave a heavy sigh, looked to Maggie and said, "Yes, Detective McClinton, I am. But I hope you'll excuse me for saying that if you're now suggesting that I killed my wife for her money, you are completely nuts. And if that's the way you people are going to go about trying to solve this case, then the son of a bitch who actually did kill her is never going to get caught."

"Again, sir, we regret having to ask these questions," Maggie replied. "But, as Detective Richardson said, these are simply routine questions."

Miller glared at her for a long moment and then turned to me. "Do you need anything else this morning, Detective?"

"No, not at the moment, sir."

I picked up the computer and Miller walked us back downstairs without saying another word. At the door, Maggie and I again expressed our sympathy and promised him that we'd be in touch as soon as we had any news.

## 9

On the afternoon of March third, Cathy Stanton apparently gave Walter an ultimatum. She reinforced it later that night in an e-mail message, bluntly warning him not to call her or to come "sniffing around my apartment until your ready to tell that bitch good-by."

Walter responded to the message, pleading with Stanton to "please understand the situation I'm in. As I've told you over and over, much of the money that went into my business came from my wife. If I leave her, she will pull her money out of the business and some damn judge will probably give her the house and most of my other possessions as well. I can't afford that. And if it happened, I certainly wouldn't be able to support you in the style you desire.

"You know that I love you and that I love being with you. But if you can't learn to accept the situation for what it is, at least for a little while longer, you leave me no choice. I will have to do as you ask and not see you anymore."

Reading the exchange, Becky nodded her understanding. Indeed, her husband *was* between a rock and the proverbial hard place. She was pretty sure now that Walter was not simply stringing Stanton along — that in fact he *was* strongly attracted to her, and that all other things being equal, he might actually think about leaving Becky for Stanton. But, of course, as Walter tried to tell Stanton, all other things were definitely not equal.

When Becky's widowed mother died seven years earlier, she had left Becky stocks and other investments worth a little over a quarter of a million dollars. The sale of her mother's house, which was located in an exclusive gated community in north Scottsdale, netted another four hundred thousand, putting Becky's total inheritance at around six hundred and fifty thousand dollars.

Becky's mother endured a disastrous marriage before being abandoned, virtually penniless, by her first husband. In the wake of that experience she scrimped and saved, determined that she would never again be financially dependent on any man, no matter how much she might think that she loved him.

She carried that spirit into her marriage to the man who would become Becky's father and insisted that she would maintain at least some money of her own apart from her husband's funds and from their joint marital assets. She proved to be a shrewd investor, and from the beginning she drilled into her daughter the principle that every woman, married or single, should be financially independent. As she neared her death, she insisted that Becky should use her inheritance to secure that independence.

Becky took her mother's advice and her experience to heart. From the beginning of their marriage, she and Walter pooled money from their salaries for common household expenses and for other joint investments. But each of them also retained some of their earnings for their own individual use.

Walter was somewhat less disciplined than Becky in the use of his personal funds, spending fairly freely on clothes, cars, and other toys. Becky was certainly no ascetic; she particularly enjoyed shopping for books, clothes, and jewelry, for example, but she allocated a portion of her personal money every month for savings and investment. As a result, even before her mother died, Becky had begun to accumulate a growing nest egg in her own right.

When her mother's estate was settled, Becky invested about a hundred and fifty thousand dollars of the money in blue chip stocks, but she let Walter talk her into putting the rest of the money into his growing business. Still her mother's daughter, however, Becky refused to simply give her husband the money with no strings attached. She also refused his offer to make her a silent partner and to give her a percentage of the business in return for her investment. Rather, she gave him the money as a loan.

Becky insisted that they go to an attorney and draw up a contract, formalizing the agreement, even though Walter was unhappy about the idea. Didn't she trust her own husband? Did she not love him enough to give him the money without forcing him to jump through all these hoops? Had she no confidence in him?

Becky tried as best she could to soothe his feelings. It had absolutely nothing whatsoever to do with trust, love, or confidence, she told him. This was simply good business, and it was what her mother would have expected of her. Walter spent another couple of weeks pissing and moaning about the idea, but he really wanted the money and so in the end, he went to the lawyer's office with her.

Becky loaned her husband five hundred thousand dollars at three percent a year — a much better interest rate than Walter could have gotten at any bank, and a much smaller rate of return than Becky might have gotten had she invested the money elsewhere. Certainly, she thought, that should be some proof of her love for him.

The schedule for the repayment of the loan was generous, but the contract provided that if Walter should ever miss a payment, Becky had the right to demand that the entire balance be repaid within sixty days. Such a demand would force Walter either to liquidate a significant portion of his holdings or go hat in hand to the bank and attempt to borrow the money at prevailing rates.

Anxious to get his hands on the money, and confident in his own ability to grow the business, Walter did not protest the terms of the contract. Then, a year after getting the loan, he had an opportunity to acquire another prime property, expanding the business to a fourth location. The financing was tight, and with Becky's permission, Walter missed two loan payments.

She assured him that she understood his situation, and that this was no big deal; he could make up the payments whenever he was able to do so. But this was an informal agreement; they put nothing in writing, and Walter never got around to making up the two missed payments.

Becky did love her husband, and she did have faith in his business acumen. But the fact remained that he was now in violation of the contract. And while she could never imagine doing such a thing, at any time she felt moved to do so, Becky could demand that Walter repay the balance of the loan immediately.

She was quite certain that, no matter how intoxicated he might be with Cathy Stanton, Walter would not come begging for a divorce, knowing that Becky could — and would — demand immediate payment of the loan. All of which made her wonder just exactly what Walter had in mind when he had asked Stanton to accept the limits of their relationship for at least "a little while longer."

# 10

While Maggie went off to interview the staff of the bookstore where Becky Miller had worked part-time, I decided to spend some time rooting through the victim's computer before turning it over to the techs. I hung up my suit coat, dug a Coke out of my small office refrigerator, and dropped into my desk chair. Miller's computer booted, showing a plain blue desktop with a handful of icons. I clicked on Internet Explorer and the screen refreshed, taking me to her MSN home page.

In a stroke of luck, I discovered that Miller had instructed the program to remember her screen name and password, and I clicked on the mail prompt. She had organized her correspondence into several folders, and I spent the next hour or so reading messages that she saved to and from a variety of people.

A few of the folders held e-mails relating to business matters, and I found a number of messages to and from Miller's stockbroker. She also carried on a fairly detailed electronic conversation with her landscaping and yard maintenance service. But most of the correspondence was between Miller and a number of female friends. The exchanges were all seemingly innocuous and involved discussions of books, movies, shopping excursions, luncheon plans and the like. None of them suggested that Miller had any serious problems, that she might be under pressure of any kind, or that she was unhappy for any particular reason. And none of the messages even hinted at the prospect that she might be thinking of abandoning a life that she apparently enjoyed very much.

I saved for last the folder labeled "Jennifer." In it I found a large number of messages between Miller and Jennifer Burke. Skimming through them, I saw that the subjects were generally of the same sort I saw in Miller's correspondence with her other female friends. They were distinguished only by the fact that the messages were more numerous and generally more detailed.

I began reading more carefully as I reached the messages that passed between the two women within the last few weeks of Miller's life. Again, I saw nothing that appeared to be of any consequence until a message from Burke to Miller, dated May thirteenth. After an extended commentary about a book that Burke wanted to recommend for their book club, Burke wrote, "With regard to the subject that we discussed at lunch last week, any developments or further thoughts?"

Miller responded to the message, agreeing that the book would be a good choice for the club. In closing, she wrote, "As for the other item you mentioned: still nothing more than a vague feeling. I'm probably just imagining things."

***

Finding nothing else that caught my attention, I made a note of the two comments and then exited the e-mail program. Back at Miller's desktop, I saw that she'd loaded a calendar program onto the computer, and I clicked on the icon to open it.

The calendar reflected the schedule I found in her e-mail correspondence. She'd blocked out the days that she worked at the bookstore and noted a number of birthdays. She cataloged a variety of engagements with her female friends as well as social obligations that she and her husband scheduled with a number of other couples.

According to the calendar, Miller had a one o'clock appointment at her salon on the first Wednesday of every month and she worked out with a personal trainer on Mondays. She'd had a dentist appointment six weeks before her disappearance and had scheduled a meeting with "Ted Lane, Western Mutual Insurance," on the day after the dentist appointment.

I remembered seeing a file folder in Miller's desk labeled "Western Mutual Insurance," so I turned to my own computer, googled Western Mutual, and then called the number. A perky female voice answered the phone and I asked for Ted Lane. When he came to the phone a moment later, I identified myself and explained that I was investigating the death of Becky Miller.

Lane's hearty insurance salesman's voice melted away. Sounding genuinely saddened, he said, "I just can't believe it,

Detective. Becky was such a fantastic woman. What sort of a world do we live in where something like this can happen?"

I assumed that he wasn't expecting an answer to the question, and so waited for a moment, then said, "I'm sorry to bother you, Mr. Lane, but I was just checking Mrs. Miller's calendar, and I see that she scheduled an appointment with you on April fifteenth. Can you tell me why she wanted to see you?"

The silence built for several seconds and then Lane said, "Well, my agency handled all of the Millers' insurance, both business and personal. Naturally I dealt with Walt regarding his business insurance, but Becky handled the household side of things — their home insurance policy, her auto insurance, and the like."

"So, she came to see you about her household insurance?"

After another long pause; Lane sighed heavily. "No, Detective. Actually, she came in to sign an application for a life insurance policy."

"A policy on her own life?"

"Yes."

"And how did that come about — had you suggested that she should have such a policy?"

"No, actually, I hadn't — at least not recently. Several months ago, I met with Walt and Becky for a periodic review of their personal insurance needs. I was mostly concerned with updating their home insurance policy, but as a part of the review, I also suggested that they consider life insurance for Becky. But it was really just a pro forma suggestion.

"In the case of some families, life insurance for the wife does make very good sense, even if she doesn't work outside of the home. But in Becky's situation, there really wasn't any apparent need. Since leaving teaching, Becky had very little income from wages, and in the event of her death, the loss of that income would have no effect of any consequence on Walt's financial situation. They had no children, and so he would not have needed additional money to pay for childcare. Again, I really couldn't see a reason why she might need life insurance, but I suggested it, just in case for some reason they did want to think about it."

"And at that point, I take it that they declined?"

"Yes."

"Why did they change their minds?"

Again, Lane took his time about answering the question. Speaking very deliberately, he said, "This is a question that you should doubtless be asking of Walt, rather than of me. Certainly, he would know much better than I the reasoning behind the decision."

"They didn't tell you why they'd changed their minds?"

"Only very generally. A couple of days before Becky's appointment, I got an e-mail message from Walt saying that they'd been thinking about the idea. He asked me to call Becky with some quotes. I did as he asked and Becky said that she and Walt would talk about the numbers. Two days later she called and made the appointment to come in and see me.

"To be honest, she didn't seem very happy about the idea. But Walt apparently convinced her that the premium was fairly nominal relative to the benefit in case some tragedy should befall her. He's fairly heavily insured himself and decided that it would make sense to have at least a small policy on her life as well. Anyhow, she came in on the fifteenth, signed the application, and wrote me the check for the first year's premium. And then six weeks later ..."

"How much was the policy for, Mr. Lane?"

"One hundred thousand dollars.... And the policy pays double indemnity, so in this case, we're looking at two hundred thousand."

"And I take it that there was no contingency regarding the length of time the policy had to be in effect before a payment would be made?"

"Only in the case of suicide."

"And the beneficiary is Mr. Miller?"

"Yes, Detective, it is."

11

In the wake of the ultimatum she delivered early in March, Cathy Stanton refused to see Walter for a week and a half. During the intermission in their physical relationship, the two continued to exchange e-mail messages, and Walter finally convinced Stanton to let him back into her bed. On the evening of March fifteenth, Stanton wrote Walter, describing in explicit detail how much she enjoyed the afternoon. In concluding the message, she suggested that "If only a certain other person wasn't around any longer, I could be getting you off like that EVERY night ☺"

Walter replied, indicating that he also enjoyed the afternoon, "especially since it's been so long." He told Stanton that he was looking forward to seeing her again in a couple of days, then chided her for "the suggestion that you made as I was leaving this afternoon. Even joking around, you shouldn't even think something like that, not to mention saying it out loud."

On March sixteenth, Stanton assured Walter that she too was looking forward to their next afternoon together and promised that she had something "especially naughty" that she wanted to try with him. "As for the other," she wrote, "I wasn't joking and you know it. We would BOTH be a hole lot better off."

Sitting at her desk in the bedroom, Becky read the exchange twice, then dropped her head into her hands and sighed heavily. Was Cathy Stanton a complete moron? Did the woman not understand *anything* about how the Internet worked? Did she not realize how easily these messages could be intercepted, forwarded, or otherwise read by someone other than Walter?

It was bad enough that Stanton was broadcasting the intimate details of her sexual relationship with Walter for any pimply-faced hacker to get off on. But even worse, the ditzy woman was actually suggesting in writing that she and Walter should take steps to eliminate Becky from the picture. And from the tone of the messages, Becky clearly understood that Stanton was not suggesting that Walter should simply file for a divorce.

Becky couldn't decide if she was angrier because Stanton dared to make the suggestion or because Walter made such a tepid response to it. Becky didn't believe for a moment that Walter would actually consider the possibility of killing her, but she was furious about the fact that he didn't break off his relationship with Stanton the moment that the woman even hinted at such a thing.

Staring back up at the computer screen, Becky decided that this had gone on long enough. It was time to teach Walter and his dopey girlfriend a lesson they would never forget.

## 12

While the techs began rooting through Becky Miller's computer, I decided to have another talk with Jennifer Burke. She met me at the door of her condo wearing shorts and a dark blue tee shirt. She'd obviously been crying and was clutching a wad of tissues.

She led me up the stairs into her living room, and we took the same seats we'd each occupied a few days earlier. When I expressed my condolences, Burke sniffled and said, "When I talked to you the other day, I thought I had braced myself for the worst possible news. But when I heard that the body had been identified as Becky …"

"I understand, Ms. Burke. And again, I'm very sorry."

She nodded, and I said, "I know that this is a difficult time for you, and I'm sorry to bother you again, but now that we've identified the victim as Mrs. Miller, I wanted to ask you a few additional questions."

"Of course. What do you need to know?"

"A couple of things. When we talked earlier, I asked you if there were any problems in the Millers' marriage. You seemed to hesitate for a moment before responding and then gave me an answer that was fairly non-committal. I was hoping that you might now be willing to answer the question a bit more directly."

Holding my eyes with hers, she said, "Why? Do you have some reason to think that Walter might have killed her?"

I shook my head. "No, none at all. We're simply trying to understand as best as we can what was going on in Ms. Miller's life over the last few months in the hope that the knowledge will point us in the right direction."

She nodded and then broke the eye contact. Looking down at the carpet rather than at me, she said, "In fairness, Detective, I should tell you that I've never been a big fan of Walter's. My impression is that he's one of those college jocks who peaked in his early twenties and who's spent the rest of his life living off of the memories.

"There's no doubt that he was a fairly gifted athlete, and I think that he has been reasonably successful as a businessman. But even there, to a considerable extent, he's been trading on the reputation that he made when he was twenty-two or twenty-three years old."

She paused for a moment and then continued. "I really don't have a problem with that, I guess. But what I do have a problem with, though, is the fact that he never grew intellectually beyond his glory days on the basketball court.

"Walter doesn't read much, except for the sports pages of course, and he knows nothing of the world except for what he sees on television. So, unless you're interested in talking about sports, it's virtually impossible to have a conversation with him about anything of any consequence.

"Becky, on the other hand, was a very vital person. She had an unceasing curiosity. She read widely, and she was active in a number of social and political causes. While Walter was basically drifting cluelessly through the world around him, Becky was *involved* in the world, and inevitably that created something of a gulf between them. They no longer had much in common, and increasingly, they each went their separate ways."

"But," I pointed out, "they did stay married for fourteen years."

Burke shrugged slightly. "Lots of people stay married for one reason for another even when there would seem to be no logical reason for them to do so. I think in the case of Becky and Walter, a kind of inertia took hold. They didn't argue. Neither of them was abusive toward the other, and while neither of them was particularly happy in the marriage, neither was sufficiently unhappy to want to end it."

"Do you know if either of them was involved with anyone else?"

She hesitated for a moment, then shook her head. "Becky wasn't, I'm sure of that, Detective. As for Walter ..."

"What about Walter?"

Again she shook her head. "I don't know. A few weeks ago, Becky told me that she suspected that Walter was having an affair. I asked her how she knew. She said that she didn't know for sure and that she couldn't even point to any concrete clues. It was just something that she felt — something about the way he'd been behaving lately that made her wonder about the possibility."

"Do you know if she ever confronted him with her suspicions?"

"No — at least not as far as I know. We talked about it a couple of times after that, but she said that she still didn't know for sure that he was cheating on her, and she didn't want to raise the issue with him unless and until she did have some hard evidence."

"But as far as you know, she didn't have any?"

"No, I don't think so."

"Did she tell you how she proposed to search for that evidence? For example, was she thinking of hiring a private investigator to check up on her husband?"

Burke shook her head. "I don't know. I think she simply intended to pay close attention to Walter's behavior. He's a pretty transparent guy, and Becky assumed that if he was involved with another woman, he wouldn't be able to hide the fact for all that long."

"And if she had confronted him with her suspicions, she would have told you?"

"Yes, I'm sure of that."

"And again, she'd said nothing to that effect, and had given you no indication of the fact that she might have found the evidence she was looking for by the time you said goodbye to her the night she disappeared?"

"No, she hadn't."

"And if Ms. Miller had discovered that her husband was having an affair?"

"I can't know for sure, Detective, but my instinctive reaction is to say that she probably would have divorced him. As I said earlier, Becky was neither particularly happy nor unhappy in her marriage. But I think that she was sufficiently disillusioned with Walter and with the state of their relationship that under those circumstances she would have decided to call it quits and make a fresh start."

"And how do you suppose Mr. Miller would have reacted to that?"

Burke leaned forward in her chair, resting her elbows on her knees and tenting her fingers together over her lips. After a moment, she lifted her head and looked up to meet my eyes. "I imagine that Walter would have been very conflicted, assuming, that is, that he actually cared about the woman he'd become involved with. On the one hand, if he loved the woman, he might have been happy to be free of Becky so that he could establish an open relationship with the other woman. But divorcing Becky would have been a very expensive proposition, and Walter would not have been at all happy about that."

"How so?"

Burke let out a long sigh and leaned back in her chair. "Becky inherited a large sum of money from her mother. She then loaned most of it to Walter so that he could invest it in his business. If she did divorce him on the grounds of infidelity, not only would he stand to lose a large share of their marital assets, but he would also have to repay the money Becky had loaned him."

She looked away for a moment, then turned back to me. "Even if Walter was not having an affair, Detective, Becky's death will provide him with a significant financial windfall. But if he was having an affair, and if Becky would have divorced him as a result, then, financially at least, Walter will benefit enormously as a result of her death."

## 13

Becky Miller spent three days working out a plan to scare the living bejesus out of her husband before she divorced him, stripped him of virtually everything he owned, and left him to the tender mercies of the mental midget he'd been screwing behind her back.

On a Monday morning, she kissed Walter goodbye when he left for work as though she hadn't a care in the world. After waiting for fifteen minutes to make sure that he was actually gone, she went up to his study and booted his computer. She then logged onto his regular e-mail account, using the sign-in name and password that she'd captured earlier with the spyware program she'd installed on the machine.

The mail program indicated that Walter had three new messages. Ignoring them, Becky opened the window to compose a new message and typed the e-mail address of their insurance agent in the "To" box.

Tabbing down to the message window, she wrote: "Ted, After thinking about it, Becky and I have decided that it *would* be a good idea for us to take out a small policy on her life. We think that 100K would be about right, probably with a clause for double indemnity. Becky will take care of the details. Will you put some numbers together and give her a call? Thanks Buddy."

Becky typed Walter's name at the bottom of the message, read through it once again and clicked the "Send" button. She remained at the computer, sipping a cup of coffee and keeping her fingers crossed, hoping that Lane would respond to the message quickly, so that she would have the opportunity to intercept the reply before Walter could find it in his mail box.

Fortunately, the agent was apparently at his desk and paying attention to his e-mail. Twenty minutes after Becky sent the request, a new message popped into the inbox and Becky opened it to find a response from Lane, assuring Walter that he would do as Walter had asked. Becky nodded, deleted the message, then went to the "Trash" folder and deleted the message from there as well before shutting down the computer.

Two days later, Lane called the house in the middle of the afternoon. Becky answered the phone and when the insurance agent identified himself, she summoned up the most frigid voice she could manage and said, "Hello, Ted."

Lane indicated that he'd received Walter's e-mail about the life insurance policy and that he'd put together some figures as Walter had requested. "Okay," she replied curtly.

Sounding clearly defensive, Lane gave her the numbers. Becky let him hang for a few seconds, then sighed and said, "What do I need to do?"

Lane explained that they would need to get together so that she could sign the papers. She would need to pay the first year's premium and they would be in business. They scheduled an appointment for three days later, and Becky drove down to Lane's office where she completed the paperwork and wrote a check from the household account to cover the premium.

Lane appeared distinctly uncomfortable in the face of Becky's cool demeanor and her obvious reluctance about the transaction. As Becky handed him the check, Lane thanked her and told her that she should expect to receive the policy within a couple of weeks or so. Refusing to make eye contact, Becky put her pen and checkbook back in her purse and stood to go. Sighing heavily, she finally looked at him, arched her eyebrows, and said, "Well, I'm sure Walter will be happy to have it taken care of." Then she said a quick "Goodbye," and was gone.

Becky hoped that Lane would clearly get the message that the life insurance policy was a sore subject in the Miller household and that he thus would refrain from mentioning the issue if he should run into Walter somewhere. And when the policy arrived two weeks later as promised, Becky took it upstairs and hid it temporarily in the bottom drawer of her desk.

## 14

On the basis of my conversation with Ted Lane, the insurance agent, a judge issued a warrant, authorizing us to search the Miller home for evidence of the life insurance policy that Walter Miller insisted did not exist. When Maggie and I appeared on his doorstep early the next morning, Miller greeted us by asking if there had been a break in the case.

"In fact, there has," I answered as he ushered us into the living room.

Miller looked at us expectantly and Maggie said, "When we talked to you earlier, sir, we asked if there was a life insurance policy on your wife. You told us that there wasn't."

"What about it?" he replied, apparently puzzled.

I let him think about it for a couple of seconds and then said, "Well, Mr. Miller, it's just that your insurance agent, Ted Lane, tells us that, in fact, there is such a policy and that you're going to collect two hundred thousand dollars."

"You're fucking kidding! Why the hell would I lie about something like that?"

"Why don't you tell us?" Maggie asked.

Miller shook his head, looking back and forth between us. "I'm not lying. I'm telling you there is no such policy. Why the hell would Ted tell you that there was?"

"In looking at your wife's computer," I said, "we found the calendar that she kept there. She had an appointment with Mr. Lane on April fifteenth. He told me that he received the e-mail you sent, indicating that you and Mrs. Miller had changed your minds and that you did want to insure her life after all. As you asked, he called your wife with the numbers, and she went in and signed the papers and paid the premium."

Miller simply stood and stared at me. After a moment, he shook his head again. In a distinctly softer voice, he said. "No. That's absolutely crazy. We never changed our minds, and I sure as hell never sent Ted any e-mail saying that we had."

"Mr. Lane is lying?" Maggie asked. "Why would he do that, sir?"

Miller sank into a large upholstered chair. "I have absolutely no idea. He says that Becky came in and signed the papers — that she paid the premium?"

"That's right, Mr. Miller," I replied.

"And she named me the beneficiary?"

"Yes, she did."

He stared at the floor for a long moment, then looked up to me. "I don't know what to say. This is all news to me, and it makes no sense at all. If what you say is true, then where's the policy?"

"That's what we're looking for this morning," I said.

I pulled the warrant out of my pocket and handed it to him, explaining that it authorized us to search for and to take possession of any evidence relating to the life insurance policy. Miller gave the document a cursory look, then said in a bewildered voice, "Be my guest, but I can't imagine what you think you're going to find."

Miller followed us up the stairs and into the sitting room where his wife's desk was located. Sitting at the desk, I opened the file drawer and retrieved the Western Mutual Insurance folder that I noticed when we initially went through the desk. I dropped the folder on the desk and opened it. It held a number of statements, filed in chronological order, and at the back of a file was a piece of notebook paper.

Written on the paper in a neat feminine hand was a list of insurance policies and the locations where they were kept. It indicated that the automobile policies and the home insurance policies were "in Walter's office safe." Two life insurance policies on Walter's life were "in Becky SDB." The last line on the page, written in the same hand, but in a different color of ink, noted that "Becky life insurance policy" was "in Walter's safe."

I handed the note to Miller who simply stared at it, shaking his head in apparent disbelief. Still holding the note, he finally looked at me. "I don't understand this at all. We never had any discussion about this, and I never sent any e-mail message to Ted Lane. I swear to God, this is the first I ever heard of this policy. And I flat out guarantee you that there's no such policy in my safe."

I took the note back from him, put it back into the file, and closed the folder. In the file drawer, I found Becky Miller's bank statements and dropped that folder on top of the other. Looking carefully through the rest of the folders, I saw nothing else that I thought I could legitimately claim as evidence of the insurance policy and closed the drawer.

Rising to my feet, I asked Miller where his home computer was. Now clearly on the defensive, he said, "In my office. Why?"

"I'm afraid that we'll have to take that with us as well," I answered.

"What the hell for? I need that computer."

"I'm sorry, Mr. Miller, but the warrant authorizes us to seize any evidence related to the insurance policy. Mr. Lane tells us that he received an e-mail from you directing him to call your wife about the policy. You insist that you sent no such message. We'll need to have our technicians look at your computer to see if there's any evidence of the message on the machine."

"No, you can't do that. I *need* that computer. Besides which, it's my private property. You have no right to go rooting around in it."

"Sorry, but the warrant says that we do have that right, Mr. Miller. Do you want to show us where it is?"

A tumult of conflicting emotions showed in his face until finally a look of resignation won out. "Jesus Christ," he said, sadly, "I'm the *victim* here. Some asshole killed my wife. And instead of being out there looking for him, you're hassling me. Are you telling me you think I had something to do with Becky's death?"

"We're making no such suggestion," Maggie said. "But clearly you can see that we have a problem with this insurance business. And the sooner we can get it straightened out the sooner we can be directing our attention elsewhere."

Miller shook his head, but said nothing more. He led us down the hall to his study and stood to one side as I disconnected his computer and wrapped up the cords. Maggie wrote him a receipt for the items that we were taking and Miller stuffed the receipt into the front pocket of his jeans. Then he grabbed a set of keys from the top of the desk.

"I want you to follow me over to my office," he said. "I'm going to open the safe and let you go through it. I want you to see for yourselves that there is no goddamn life insurance policy in there."

*\*\**

Twenty minutes later, Maggie and I followed Miller into the parking lot of the sports bar where we first interviewed him. We understood, of course, that even if Becky Miller's life insurance policy had been in her husband's safe, he would have had ample opportunity to remove it by now. But if Miller was going to give us carte blanche to root through his safe, we were more than happy to take him up on the offer.

I parked next to Miller immediately in front of the bar, which was not scheduled to open for business for another couple of hours. Miller unlocked the door, ushered us in, and then locked the door behind us again. An elderly Hispanic couple was in the process of cleaning the place. Miller walked across the room, bid the two a good morning, and then led us down the hall to his office.

Sorting through his keys, he unlocked the door and flipped on the lights. Moving around the desk, he stepped over to a safe that had been built into the wall immediately behind the desk. Maggie and I looked away for a moment while Miller spun the dial on the front of the safe through the sequence of numbers that would open the door. He stopped at the last number and then turned to me. "There's a loaded revolver right behind the door," he said. "You open the door and take out the gun, then I'll show you what else is in there."

I nodded, stepped up to the safe and pulled the door open. The safe was about three feet square, divided into four separate compartments, and the revolver was sitting at the front of the safe exactly as advertised. I took the gun out, broke it open, and set it on the desk. Then Miller moved in beside me. He pulled a large leather bag out of the front of the safe, unzipped the bag, and held it out in front of him.

"Last night's receipts," he said, giving us a look at the currency and credit card receipts in the bag.

Setting the bag on the desk next to the .38, he methodically went through the remaining contents of the safe, showing us backup computer discs, insurance policies on his and his wife's automobiles, their home and his business establishments, and a variety of other business documents. Then he reached into the back of the safe and came out with a stack of maybe thirty baseball cards, bound by a thick red rubber band. "The cream of my childhood collection," he said with a sad smile.

Holding the baseball cards, he stepped aside and gestured toward the safe. "See for yourselves, detectives. No life insurance policy."

Maggie and I stepped up and peered into the empty safe. Then I turned to Miller. "Okay, sir, we're satisfied. There is no life insurance policy in the safe. But that hardly means that there is no life insurance policy."

Miller looked down at the baseball cards, gently turning the pack over in his hands. Then he looked up at me and shook his head. "Obviously, I'm going to call Ted and find out what the hell is going on here, but I'm telling you, there is no policy. Period. End of story."

We thanked Miller for his time, promising that we would be in touch. Then we left him to his apparent confusion.

# 15

Walter's other safe was hidden in the wall of his home office, behind a large framed poster of the Arizona State Sun Devils from Walter's last season as a member of the team. Only Walter and Becky knew that the safe was there, and only Walter knew the combination.

Becky was more than a little annoyed when Walter had the safe installed and then refused to trust her with the combination. He tried to make a joke out of it, insisting that there was nothing of any consequence in the safe — only some personal items that he treasured and did not want to lose to burglars or to a fire. "I'll leave a couple hundred bucks in there," he said laughing. "That way when I croak, you can have the stupid safe drilled and pay the guy on the spot."

Becky had no idea *what* Walter was planning to keep in the safe, but she was pretty damned sure that it was more than just his friggin' baseball card collection. Then one night, a couple of months after the safe was installed, Becky went into the study to ask Walter a question about the cable television bill. She found him counting a small stack of currency, and the door of the safe was standing open. When Walter looked up and saw her walking through the door, he shoved the money into a small zippered bag and set it on the floor beside him.

Becky pretended not to notice. She asked her question, and Walter said that, yes, he had called the cable company and asked them to add the Golf Channel to the sports package that they were already getting. And so, yes, there should have been a small bump in the monthly bill.

Becky simply nodded and returned to her own desk, realizing that Walter had almost certainly installed the safe in his home office so that he could skim cash from his bars and hide it somewhere other than in his office safe.

She was fairly certain that if she raised the issue, Walter would simply deny it, and so she decided not to worry about it. Because of the complexity of his business operations and of her own individual investments, she and Walter filed separate income tax returns. She was confident of the fact that if he screwed up and got himself arrested for income tax evasion, there was no way the government could ensnare her as well.

***

Four days after vowing to teach Walter and his girlfriend a lesson, Becky armed the perimeter alarm of their home security system so that she'd have a couple of minutes warning if her husband should come home unexpectedly in the middle of the afternoon. Then she went into his study and set the basketball poster on the floor, exposing the small wall safe.

For a minute or so, she stood in front of the safe, staring at the dial in the center of the safe's door, as if willing the safe to give up its combination. Then she started with the most obvious possibilities. First, she experimented with the numbers that composed Walter's birth date. When that didn't work, she went on to the date of their marriage and then to her own birth date.

She tried using the numbers from Walter's license plate, from his code for the home security system, from his social security number, and from their home address. But after an hour and a half, she was compelled to accept the fact that there were simply too many possible variations of too many possible numbers. And even if Walter had selected a string of numbers that would be easy for him to remember, she wasn't going to stumble onto it like this.

Before starting her experiment, she noted that the dial had been set at the number 43. Just in case Walter might be astute enough to notice, she set the dial at 43 again. Then she hung the poster back in on the wall and checked to make sure that it was level.

The next morning, Becky drove over to an electronics store in Glendale and told the clerk that small items were disappearing from her dresser. She was afraid that the women from the cleaning service were pilfering the items, but she didn't want to accuse them of stealing and get herself sued for slander without some hard evidence to support her claim.

The clerk was very sympathetic and extremely helpful. He sold Becky a tiny video camera with a small antenna. Once the camera was secreted somewhere with a view of the dresser, and once Becky installed the software on her computer, the camera would send video to the computer, allowing Becky to confirm her suspicions, record the evidence, and present it to the cleaning company.

Back at home again, Becky grabbed a small stepladder from the kitchen pantry and went up to the study. Walter had installed track lighting to highlight the items on his ego wall, including the poster in front of the safe. Becky opened the ladder under the light can that shined directly on the poster.

There was about an inch of space between the rim of the fifty-watt Halogen bulb and the wall of the can itself. Becky unscrewed the bulb, stepped down from the ladder, and set the bulb on Walter's desk. Climbing the ladder again, she used two small pieces of black electrical tape to secure the video camera to the inside of the light can.

She retrieved the light bulb and began screwing it back into its socket. Just as the bulb was securely seated, it suddenly struck her that it would be most unfortunate if the bulb should burn out, causing Walter to have to replace it while the camera was still in the fixture.

She climbed down from the ladder again, went downstairs to the pantry and returned with a new bulb. She screwed it into the socket then stepped down from the ladder and looked up at the fixture. Looking closely, with the light turned off, she could see the camera peeking out from the edge of the bulb. But it was not all *that* obvious.

She walked across the room, flipped on the track lights, and stood under the fixture again. Looking directly into the light, there was no way you could see the camera. Satisfied, Becky folded up the kitchen ladder and carefully brushed the footprints of the ladder out of the carpet. She returned the ladder to the pantry, pitched the old light bulb into the garbage can and then went up to her own study.

As the clerk had promised, the software installed itself automatically once Becky had inserted the CD into her disc drive. Once the installation was complete, she removed the disk and ran it through the shredder that was sitting by the side of her desk. Then she launched the program and when the screen refreshed she found herself staring into the faces of Walter and his fellow Sun Devils.

\*\*\*

For the next three nights, Becky set the program to record whatever the video camera was seeing from seven p.m. to midnight, and on the two mornings following, she fast-forwarded through the images seeing nothing but the poster. Finally, on the third morning, she was halfway through the digital recording when the poster suddenly appeared to jump up in front of her before disappearing from view. Becky slowed the recording to regular speed and watched as the back of Walter's head appeared in front of the camera.

Becky cursed under her breath, fearing for a moment that her husband's stupid head would block her view of the dial in the door of the safe. But then, almost as in answer to her prayer, Walter moved slightly to his left as he brought his right hand up to the dial.

Becky now had a direct, clearly focused view of the dial. She watched as Walter spun it three times to the right before stopping at the number thirty-seven. More slowly now, he rotated the dial to the left, making two full turns before stopping at nineteen. One full rotation back to the right, and he stopped at five. Then he turned the dial left again, stopping as soon as the dial reached the number twenty-eight.

The sequence of numbers meant absolutely nothing to Becky, and she realized that she could have stood in front of the damned safe for the next fifteen years without coming up with the combination. But that made no difference now. On her way through the bedroom door, she again thought to set the perimeter alarm and then made her way to Walter's study. There, she carefully took down the poster and tried the combination that she had written on a slip of paper.

The safe opened on the first try, and the first thing Becky noticed were the stacks of hundred-dollar bills. There were five of them, one slightly smaller than the others. Riffling through one of the larger stacks, Becky estimated that there were about fifty bills in it. Quickly doing the math, she realized that Walter had stashed close to twenty-five thousand dollars in the safe. Almost certainly the money was unrecorded and unreported, and Becky smiled at the thought.

At the back of the small safe, she found a pile of documents, about four inches thick, and bound with a rubber band. The papers included Walter's birth certificate, his high school and college diplomas, three hand-written letters that Walter saved from his father who was long deceased, and a few other personal items.

Becky left everything in the safe exactly as she had found it, then she closed and locked the safe. She tried the combination two more times just to make sure. Then she returned the poster to its proper place and removed the video camera from the light can above the safe.

# 16

Back at the station, I took Walter Miller's computer to the Property Management Bureau where it was officially logged into evidence and tagged with a bar code. Then I walked it over to the crime lab and handed the machine to Andy Sheldahl, the head of the computer investigative staff. I explained that I was looking specifically for evidence of an e-mail from Walter Miller to his insurance agent, instructing him to call Becky Miller regarding the life insurance policy. Sheldahl nodded, pushing his glasses up on his nose. "You realize, obviously, that even if we do find such a message, there's no way of proving that Miller actually sent it."

"Yeah, I know. But he told us very clearly that he and his wife used separate computers. That doesn't seal the deal, of course, but it does give him something else to explain. Speaking of which, have you gotten anything out of her computer yet?"

Sheldahl shook his head and gestured in the direction of a technician at a workstation on the other side of the room. "Nothing so far. Bill's working on it now, and we'll have a preliminary report for you by the end of the day."

\*\*\*

Back up on the third floor, I dropped my suit coat in my office, then walked across the hall to Maggie's. I found her on her cell phone, just concluding a conversation. Her tone of voice was decidedly unhappy and as she disconnected, I dropped into the chair next to her desk. "So, what's wrong now?"

She shook her head and dropped the phone back into her purse. "Patrick. He called me last night and asked if I'd be willing to go out to dinner. Being too much of a chickenshit to simply tell the guy that it wasn't going to work between us, I told him I needed a little more time apart. While we were talking, Yolanda came into the room and realized that he was on the phone with me.

"She wanted to say hello and so Patrick gave her the phone. She told me how much she was missing me and said that she hoped she would see me real soon. I basically waltzed around the question, feeling like the jerk of the century, and told her that I missed her too. She gave the phone back to her dad, who said a quick and cold goodbye.

"This morning, he called to say that he wanted to break it off. He said it was pretty clear that I didn't have the same sort of feelings for him that he did for me and that he didn't want to drag things out any longer. He also said that he didn't want to have his daughters any more hurt and confused than they already were."

"That's kind of hitting below the belt, isn't it?"

"Probably not, actually."

"Bullshit, Maggie. You were upfront with the guy right from the start about the fact that you weren't willing to give up your job and that you needed somebody who could go with the flow. Meantime, he's Mr. Sweetness and Light, boasting about his flexible schedule and about how the job wasn't going to be a problem.

"As I also recall, *he* was the one who insisted on the two of you spending time with his daughters even though you told him it might not be a good idea that soon. If anything, he used Yolanda and Claire to try to strengthen your attachment to him and to them, and if anybody needs to be feeling guilty about that, it's certainly not you."

"Yeah, well, I *do* feel guilty about it, Sean, and I suspect that I'm going to for a while."

She stood quietly for a minute or so, lost in her thoughts, then turned back to her desk and picked up a file. "Meanwhile," she said, "here's something you'll find interesting."

"What's that?"

"I've been going through Becky Miller's bank statements. Six weeks ago, she wrote a check for eight hundred bucks to a firm of private detectives."

"Anybody we know?"

"No — at least nobody that *I* know. It's an outfit called Malcolm & Associates Confidential Investigations. Their office is in a strip mall in Glendale, and their ad in the Yellow Pages says that they specialize in 'domestic work.' It promises that they're discreet, confidential, and that by consulting them you can find peace of mind."

"Well, Jesus, I could sure as hell use a little peace of mind. Let's go see them."

\*\*\*

We walked out of the building into the blistering heat. Although it was only the middle of June, the metro area had suffered through four days in a row of temperatures in excess of a hundred and ten degrees, and there was no relief in sight.

As we stepped through the door, I slipped on my sunglasses, took off my suit coat, and threw it over my shoulder. Maggie was dressed more appropriately for the heat in a pale green blouse and a skirt that ran out of fabric just above her knees. A month past her thirty-ninth birthday, she was a very attractive woman who ate carefully and exercised rigorously. As a result, she had a body that many women ten years younger would have envied, and looking at her I could almost feel some sympathy for Patrick who would doubtless be missing her attention. She put on her own sunglasses and said, "I'd offer to drive, but the air conditioner in my car sucks, so you're driving."

Given the fact that in the nearly two years since she'd joined the unit Maggie had never once offered to drive, this hardly came as a revelation. The temperature inside my Chevy must have been least a hundred and thirty degrees. I slipped in and cranked the AC to high, then got back out of the car. I threw my coat into the back seat, and we stood there for a couple of minutes with the doors cracked open while the cooler air flooding from the air conditioning vents pushed some of the warmer air outside.

Once we judged that the car was as cool as it was likely to get any time soon, we settled gingerly into the hot seats. I hit the "Play" button on the iPod that I'd wired into the car's radio, and Brian Chartrand's "How Thin These Walls" cascaded out of the speakers. "Nice choice," Maggie said.

She leaned over and cranked up the volume as I pulled out of the lot and accelerated into traffic.

***

Glendale, a city of about two hundred and twenty-five thousand people, borders Phoenix on the northwest. As Maggie told me, Malcolm & Associates was located in a small strip mall that had clearly seen better days. The office sat between an Asian massage parlor on one side and a used CD store on the other. The window fronting the detective agency had been painted white, perhaps to provide some measure of confidentiality for its clients. The firm's name was stenciled on the pebbled glass of the door, and a sign hanging in the middle of the door indicated that the agency was open.

We pushed through the door to find a short, heavy-set man sitting with his feet propped on a desk, reading a magazine. He was somewhere in his late forties or early fifties with thinning brown hair that was artfully arranged in a less-than-successful comb over.

The guy had the ruddy complexion of somebody who thinks that it's always the cocktail hour somewhere. He was dressed in a pair of pleated chinos, a white shirt that had been worn and washed a few too many times, and a regimental tie that hung loosely around his neck. The office was small — just large to accommodate the desk, three chairs, and a couple of file cabinets. Even at that, the air conditioner was losing its battle against the late afternoon heat, and the man at the desk was perspiring.

As Maggie and I stepped through the door, the guy dropped his feet to the floor and slipped the magazine into the top drawer of the desk. He rose to his feet and looked from me to Maggie, making a long and obviously interested appraisal. Then he turned back to me and said, "Help you?"

We gave him a look at our shields and IDs. "Are you Malcolm?" Maggie asked.

The guy shrugged. "That's what it says on the door, isn't it?"

I looked around the office and then back at the detective. "Where're you hiding the Associates?"

86

Malcolm gave me what appeared to be his best effort at a hard stare, then said, "There are no associates at the moment. Things are a little slow these days."

Maggie produced the copy of Becky Miller's cancelled check and set it on the desk in front of him. "Two months ago, you did a job for a woman named Becky Miller. Tell us about it."

Malcolm drew himself up and gave her a little wink. "Sorry, Darlin'. That's confidential."

Maggie slapped her hand down on the desk and the fat man flinched. "Bullshit, Malcolm. You've been reading way too many crappy private detective novels. Becky Miller is a murder victim and we're investigating the case. You *will* tell us about the job you did for her. You *will* show us the paperwork, and you will damn well do it right now or your license to practice will be gone by the close of business. In addition to which, we may run your flabby ass downtown and charge you with obstruction."

"You can't do that," he said, without much conviction.

"Try me, asshole."

Malcolm glared at her for another couple of seconds, and then threw up his hands. "Okay, Jesus! We're all professionals here. You could at least ask nicely."

Maggie rolled her eyes and I said, "What was the case, Mr. Malcolm?"

He shook his head. "Just your normal domestic thing. The woman thought that her husband was cheating on her and she hired me to get the goods."

"And did you?"

"Yeah. Hell, it was so easy a girl scout could have done it. Her husband is one of those guys who apparently thinks he's bulletproof or some fuckin' thing. He was screwing a cocktail waitress and he didn't even try to be discreet about it. I got pictures of the two of them having lunch together, of them going into her apartment, and of him kissing the broad goodbye at the door. I'm good enough that I could've gotten pictures of the two of them in the sack, but the wife said that wasn't necessary. She took copies of the pictures I had and called me off."

"Of course, you kept copies of the pictures for yourself," Maggie said.

He hesitated a moment, then gave a slight nod. "Yeah. They're in the file."

Malcolm showed us the file, which included his report and several photographs of Walter Miller with a woman who appeared to be somewhere in her middle thirties. Her light blonde hair was cut short and she had a very good figure, but her face was all angles and sharp lines, giving her a distinctly hard look.

I jotted down the basic details of the slim report and we confiscated a couple of the photographs. As we left, Maggie tapped the desk. Malcolm looked up at her and she said, "Okay, Ace. You can go back to playing Sam Spade now. As of this moment, your investigation *is* confidential again, and you don't discuss it with anyone. Understood?"

The detective made one last stab at his hardened, tough-guy stare, but when Maggie refused to blink, he looked over to me and said, "Yeah, I understand."

17

Becky Miller went to three private detective firms before finding the one she thought would best suit her purposes.

The first three agencies all looked way too professional. Becky was certain that any one of them could get the goods on Walter and his girlfriend without breaking a sweat, especially since Becky was ready to provide them with Cathy Stanton's name and home and work addresses. All three agencies promised confidentiality, and Becky's concern was that they might actually try to deliver on the promise. She had no idea how easily a firm of private investigators could be compelled to give up its records for a police investigation, but she didn't want to hire any agency that looked like it might even *think* about putting up a fight before doing so.

Malcolm and Associates was the fourth firm on her list, and even before getting out of her car in front of the place, Becky was virtually certain that she'd hit pay dirt. The strip mall in which the agency was located looked to be only about sixty percent rented. The remaining spaces sat vacant, looking particularly sad and empty.

In two or three cases, the management company had removed the signage and cleaned up the spaces in anticipation of renting them out again. At some point though, they'd apparently thrown in the towel. In several of the vacant offices and stores the signs remained in place, although clearly business was no longer being conducted there. Through the windows fronting the spaces, Becky could see the detritus of the failed establishments looking almost pathetically abandoned, like the last tenants had simply locked the door one day and then walked away, never to return.

Most of the businesses that still survived in the strip mall looked like they were close on the heels of their former fellow tenants. There were only a handful of vehicles in the littered parking lot, and Becky figured that once you subtracted the ones that belonged to the owners and employees, there were precious few left that might actually belong to customers.

Malcolm and Associates looked as forlorn as its neighbors, and as Becky walked through the door, her first impression was that the operation looked even less prosperous on the inside than it did on the outside. A florid-faced, overweight man sat behind a desk in the middle of the office. Becky closed the door behind her and the man rose slowly to his feet, looking her over very thoroughly as he did. Becky stepped into the office and said, Mr. Malcolm?"

"Yes Ma'am," the guy replied. He invited her to take a chair in front of the desk. When they both were seated, he said, "How can I help you?"

Feigning nervousness, Becky clutched her purse in her lap. Looking at the purse, rather than at Malcolm, she swallowed hard and said, "Forgive me, Mr. Malcolm, this is a little difficult."

The detective leaned forward in his chair and clasped his hands on the desk in front of him. "Don't worry about it at all, Ms. ...?"

"Oh, I'm sorry," Becky said, appearing flustered. "It's Miller ... Becky Miller."

"And what's the problem, Ms. Miller?"

Her hands still in her lap, Becky made a show of turning her wedding ring around her finger. Finally, still not meeting Malcolm's eyes, she said quietly, "Well, Mr. Malcolm, it's my husband."

The detective leaned back in his chair and sighed heavily, suggesting that he knew all too well the ways of the world. "It usually is, Becky. It usually is. Let me guess. He's cheating on you?"

"Yes ... maybe ... I don't know for sure."

Now she finally looked up to meet Malcolm's eyes, hoping that he would see in her face the despair, pain, and betrayal that she was attempting to project. "I've suspected it for a couple of months now," she said in a breaking voice. "At first, I thought I'd be better off not knowing if he really was having an affair, but I find that I can't stand *not* knowing for sure. It's tearing me apart, and I have to know the truth, no matter how painful it might be."

Malcolm shook his head and gave her his most sincerely sympathetic look. "I'm very sorry for your troubles, Becky. And for what it's worth, I'd just like to say that your husband — or any other man — would have to be out of his mind to cheat on a woman as attractive as you are."

"Thank you. You're very kind."

"Well, I'm just stating the obvious."

Malcolm leaned forward again. "I take it you'd like me to investigate the situation and determine if your husband is involved with another woman?"

Becky nodded. "I can give you the woman's name and address. Can you give me some idea how expensive this might be?"

Malcolm spent another few seconds sizing her up again, then said, "My normal rate is five hundred dollars a day plus expenses."

Becky looked back down into her lap, biting her lip as if thinking about whether she could afford to pay five hundred dollars a day. After a long minute had passed, Malcolm got out of his chair, walked around, and sat on the corner of the desk almost directly in front of Becky. At this close range, his stale breath almost repelled her back, but she held her ground. Malcolm reached out and laid his hand on her shoulder.

Becky flinched slightly, not having to fake it at all. Malcolm squeezed her shoulder lightly. Again using his sympathetic voice, he said softly, "Look, Becky, with the woman's name and address, this case should be a bit simpler than most, so I can probably give you a bit of a break on the fee. Why don't we say four hundred a day and I'll eat the expenses myself. You can give me eight hundred as a retainer and I'll start first thing in the morning. Depending on what I come up with the first couple of days, we can decide where we want to go from there."

Becky appeared to think about it for a moment, then nodded. "Okay. If in that time you come up with some evidence that Walter is cheating on me, I'll decide whether I want to pursue it any further. If not, I guess I'll assume that I was just imagining things."

With some apparent reluctance, Malcolm removed his hand from Becky's shoulder and returned to the chair behind his desk. He pulled a blank contract from the top drawer, filled in the details, and turned it around for Becky's signature. She read the document carefully, then wrote Malcolm a check for eight hundred dollars.

Malcolm slipped the check into the top drawer of the desk. "As I said, Becky, I'll start your case officially tomorrow. However, I might try to get an early start and put in some time on it tonight. But anything I do tonight will be gratis."

"Thank you, I appreciate it," she replied in a grateful tone of voice.

Becky gave the detective a photo of Walter, the address of his office, and Cathy Stanton's name and home and work addresses. She told Malcolm that she would call him for his report, since she did not want an unfamiliar number to appear on her caller I.D. where her husband might see it. Malcolm told her that he understood completely and insisted that she could rely on his total discretion. "I've had a lot of experience in these kinds of matters," he assured her.

As Becky got up to leave, the detective rose again from his desk and walked over to meet her at the door. Invading her personal space, he touched his hand softly to her back. "Please don't worry about this any longer, Becky. From now on, it's my job to worry about your husband and his girlfriend."

"Thank you, Mr. Malcolm. Again, you're very kind."

Malcolm moved his hand gently across the top of her back. "Please," he said, "call me Jerry." He hesitated for a moment, and then moved even closer. In a softer voice he said, "Is there anything else I can do to help?"

Reaching for the door, Becky said, "No, thank you, Mr. Malcolm … Jerry. I'll call you in a couple of days to see what you've discovered."

Before the detective could paw her any more, Becky pulled the door open and walked out into the bright sunshine. Malcolm stood in the door, watching her into her car and out of the parking lot. As Becky pulled out into the street, she watched in her rear-view mirror as he slowly retreated back into his office and then closed the door behind him.

## 18

According to the report that Jerry Malcolm prepared for Becky Miller, Miller's husband was involved with a woman named Cathy Stanton. The report indicated that Stanton lived in an apartment in northeast Phoenix and that she worked as a waitress at a trendy restaurant and nightclub in north Scottsdale.

His first day on the case, Malcolm trailed Walter Miller to Stanton's apartment. From there Miller drove Stanton to a small, quiet restaurant where they enjoyed an intimate lunch. The detective then followed the pair back to Stanton's apartment and waited outside. When Miller emerged ninety minutes later, Malcolm ran off a succession of photos of Miller kissing the woman goodbye.

Maggie and I decided to brace Stanton first, before confronting Miller with our discovery, and so drove over to her apartment complex on North Scottsdale Road. Signs outside the complex promised luxury apartments and generous move-in bonuses. We drove in through the security gates that were standing wide open, thus failing to provide even the illusion of security, and found Stanton's unit near the pool in the middle of the complex.

The unit appeared to be a two-story model, and we parked directly in front of the door. I rang the bell and we stood for a minute or so, sweltering in the hot sun, without getting an answer. I then tried knocking on the door a couple of times, but that produced the same result. Looking at her watch, Maggie said, "It's nearly four o'clock. She could be at work by now."

"Maybe. Let's give that a try."

Less than ten minutes later, we walked through the huge double doors of the restaurant where Stanton worked and stepped up to the hostess station. At some point when I must not have been paying attention, the city of Scottsdale had apparently passed an ordinance requiring that the hostesses in all of the city's upscale restaurants must be tall, beautiful, and impossibly thin. The young woman who greeted us was no exception to the rule. We asked to see the manager, and the hostess escorted us to an office in the back.

As we walked through the restaurant, the staff was busy setting up for dinner which would begin in an hour or so and last until ten thirty. At that point, the staff would quickly clear the tables from the dance floor; the house band would take the stage; and the place would be transformed into one of the city's most popular dance clubs. The hostess stopped in front of the open office door and said, "Mr. Abernathy?"

A man in his late forties looked up from the computer in front of him and said, "Yes, Amber?"

Abernathy was dressed casually in a silk shirt, dark pants, and a pair of well-polished black loafers. I guessed that the outfit must have set him back at least twelve hundred bucks, not counting the slim gold watch on his left wrist. His dark hair was of medium length and expensively cut, but there was nothing ostentatious about the guy. Clearly, he was one of those increasingly rare men who had excellent taste in clothes and who still preferred to dress well while most of those about him were content to appear virtually anywhere in jeans, flip-flops, and raggedy tee shirts.

The hostess said, "These people would like to see you."

Without waiting for an invitation, Maggie and I walked into the office. "Mr. Abernathy," I said, "I'm Detective Sean Richardson of the Phoenix PD, and this is Detective Maggie McClinton."

Abernathy took a brief look at our badge wallets then rose from his chair and said, "What can I do for you?"

"Well, sir," Maggie replied, "We'd like to speak to one of your employees, a Cathy Stanton."

Abernathy gestured in the direction of the two chairs that sat in front of the desk and returned to his own seat. "Well, Detective," he said, "that makes at least three of us."

"Sir?" I said.

Abernathy exhaled. "Cathy quit on us a week and a half ago. She didn't show up for her shift one night, and the next day she sent me an e-mail announcing that she was quitting for 'personal reasons.' I haven't seen or heard from her since."

"How long had she worked here?" Maggie asked.

"About four years. She started as a second shift cocktail waitress and then a year or so ago, she made the transition to the first shift in the dining room."

"That was a promotion?" Maggie said.

Abernathy fluttered his hand. "It's the logical progression here," he answered. "The second shift is the late-night dance crowd, and we usually assign the younger employees to that shift. It's a better fit with customers we attract at that hour. The first shift is a more mature crowd, thirties and on up, who come in for dinner and maybe stay for a little while after the band comes on. A waitress can make pretty good money on either shift, but at her age, even though she's still a very attractive woman, Cathy more properly belonged on the first shift."

"When was the last night she worked?" I asked.

Abernathy pecked at his keyboard, looked at the monitor for a moment, and said, "Tuesday, June first. She was scheduled to work the following night as well, but as I said, she didn't show. On that Thursday, I got her 'resignation'."

Maggie nodded. "Did you save a copy of it?"

"Sure."

Abernathy turned to a bank of file drawers behind the desk, pulled open a drawer and extracted a file. He turned back, set the file on the desk, and opened it. He pulled the top sheet from the file and turned it around for us to see. The message was short and to the point.

> Dear Steve: Im having some personel problems that I cant really talk about in a message like this. I apologise, but I am going to have to quit work at least for a while. Sorry not to give you more notice. Will you please mail my last check to my apartment? Thanx, Cat. PS Im really sorry.

I looked up from the message. "Were you surprised at this?"

Abernathy leaned back in his chair and tented his fingers under his chin. "Yeah, as a matter of fact I was. As you can imagine, in an operation like this, no matter how carefully we try to screen applicants, we inevitably wind up occasionally hiring staff whose self-discipline and sense of responsibility aren't all that we would like. But Cathy had been with us for what amounts to a long time in this business, and she was normally very responsible. So, yes, I was surprised."

"How did she seem in the nights before she quit?" Maggie asked. "Did she appear troubled or worried about anything?"

Abernathy shook his head. "No, not at all. She seemed perfectly fine — just like her usual self."

"I gather she was single," I said. "Was she seeing anyone?"

"Divorced, actually. As to the question of whether she was seeing anyone or not, I have no idea."

"Was she particularly close to any other employees?" Maggie asked.

Abernathy nodded. "There are a couple of women who've been here nearly as long as Cathy. They might be able to give you a better idea than I of what's going on in her life. But if I may ask, why are you looking for her? Is she in trouble of some kind?"

"No, not at all. We think that she may be a witness in a relatively minor matter that we're investigating. We were simply hoping to talk to her about it."

\*\*\*

Abernathy walked us out into the restaurant and introduced us to Jennifer Johnson, a tall brunette who was sporting what was, even for Scottsdale, a pretty outlandish set of breast implants. Johnson told us that she too was surprised when Stanton quit so abruptly. "She never said a thing about it to me. One night she seemed perfectly fine, and then the next night she didn't show up."

Johnson indicated that, after playing the field for some time, Stanton had recently become involved with someone. However, Stanton had said virtually nothing about the new man in her life. Shaking her head, Johnson suggested that the guy was probably married and that Stanton was protecting his secret.

The other waitress with whom Stanton had apparently been close was not scheduled to work today. Abernathy gave us her name, number, and address, and we thanked him and Johnson for their help. Once back in the car, Maggie turned to me and said, "Well, the plot thickens. Stanton fails to show up for work the night that Becky Miller disappears. She quits the next day, and nobody's seen her since. What the hell do you suppose that means?"

"Damned if I know, Maggie. But I do think it's time to make another call on the grieving widower."

19

Three days after she had retained Jerry Malcolm, Becky Miller called the detective and asked for his report. Malcolm sighed sympathetically. "I really am sorry to have to tell you this, Becky, but I'm afraid that the situation is as you feared. Your husband *is* having an affair with the Stanton woman."

Becky paused for a moment as if fighting to control her emotions. Then, her voice breaking, she asked, "What evidence do you have of this, Mr. Malcolm?"

Malcolm explained that he had followed the couple to lunch and that he managed to surreptitiously get pictures of them at lunch and then again at Stanton's door. In retelling the story, he made it sound as if the task had been a lot more difficult than it really was, suggesting that only a very talented investigator could have pulled off such a coup.

Becky listened and then again hesitated for a moment. Finally, she said into the phone, "Well, I guess that's it, then. Now I know."

The detective cautioned that, while his observations and the photographs he had so cleverly managed to take certainly *suggested* that Becky's husband was having an affair, it wasn't concrete proof. He apologized for being so indelicate at a time when Becky had suffered such a harsh emotional blow. But he suggested that if Becky intended to sue Walter for divorce, she'd have a much stronger case if Malcolm remained on the job and got photos of Walter and Stanton in *flagrante delicto.*

Becky held the phone away from her ear and stared at it for a moment, unable to believe that a schmuck like Malcolm had actually used the term *flagrante delicto.* Returning the phone to her ear, she said, "Uh, you mean pictures of them actually having sex together?"

"Yes," Malcolm replied, in a tone suggesting that he too was shocked by the thought. "I know how horrible it would be for you to see pictures like that. And frankly it would be extremely difficult and, I'm afraid, fairly expensive to have me get them for you. But believe me, it would be well worth it once you get into court. Your husband might be able to explain away the pictures of the two of them at lunch and at Stanton's door, claiming that they were just friends or something like that. But with the other, if you'll excuse my being so blunt, you'd have him by the short hairs, no question about it."

Becky pretended to think it over for a few moments. Finally, she made an attempt at an anguished voice and said, "Even though I suspected it, this is still such a shock. I just don't know what I should do about it at this point. Please send me a copy of the report and of the pictures that you took. Once I've had an opportunity to digest that much, I'll decide if I want you to go any further."

Malcolm made a valiant effort to convince her that time was of the essence, and that Becky should strike while the iron was hot. Two or three clichés later, she finally cut him off at the pass, insisting that she really did need some time to think about what she was going to do next.

Malcolm offered to deliver the report in person, but Becky demurred, insisting that she just couldn't face anyone at the moment. Couldn't he please just put the report in the afternoon mail so that she would get it tomorrow?

The detective finally surrendered and agreed to do as she asked. "Just remember, though, that I'm here for you. I know exactly what you're going through, and so if there's anything I can do for you Becky — and I do mean *anything* — please let me know."

Becky thanked him again for his efforts and promised that she would keep his offer in mind. Then she disconnected from the call and gingerly set her cell phone down, feeling like she should spray it with a heavy dose of disinfectant.

20

Just after five o'clock, Maggie and I found Walter Miller in his office. He was sitting behind his desk, staring off into space when I startled him out of his reverie by tapping on the open door. He rose to his feet as we walked over to the desk. "Detectives?" he asked.

Dispensing with any opening pleasantries, I said, "Mr. Miller, why don't you tell us about your relationship with Cathy Stanton?"

The man seemed to collapse into himself like a balloon that had sprung a fatal leak. Shaking his head, he sunk back into his chair. After a long minute, he looked up to Maggie and me. "She's a waitress at a place down Scottsdale Road. We've been seeing each other for a couple of months."

"Did your wife know about your affair?" Maggie asked.

Miller shook his head. "No. Cathy and I were very careful and we only ever saw each other in the middle of the day. I don't think Becky ever suspected a thing."

Maggie nodded. "When was the last time you saw Stanton?"

"Two days before Becky ... two days before she disappeared. I haven't seen Cathy since."

"And where do you suppose Ms. Stanton is at the moment?" I asked.

Miller looked at his watch. "She'd be at work now. Her shift starts at four thirty."

Maggie made a show of jotting something in her notebook, then looked to Miller. "How serious is your relationship with Stanton — were you planning to leave your wife for her?"

Again Miller shook his head. "Christ, no," he said in a soft voice. "Cathy's a nice girl, but she's not in Becky's league — not even remotely. I never thought of leaving Becky for her."

"Did Stanton want you to leave your wife?" I asked.

"Yeah, she did."

"And did you encourage her to believe that you *would* leave your wife for her?" Maggie asked.

Miller hesitated for a moment. Then, looking at the desk and not at Maggie, he said, "No. ... Well, to be honest, maybe a little, I guess. I certainly never told her that I *would* leave Becky, but I did tell Cathy that I loved her, and I guess I led her to believe that if things were different ..."

"If what things were different?" I asked.

"It's complicated, Detective. I told Cathy that Becky had loaned me money for my business and that I couldn't afford to divorce her. That was technically true, but even if it wasn't, I still would've never left my wife for her."

"But you would screw around behind your wife's back," Maggie observed.

Miller glanced up at her. "Look, Detective McClinton, I understand that you think I'm a total asshole. But believe me, you can't think any worse of me than I do of myself right now. I hate myself for having betrayed Becky and whether you believe me or not, I will never forgive myself. And I'm not attempting to excuse what I did. I can only say again that the situation was more complicated than it appears on the surface."

"Was Ms. Stanton getting impatient with you?" I asked.

Miller nodded. "A little, I guess. She told me I needed to make up my mind. She said that she wouldn't go on seeing me if I didn't leave Becky."

Maggie made another note. Then after a moment, she said, "Did Stanton ever suggest taking more drastic action?"

Miller held Maggie's eyes for a moment then looked down at the floor. "Yeah, she did," he said quietly. "But I know she wasn't really serious."

"Exactly what did she suggest, Mr. Miller?" I asked.

Again, he waited a moment before responding. "A few weeks ago, she said that we'd both be a lot better off if Becky was completely out of the picture."

"And what, exactly, did she mean by that?" Maggie asked. "Completely out of the picture how?"

He sighed. "I don't know. She didn't say."

"Wait a goddamn minute," I said. "You're having an affair with the woman. She tells you that you'd both be better off if your wife was out of the picture, and you don't ask her what in the hell she means?"

Miller threw up his hands. In a resigned voice, he said, "I told her not even to joke about something like that."

"And how did Stanton respond to that?"

"She said she wasn't joking."

"This was a few weeks ago," Maggie said. "Did she ever raise the subject again?"

Miller shook his head.

For thirty seconds or so, Miller stared at the floor while no one said anything. Finally, he looked up again and I said, "Let me make sure I understand this, Mr. Miller. You're having an affair with Cathy Stanton. A few weeks ago, she suggests that you'd both be better off if your wife were out of the picture. She tells you she's not joking about it. Then your wife disappears and turns up murdered. And you don't think this is something you might have mentioned to us?"

The man sighed heavily. "I'm sorry. I guess I should have said something. But I know that Cathy wasn't *really* serious. I can't believe that she had anything to do with Becky's death."

"Well," Maggie said, "would you believe that Stanton quit her job and disappeared the day after your wife went missing, and that nobody's seen her since?"

Miller paled and his mouth dropped open. "You've got to be shitting me."

I said, "Not a chance, Mr. Miller. Your wife's dead and your girlfriend is in the wind."

## 21

Maggie and I left Miller stewing in his confusion and fought our way through the end of the evening rush hour traffic back to Cathy Stanton's apartment complex. The rental office was still open, apparently in hopes of attracting any prospects that might be spending the early evening hunting for a new apartment. I parked in front of a sign indicating that the spot was reserved "For Future Tenants," and we walked into the air-conditioned office, grateful to be out of the heat.

The office was cool, spacious, and tastefully decorated. A scale model of the complex sat on a pedestal in the middle of the room, showing the relationship of the various apartments to the pool, clubhouse and fitness center. The saleslady was equally decorative — an attractive young redhead dressed in a skirt, heels, and a blouse that was unbuttoned just to the point where things began to get interesting. As Maggie and I walked through the door, she rose from the chair behind her desk, gave us a broad smile, and said, "Good evening. Welcome to The Oasis. I'm Megan."

Opening her ID wallet, Maggie said, "Megan, I'm Detective Maggie McClinton of the Phoenix P.D. This is my partner, Sean Richardson."

The young woman's smile dissolved into a mixture of confusion and apprehension. She looked from Maggie to me and said, "Is something wrong? Has something happened?"

"Nothing that concerns you personally, Miss," I answered. "But we are anxious to get in touch with one of your tenants."

"Which one?"

"Cathy Stanton, in 2912," Maggie said.

The saleswoman shook her head. "I don't know her. I've only been working here for four months, and so I don't know a lot of the residents who have been here for longer than that."

"Can you check her record for us?" I asked. "She isn't answering the door at her apartment and she quit her job a couple of weeks ago. We're wondering if she might have made any arrangements about her apartment."

"Well, I can check the computer."

We followed her back to the desk and I stood at the corner of the desk where I could get a look at the monitor while the woman typed Stanton's name into the computer. The screen refreshed, and the data indicated that Stanton had been living in unit 2912 for a little over two years. Her rent was due on the tenth of each month and was automatically deducted from her checking account. She'd listed the restaurant as her employer, and the form indicated that she owned a three-year-old blue Buick Regal.

I jotted down the make, model, color and plate number of the car. The young woman looked up from the monitor and shrugged, "Everything looks normal here. Her rent is current and she's given no notice that she might be leaving."

I slipped my notebook back into my pocket. "Well, here's our situation, Ms. ...?"

"Sutherland — Megan Sutherland."

"Right. Okay, Ms. Sutherland, Ms. Stanton is as important witness in a matter that we're investigating. We discovered earlier this afternoon that she had unexpectedly quit her job and apparently no one has seen her in the last two weeks. Our concern now is that something might have happened to her. We'd like to have you accompany us to her apartment with a passkey, go in and take a look to make sure that she isn't in there."

The young woman paled and put her hand to her throat. "Oh jeez, you mean you think that she might be lying dead in there or something?"

"No, we have no reason to think that," Maggie said. "But under the circumstances, we would like to know that everything is okay in her apartment."

Sutherland nodded and pulled a ring of keys from the desk drawer. She hung a sign in the door, indicating that she would return in ten minutes, then followed Maggie and me out the door and locked it behind us. She led us to a golf cart that was parked in front of the rental office and ferried us a couple hundred yards to Stanton's building.

I punched the doorbell and we listened to it ring inside the unit. I waited thirty seconds, punched the bell again, waited another thirty seconds, and then knocked loudly on the door. I succeeded only in annoying what sounded like a particularly large dog in the unit next to Stanton's, and he or she began barking loudly. Turning to Sutherland, I said, "It doesn't appear that anyone is going to answer. Why don't you go ahead and open the door?

She nodded, turned the key in the lock, and stood aside. "Why don't you go in first?" she said. "If there's anything wrong in there, I'd rather that you guys find it."

I nodded and opened the door. Still standing outside, I called Stanton's name. When no one replied, I said in a loud voice, "This is the police. Is anyone home?"

Again, there was no answer, and so I stepped across the threshold, followed by Maggie and a nervous Megan Sutherland. Sutherland closed the door, leaving it slightly ajar. The apartment was virtually dark, save for the light that was filtering in through the closed drapes and blinds that covered the windows. I flipped on a light switch and we moved from a small foyer into a living room on our left. Turning to Sutherland, I said, "How is the unit laid out?"

In a whisper, she said, "There's a living room, kitchen and bath downstairs and two bedrooms and another bathroom upstairs."

In the living room, a couch sat under the window with a love seat at a right angle to the couch on the far wall. A corner table between the couch and the love seat held a large table lamp. In front of the couch was a large, square, glass-topped coffee table which held a couple of magazines, a few candles, and a box of matches from Mastro's Steakhouse. On the wall opposite the couch was a home entertainment center that housed a television set, CD and DVD players, and a couple rows of CDs and DVDs. A light layer of dust had settled over the furniture, but otherwise the room was neat and in good order.

An archway to the left of the home entertainment center led into a large kitchen with a breakfast bar that separated a table and four chairs from the work area. Like the living room, the kitchen was clean and tidy.

Maggie pulled open the doors to a huge, side-by-side refrigerator/freezer. The freezer compartment held a few frozen dinners and a couple of pizzas. On the refrigerator side, we found some vegetables that were clearly going bad, some condiments, half a loaf of wheat bread, and a few cans of diet pop.

Things were much the same upstairs. Both bedrooms and bathrooms were neat and clean. Stanton had put a desk in the smaller bedroom, and on the desktop were a lamp, a cup with some pens and pencils and a couple of photographs that looked like they might be of Stanton's parents. The space in the center of the desk immediately in front of the chair was empty. A blue cable modem lay on the floor under the desk. An Ethernet cable was connected to the modem and lay across the top of the desk, suggesting that it had probably been disconnected from a laptop computer.

In the larger of the two bedrooms, a king-size bed was made up with a number of pillows resting on a green comforter with a floral print. A glass door fronted the closet and I slid it open to discover that the closet was about half full of clothes. Checking the bathroom, Maggie said, "There's only a few toiletries and cosmetics in here, and the medicine cabinet and the drawers are basically empty."

Megan Sutherland had trailed us up the stairs, keeping her distance as she had downstairs, in the event that we might find Stanton's body decomposing somewhere in the apartment. Maggie and I walked out of the bedroom and I flipped off the light. Sutherland said, anxiously, "Is everything all right?"

"It appears to be," Maggie answered. "It looks like Ms. Stanton cleaned the apartment, packed a few clothes and toiletries and left. I only wish we knew where she might have gone.'

Back downstairs in the foyer, I pointed to a door on my left. "Does this open into the garage for the unit?"

Sutherland nodded and I opened the door. A few boxes were neatly stacked on some shelves at the front of the garage and a mountain bike hung from a hook in the ceiling. Otherwise, the garage was empty. Neither Cathy Stanton nor her Buick Regal were anywhere in evidence.

***

Once back at the office, Maggie left for the evening. I spent some time moving paper between my "In" and "Out" baskets and finally got home a little after nine o'clock.

As had been the case every night for the last two and a half years, I arrived to find the house empty and dark. By now, of course, I was accustomed intellectually to the fact that Julie would not be there to greet me. But even after all this time, I still hadn't completely adjusted to the idea emotionally. Scattered all through the house were dozens of tangible reminders of the time we had spent together here, from all of the decorating choices we had made down to the smallest kitchen utensils that Julie had considered indispensable. And even though I'd now disposed of her clothes and most of her jewelry, her presence still permeated every room.

During the time she'd been hospitalized and for the first few months after her death, the house had been my refuge — a sanctuary where I could hold tight to my memories and feel her physical presence long after the morning she had kissed me goodbye on her way to work, never to return again. And during that time, I could never have imagined living anywhere else.

In the last few months, though, I'd finally begun to wonder if it wasn't time to sell the house and move to someplace more suitable for my new life alone — somewhere smaller that would be easier to maintain and that wouldn't smack me in the mouth every time I walked through the door, reminding me of the life that had so abruptly been ripped away from me.

When the notion first occurred to me, even before I'd met Stephanie, I felt guilty as hell, as though I were turning my back on Julie and attempting to push her out of my life. Intellectually, I knew that the thought was ludicrous, but emotionally it was another matter altogether and I shelved the idea almost as quickly as it had popped into my mind. Gradually, though, I was coming to grips with it, and even though neither Stephanie nor anyone else would ever displace Julie from the center of my heart, I knew it was time to be thinking more seriously about moving on.

I hung my suit in the closet and pulled on a pair of jeans and a tee shirt. On my way back through the bedroom, I paused for a moment to look at the picture of Julie that sat on my nightstand. I'd taken it in the summer before Julie's accident, on a vacation to the Flathead Valley in northwestern Montana. In the photo, she stood, smiling into the camera, leaning against the rail of a deck that hung out over the lake with the magnificent Mission and Swan Mountains in the distance behind her. It was my favorite memory from what had been the best vacation of our lives, and slowly shaking my head at the recollection, I drifted off toward the kitchen in search of another dinner alone.

It *was* time to be thinking more seriously about moving on, but maybe not just yet.

## 22

When Becky Miller began keeping a diary on her laptop computer, she created a password consisting only of her first name and the year of her birth. She hoped that the password was simple enough that any reasonably competent computer technician would easily figure it out. Failing that, she trusted that the police department's computer people would know how to break into a Microsoft Word file that was protected only by a simple password, even if they didn't know what the password was.

She was confident of the fact that, once she disappeared, the police would confiscate her computer and dig through it, hoping to find some evidence of what might have befallen her. Having found and opened the file, they would discover that Becky suspected her husband of cheating on her for quite some time.

They would also learn that she hired a detective who had confirmed her fears. And just in case the police hadn't tumbled to the obvious clue she left for them in her checkbook, she made sure to mention Jerry Malcolm's name in the diary. To her diary, she confided, "I'm so confused, and so uncertain as to what to do next. I've put the detective's report in my safe deposit box so that Walter can't find it until I've made up my mind."

Becky also expressed her concern about the fact that Walter encouraged her to take out a life insurance policy on herself after he started his affair with "that miserable slut." Was this only a coincidence, or was it something more sinister? Then: "Jesus, Becky, get a grip. The guy's a prick but not *that* much of a prick. You've been reading too much James M. Cain."

She worked on the document on and off for four days, dating the first entry about six weeks before she hired Jerry Malcolm. She created entries for two or three days of each of the weeks after that, describing her suspicions and pretending to argue with herself about whether she was simply over-reacting to the fact that Walter seemed more distant and to the fact that he was away from the house more than usual lately.

In the days after the detective confirmed Becky's "suspicions," she vacillated back and forth in her feigned reaction to the news. In some entries, she claimed to be mad as hell and blamed Walter alone for having destroyed their marriage. In a couple of entries, though, she confessed to the diary her fear that maybe she had not been a good enough wife to Walter. Perhaps she had not paid him sufficient attention. Maybe she had given him reason to stray.

In the end, though, she rejected that argument. If Walter was unhappy with the state of their marriage, he should have talked to her about it. Perhaps they could have gone to a marriage counselor. Ultimately, there was *no* legitimate excuse for what he did.

Obviously, she wrote, her pride would never allow her to stay with Walter after learning of his betrayal. But where would she go? What would she do? How hard would Walter fight her over a divorce? What would he do about all the money he owed her? And how could she ever face her friends again, even Jennifer?

Most of her friends would pity her, she wrote. But some would wonder why she had not been able to hold on to her husband. A couple of her "friends," she suspected, might even make a play for Walter once the dust had settled. This sort of thing might happen to other women, but it was not supposed to happen to her.

And Becky told her diary that she was absolutely devastated by it all.

## 23

When I got into the office on Thursday morning, I found a voice mail from Andy Sheldahl, telling me that he had a preliminary report on Becky Miller's computer. I walked downstairs and found him at his desk. We wished each other a good morning, then he swiveled his chair around and grabbed a file from the worktable behind the desk.

Turning back, he laid the file on the desk, flipped it open, and said, "We're still working on both of the Millers' computers, but Bill found something on the wife's machine that we thought you'd want to see right away."

"What've you got?"

Tapping the file, he said, "About six weeks before she was killed, she began to suspect that her husband was having an affair. She started a diary, recording her suspicions and agonizing over what she should do. It was the only file that was protected by a password, but it took Bill all of about ten minutes to break it."

I spun the file around and skimmed through the first couple of pages. "Have you found anything else of interest?"

Sheldahl shook his head. "Not yet. Nothing else on the machine would seem at first glance to have any bearing on what might have happened to her. The woman was apparently pretty compulsive. She had her financial records, her home inventory, and some correspondence on the computer. She also had databases for her book and music collections, and a fairly large file of notes on the books she'd read. She apparently enjoyed her detective fiction, but she read a lot of other stuff as well. I should have that kind of time."

"Shouldn't we all? What about the husband's computer?"

"Bill's looking at it now, but he just got into it. There's still no sign of the e-mail message you're looking for. I'll let you know immediately if and when we find it."

*\*\*\**

Maggie firmly believed that a person was much better off eating five or six small meals a day rather than two or three large ones, and back up on the third floor I found her eating an apple at her desk. In the normal scheme of things, the apple would tide her over from the small bowl of cereal she allowed herself after her early morning workout to the salad that she usually consumed during the noon hour. I dropped down into the chair next to her desk. Nodding in the direction of the file I was holding, she swallowed a bite of the apple and said, "What's that?"

"Becky Miller's diary. She started it when she began to suspect that her husband was cheating on her."

I flipped open the file, read the first page carefully this time, and handed the page over to Maggie. The diary was short — only about fifteen pages long. As Sheldahl had indicated, Miller only kept the diary for a few weeks. She wrote sporadically, sometimes skipping a day or two, and the tenor of the entries suggested that she was using the diary as a refuge where she could vent privately the anger and the pain she was feeling.

In the fourth entry, about a week after she had started the diary, Miller lamented the fact that she had no one to talk to about the situation she faced. She confided to the diary that she was too ashamed and embarrassed "even to talk to Jenn about this sordid mess. I feel like such a fool."

Over the next few weeks, Miller continued to agonize over her situation, trying to decide what she should do. By the last week of her life, however, her resolve was firming. She seemed increasingly resigned to the situation, and progressively more convinced of the fact that her husband was largely responsible for creating the crisis in their marriage.

The day before her husband reported her missing, Miller wrote that she had decided to divorce him. "I can no longer pretend that everything is normal and that I don't know what Walter is doing behind my back. And I've thought about this long and hard enough to know that I can't forgive him for what he's done. I have no idea where he'll come up with the money he owes me. I'm sure he hasn't skimmed nearly that much cash into the safe in his study, but that's his problem, not mine. I'm resolved to tell him when I get home from the book club tonight. It's time to end this charade."

I handed the last page to Maggie and waited while she digested it. After a minute or so, she looked up from the page and said, "What safe in his study?"

"My thought exactly. Remember the list of insurance policies? It said very specifically that a couple of the policies were in the husband's office safe, but it simply listed the life insurance policy as being in 'Walter's safe.' It didn't occur to either one of us to ask whether he had more than one safe."

Maggie shook her head. "Christ almighty, some detectives we are. Sounds like we need another search warrant."

\*\*\*

Two hours later, Maggie and I were standing at Miller's front door with a warrant authorizing us to search any safe in the house for the missing life insurance policy. No one answered when we rang the bell, and so I used my cell phone to track Miller down at his office. I explained that we were standing at the door of his home waiting to execute a search warrant and asked him to come let us in.

"And if I don't?"

"Then we'll have to let ourselves in Mr. Miller. And you'd probably prefer that we not do that."

Some fifteen seconds passed, and then he finally said, "I'm on my way."

Maggie and I retreated to the car and sat for the next forty-five minutes, listening to music on my iPod. The daytime temperatures had finally abated a bit, but it was still somewhere north of a hundred degrees, and even with the AC running at full blast, the car was still fairly warm and uncomfortable. Looking at her watch for the seventh or eighth time. Maggie said, "Where in the hell is this bastard? It's a ten-minute drive from his stupid bar to here. Is he playing games with us now?"

Before I could respond, two cars, one of which was Walter Miller's Lexus, pulled into the driveway beside us. Miller got out of his car and waited while a man I didn't recognize got out of a black BMW 7 Series. The second guy was wearing a well-tailored suit with a white shirt, a bright red tie, and a pair of highly polished wing tips. I was not at all surprised when Miller introduced him as his lawyer, Ted Ogilvie.

The introductions completed, Miller looked from Maggie to me and said, "I can't seem to convince you people that you're wasting a helluva lot of valuable time, harassing me when you should be out trying to find the son of a bitch who killed Becky. You're chasing your goddamn tails around in a circle while the cocksucker is getting away. I thought perhaps Ted could help me talk some sense into you."

The lawyer put his hand on Miller's shoulder. "Just hang on, Walt. Let's not make the situation any more complicated than it already is."

Ogilvie turned from his client to us. "That said, I hope you can understand that Mr. Miller is obviously feeling a great deal of frustration about the pace and the direction of your investigation."

I gave him a few seconds, then said, "With all due respect to you and your client, Mr. Ogilvie, we're actively pursuing this investigation from a variety of angles, not all of which Mr. Miller is privy to. And if he were to cooperate with us, rather than challenging our judgment at virtually every turn, we'd probably be making a lot more progress. For the moment, we have a warrant to execute. And knowing how anxious Mr. Miller is for the investigation to move along, we should probably be getting to the business at hand rather than standing out here in this heat arguing about it."

I handed the search warrant to Miller who passed it on to his lawyer. "Can they keep doing this to me?" Miller asked.

Ogilvie took a couple of minutes to read through the document then looked up to Miller and sighed. "Well, it appears that they can, at least for the moment. They have a lawful warrant and the best thing to do here, Walt, is to cooperate with them."

Miller shook his head. "So, what are you looking for today?"

"We'd like to take a quick peek into the safe in your study," Maggie replied.

Miller's eyes widened and he looked from Maggie to his attorney and finally to me. "The safe in my study? What the hell could that possibly have to do with anything?"

"We're still looking for that missing life insurance policy, sir," I replied.

"But that safe is my private property! It has my things in it, and I'm the only one who has the combination. Even Becky didn't know what it was. I've told you repeatedly that I know nothing about this goddamn life insurance policy, and there's no way it could possibly be in the safe in my study."

"Then why don't you take us up there and show us, sir," I replied. "And then we'll get out of your hair."

Miller crossed his arms, his feet firmly planted in the driveway. "I will not show you, There is nothing in that safe that is any business of yours."

Again, the lawyer touched Miller's shoulder. "They have a warrant, Walt. The judge says that they *can* look in the safe. Let's just get it over with."

Miller swiped Ogilvie's hand away and glared at me. Finally, he shook his head and said, "Let's go."

We followed him into the house and up the stairs with his lawyer trailing behind. Miller led us into his study, flipped on the lights, and walked over to a wall on the far side of the room. The wall held a number of photos and posters, most of which reflected moments apparently captured during Miller's college basketball career. He lifted a framed poster off the center of the wall and set it gently on the floor, leaning the poster against the wall. A small safe had been built into the wall behind the poster. Miller spun the dial through a series of numbers then pulled the handle to open the door of the safe.

It refused to budge. Miller shook his head and cursed softly. His hand trembling slightly, he worked the dial again, more slowly this time. Then he threw the handle and this time it released. He pulled the door open and started to reach into the small safe. "Just a moment, Mr. Miller," I said, stepping in front of him. "You need to let me do this."

He reluctantly moved away. I pulled on a pair of latex gloves and turned to look into the small barrel safe. Immediately behind the door were five stacks of bills, each stack bound by two rubber bands. Saying nothing, I stepped over and set the currency on Miller's desk. Returning to the safe, I found that the only thing remaining was a stack of documents, perhaps eight inches thick, that was also secured by a red rubber band.

As Maggie, Miller and Ogilvie watched, I moved back to the desk, removed the rubber band from the papers and began to sort through them. The document on top was Miller's degree in Business Administration from ASU. That was followed by his high school diploma and three handwritten letters. Immediately behind the letters was a plastic sleeve, perhaps five inches wide and eight inches long. And in the plastic sleeve was an insurance policy on Becky Miller's life in the amount of one hundred thousand dollars. Carefully holding the plastic sleeve by its edges, I looked to Maggie and said, "I believe this is what we came for."

"What the fuck do you mean?"

Looking genuinely stunned, Miller reached out to grab the insurance policy away from me. I batted his hand away and said, "Sorry, Mr. Miller, but this is now a piece of evidence. I can't let you handle it."

"But what is it? I swear to you that I have *never* seen that before. How the hell did it get into my safe?"

"I'm sure we wouldn't have any idea, sir," Maggie replied softly. "But you did just tell us that you were the only one with the combination to the safe."

Miller whirled to face his lawyer. "Ted, Jesus! Don't just stand there like a fucking moron. *Do* something. This is some kind of a goddamn trick. He must have brought that in here with him and slipped it into my things."

Ogilvie shook his head. "Just calm down, Walt. We all know that he didn't do that. There's got to be some other explanation."

"But what? I'm telling you there's no way that policy could have been in my safe."

"Well, clearly it *was* in your safe, Mr. Miller," I said, "and you've insisted a couple of times now that you're the only one with the combination. At this point, we'd like you to come downtown with us so we can discuss this situation in greater detail."

"You're *arresting* me?"

"No, sir, we are not arresting you. But we would like you to come down to the department for a formal interview."

"Why can't you talk to Mr. Miller here?" Ogilvie asked.

"Because, counselor, at this point, we'd like to have his answers on tape."

"You're telling me you now consider him to be a suspect?"

"No. I'm simply telling you that we have some questions that we would like to ask him downtown."

Miller looked back and forth from Ogilvie to me, watching the exchange. "And what if I refuse to go?"

"As I've told your attorney, Mr. Miller, you are not under arrest. You're free to refuse the request. But, frankly, if you do, then we've got to wonder why. You insist that you want us out looking for this mystery man that you claim killed your wife. But every time we turn around we keep bumping into things that bring us back to you. The quicker we get those things explained to our satisfaction, the quicker we can be moving this investigation in other directions."

Miller shook his head. "This is complete bullshit."

He looked away for a long moment, staring first at the open safe and then at the insurance policy that Maggie had slipped into an evidence bag. Finally, he looked back to me. "Can I bring Ted along?"

"If you like. That's your right. You can follow us downtown."

Saying nothing more, Miller gathered up the remaining documents and the cash from the top of his desk and returned them to the safe. Then he locked the safe and hung the poster back in front of it. He and Ogilvie followed us down the stairs and back out to the driveway. The two men got into the lawyer's car, backed out of the driveway and then followed us away from the house.

Maggie turned back and looked over her shoulder at the car trailing behind us. "You think he did her, Sean?"

"I don't know, Maggs. On the one hand, he's got a girlfriend who's pressuring him to do something about the wife. The wife's got him by the balls financially and has decided that she wants out. Then, coincidentally, the night that she decides to confront him with all of this, she goes missing. Add to that the business with the life insurance policy, and ol' Walt starts to look like a pretty good candidate.

"On the other hand, though, why in the hell would he lie about the insurance policy? Could he honestly be so stupid as to think we wouldn't find out about it, especially once he tried to cash it in? Even more important, where the hell is the girlfriend? In some respects, she looks like the much better candidate. She's suggested to Miller that they'd both be better off if the wife were out of the picture, and she quits her job and hits the road practically the second it happens. Hell, if Miller didn't keep stepping into another giant pile of shit every time we talked to him, she'd be the one I'd be after at the moment."

Nodding, Maggie shifted back around in her seat and tugged her skirt back down in the general direction of her knees. "So, what's your grand plan?"

"My grand plan is to get him the hell away from his house for a couple of hours or so, while we try to get another warrant. On the basis of what we've got now, a judge should let us search the house, his bars, and his vehicles for a saw and for blanket or a tarp or some such thing that he might have used to wrap up the body and dump it into the canal. On the off chance that he did kill his wife and was dumb enough to leave evidence around the house, I didn't want to leave him there with an opportunity to get rid of it now before we could get back with the warrant."

Maggie nodded and reached for her phone. "Sounds like a plan. I'll call the Sergeant and have him get somebody working on a judge."

24

Becky's Uncle Charlie was an avid coin and stamp collector, and on Becky's eighth birthday, he gave her a bag of Buffalo Nickels, a coin album, and a guide. Becky filled about half of the spaces in the album almost immediately and over the course of the next several years, she managed to fill all but four of them. Even now, nearly thirty years later, every time a clerk gave her a handful of change, Becky carefully checked the nickels, looking for the extremely rare issues that would complete her collection.

She realized, of course, that she would need some money for expenses before the divorce was final. If Walter decided to contest the divorce, she would need money for that as well. And if he did decide to fight her, Becky wanted her own personal assets well hidden in a place where Walter could never get at them.

Accordingly, in the few weeks after she'd hatched her plan, Becky converted nearly two hundred and fifty thousand dollars from her investment account into cash. When her broker asked why she was liquidating so much stock, she explained that she was going to invest the money in her husband's business. But as the checks came in from the broker, she converted them to cash and put the money into her safe deposit box.

Silently thanking her late Uncle Charlie for all of the time they spent together while he showed her his collection and helped her with her own, Becky bought a couple of current guides and spent a considerable amount of time on the Internet researching current coin prices. Armed with the information and shopping carefully, she then visited a number of different dealers, paying cash for a small number of investment grade coins. For the time being, she put the coins into a new safe deposit box at a bank different from the one where she and Walter kept their accounts. There they would be safely out of Walter's reach, and if and when she needed them, the coins would be an easily transportable, totally liquid, and completely untraceable source of cash.

On Tuesday, June first, Becky went to the bank and withdrew twenty-five thousand dollars from her money market account, leaving only a couple of hundred dollars in the account. She took the money in cash and set ten thousand dollars aside for traveling expenses. She spent the other fifteen thousand on three coins, including a beautiful 1925-S Buffalo Nickel that would have thrilled her uncle.

By the following morning, Becky was finally ready to execute the plan that she so carefully designed. By that time, she had purchased enough extra cosmetics and other personal care products to last her for a month without having to take any of the things from her bathroom that she had already opened and begun to use. She'd also picked up a few new clothes so that she could be gone for a month without having to take anything that Walter or anyone else was likely to notice missing from her closet.

By that morning, she'd fabricated the diary entries and had scattered the other clues that she hoped would lead the police to Jerry Malcolm, the private detective; to the life insurance policy; and ultimately to Walter's private safe.

A little after ten o'clock that Wednesday morning, Becky made one last entry into the diary. Then she packed the extra clothes and personal items into two large gym bags that she purchased specifically for this purpose. She counted out five hundred dollars, which she left in her purse, and then packed the rest of her cash in an envelope and slipped the envelope into the bottom of one of the gym bags. She set the bags out in the hall, returned to the bedroom and booted her computer. She updated her iPod, then copied everything except her music files onto a flash drive and shut down the computer.

She slipped the flash drive into the pocket of her jeans. Opening the file drawer in the desk, she found her mother's Visa and American Express cards. As her mother's executor, she paid the credit card bills in the wake of her mother's death, but for whatever reason, she was never been able to bring herself to close the accounts and cut up the cards. Now she slipped the credit cards into her jeans as well.

From the bottom drawer of the desk she retrieved the life insurance policy, along with the combination to Walter's safe. She walked down the hall to his study, set the poster on the floor, opened the safe, and set Walter's cash on the desk. Back at the safe, she took out the bundle of documents and slipped the insurance policy into the middle of the documents, saying a silent prayer that Walter wouldn't notice it before the police tumbled to the existence of the safe.

She returned the documents and the cash to the safe, then closed the safe and used a cloth to wipe off any fingerprints that she might have left. She hung the poster back in its proper place and wiped that down as well. Out in the hall, she picked up the gym bags, carried them downstairs, and put them into the trunk of her Audi.

Back in the kitchen she made a turkey sandwich and forced herself to eat it, even though she was so keyed up that she didn't feel hungry. She rinsed off the plate and put it into the dishwasher, then spent ten minutes going through the house watering her plants. She assumed that Walter would ignore the plants in her absence and that most of them would not survive the thirty days that she planned to be gone, but she watered them anyway.

Becky put the watering can back in the pantry, walked into the foyer, and stood there for a couple of minutes looking into rooms around her. The house was completely quiet, save for the ticking of the clock that sat on the mantle above the fireplace.

Only then, standing there alone in the silence, thinking about the years that she and Walter had spent together in this house, did she begin to have second thoughts. Maybe this wasn't the best way to approach the problem. Perhaps even Walter had not been enough of a bastard to deserve what she planned for him. But then she flashed again on the e-mail message that caused her to set this plan into motion, and she remembered the anger she felt when her husband so casually deflected his lover's insistence that they would both be better off if Becky were no longer in the picture.

Becky took one last look at the photo of her mother that sat on a table in the living room. Then she walked back through the kitchen, into the garage, and got into her car. She still had one last thing to do before leaving Phoenix.

## 25

Walter Miller and Ted Ogilvie followed us back to the department and Maggie and I escorted them up to the third floor and into an interview room. The room was equipped with both audio and video monitoring equipment and I checked to make sure that the machines were recording. The four of us took chairs around the table, and once everyone was settled, I noted the date and time for the record and identified the people in the room. Then I turned to Miller and said, "Mr. Miller, for the record, can you tell us again when you last saw your wife?"

On the ride over, Ogilvie had apparently counseled his client that the wisest course of action would be to cooperate, to answer our questions, and to lose the attitude he displayed back at his home. In a quiet voice that betrayed no anger or frustration, Miller said, "Wednesday, June second, at approximately seven thirty in the evening."

Maggie and I had agreed that in order to establish a rhythm, I would ask the bulk of the questions to open the interview. "And what was her mood like at that time?" I asked.

Miller shrugged. "Fine. She was perhaps a little quieter than usual, and she didn't eat much of her dinner. I asked if she was feeling okay, and she said that she was — that she just wasn't very hungry."

"What did you talk about over dinner that night?"

"Nothing — just the usual. I talked about how my day went. Some friends asked us to go to dinner at Eddie V's on Saturday night, and we talked about that a bit. But like I said, Becky was kind of quiet. I did most of the talking."

"Did you have an argument about anything that evening?"

For a second, the hostility returned to Miller's face, but the expression passed, and he simply shook his head. "No. We did not argue. Everything was fine."

"What did you do after dinner?"

"I went upstairs to my study while Becky cleaned up and put the dishes in the dishwasher. About seven thirty, she came up to the study to say goodbye — that she was leaving for her book club meeting."

He paused for a moment, blinking back a tear. His voice breaking a bit, he looked down at the table. "She came over to my desk and gave me a hug. I asked her if she'd be home at around the usual time, and she said that she would. I told her to have a nice evening, and she left. That was the last time I ever saw her."

"What did you do after your wife left, Mr. Miller?"

"I went back to my office and did some paperwork. I was there from a little before eight o'clock until just after ten."

"And your staff will verify that?"

"Yes."

"What did you do when you left your office?"

"I went back home. I watched the last couple of minutes of the Channel 12 News, and then watched the *Tonight Show*. When Becky hadn't gotten home by eleven, I called her cell. I didn't get an answer and that's when I started to get worried."

"And what did you do then?"

"I watched the rest of the *Tonight Show*, and then started channel flipping. I kept calling Becky's cell every fifteen minutes or so, but I never got an answer. By midnight I was starting to panic. I called Jennifer Burke, and she told me that Becky left her place at about ten thirty and that she was coming straight home. When I told her that Becky didn't come home, Jennifer started to panic too.

"I called a couple of Becky's other friends, but they hadn't seen or heard from her either. Finally, at around three in the morning, I called the police and reported her missing."

"When you were making these calls, did you use your home phone or your cell phone?"

"My cell. I hardly ever use any other phone."

I nodded to Maggie and she said, "Let's turn to the matter of the life insurance policy, Mr. Miller."

He threw up his hands. "I swear on my mother's grave, Detective McClinton, that I don't know anything about it. Becky and I never discussed it, and for the life of me I can't imagine why she would have gotten it. After you told me about it the other day, I called Ted Lane. He says that he did get a message from me and that Becky did come in and sign the papers. He says the company sent the policy out two weeks after that. But I swear I never sent him any message. I never knew that Becky went in and signed the papers, and I never saw the policy until this afternoon."

"How do you suppose that the policy wound up in your safe, then?"

He sighed loudly. "I have absolutely no idea. There is no way it could have gotten in there. Once the safe was installed, I changed the combination to one that only I would know, and I never wrote it down or told anyone what it was. I told Becky that when I died, she'd have to have it drilled." His voice started breaking as he continued, "I told her I'd leave a few hundred bucks in the safe so that she could pay the guy on the spot."

"But you see the position that leaves us in, don't you, Mr. Miller? On the one hand, you claim that you know nothing about the life insurance policy. But then we find the policy in your safe and you also swear that no one but you could get into the safe? What are we supposed to think here?"

Miller shook his head. Ogilvie leaned over, rested his hand on his client's arm and said, "What you're supposed to think, detectives, if you'll pardon my saying so, is that my client is telling you the truth here. If he were guilty of anything — which he isn't — the easiest thing in the world would be for him to tell you that Mrs. Miller had the combination to the safe and that she must have been the one who put the policy in there. There'd be no way for you to disprove his statement and no way for you to prove that he knew anything about the policy.

"His insurance agent admits that he never talked to Walt personally about the policy. Walt did not sign the application. He did not pay the premium. And the policy was not delivered to him. But instead of taking the easy way out, my client is being honest with you. And as he says and is obvious, something really odd is going on here."

Ogilvie leaned back in his chair, as if daring us to defy the logic of his argument. But letting the issue go for the moment, I said, "Let's go back to the issue of your relationship with Cathy Stanton, Mr. Miller. When was the last time you saw her?"

"June first, the afternoon before Becky went missing."

"Was that the last time you heard from her?"

Miller shifted in his chair and looked down at the table. In a quiet voice, he said, "No. The last time I heard from her was on Thursday, the third. I had an e-mail from her that afternoon."

"What did it say?"

"She told me that she was going to take some time to think things over. She said she didn't want to see me again until I agreed to leave Becky for her."

"And how did you react to that?"

He shook his head. "I didn't. By that time, I was worried sick about Becky. I didn't want to have anything to do with Cathy. If she didn't want to see me, that was fine. I sure as hell didn't want to see her at that point."

"And you've heard nothing from her since?"

"No."

"When we talked to you the other day, you told us that Ms. Stanton suggested that you and she would be better off if your wife was completely out of the picture. Tell us about that conversation."

Again, looking at the table rather than at Maggie or me, he said, "Cathy was getting increasingly impatient. She wanted me to leave Becky so that the two of us could be together permanently. I told her that I couldn't do that. As I told you the other day, I used the excuse that I couldn't afford to leave Becky — that it would destroy me financially.

"We had the argument again one afternoon last month as I was leaving her apartment. When I said that I couldn't afford to divorce Becky, Cathy said that maybe we'd have to do something else. She said it in sort of a teasing way, and when I asked her what she meant, she said that under the circumstances, we'd both be better off if Becky wasn't in the way anymore. I brushed it off, but in an e-mail that night, I told her that she shouldn't even joke about a thing like that. She sent me a reply, saying that she wasn't joking."

"Did you save those messages?" Maggie asked.

Miller nodded.

I said, "When we first talked about this, you told us that you didn't mention this conversation because you thought that Stanton wasn't serious. Are you still certain of that?"

He shook his head. "I don't know, Detective. I still believe in my heart that Becky was killed by someone who managed to get into her car while she was on her way home from the book club. That's the only thing that makes any sense to me. But I can't figure out why Cathy decided to take off, and I have no idea what the hell is going on with this damned life insurance policy."

We were interrupted by someone who tapped lightly on the door. I got out of my chair, cracked the door open, and the sergeant handed me the search warrant for Miller's home, car, and businesses. I closed the door, turned back to Miller and Ogilvie, and said, "Gentlemen, we need to take a trip back to Mr. Miller's home."

## 26

Becky Miller debated the wisdom of confronting her husband's lover before leaving town.

On the one hand, she really wanted the satisfaction of looking the woman in the eye and telling her that she was welcome to Walter. On the other, though, seeing Stanton might complicate the plan that Becky had set into motion. If, once she disappeared, Stanton stepped forward insisting that she had seen Becky and suggesting that Becky left Phoenix of her own volition, perhaps the police would believe her and would not even bother to investigate Becky's disappearance. Looking at it another way though, if Becky disappeared and Stanton suggested that she was the last person to have seen her, it might actually reinforce the impression that Walter and his lover had conspired to get rid of Becky.

In the end, Becky decided to leave it up to fate. She would stop by Stanton's apartment on her way out of town. If the woman was home, Becky would deliver her message. If Stanton was not there, Becky would simply disappear, leaving everyone to wonder what might have happened to her.

She drove into Stanton's apartment complex a little after noon. She located Stanton's unit, then parked in a visitor's slot two buildings away and walked back. The complex seemed extremely quiet, and Becky assumed that most of the residents were probably at work at this time of day. The drapes and blinds in virtually all of the apartments were closed against the blazing sun, and Becky passed no one on her way back to Stanton's door.

She double-checked to make sure that she had the right unit number and then rang the bell. She barely heard the sound of the bell ringing inside but could hear nothing else. She waited twenty or thirty seconds and then rang again. Thirty seconds after that, Becky concluded that Stanton was not at home. But just as she was turning to leave, she heard the sound of heels clicking across a tiled floor inside the apartment.

Becky turned back toward the door, and a couple of seconds later someone released the deadbolt and opened the door. Becky found herself facing a hard-looking blonde. Becky knew that Stanton was allegedly six years younger than she, but up close, the woman looked considerably older than thirty-two. She was dressed in a skirt, a top that accented the swell of her breasts, and a pair of high heels. Her makeup, Becky thought, looked a tad overdone for the middle of the day, but she realized that the total package would certainly draw the attention of a good many men. "Cathy Stanton?" she asked.

Standing with one hand on the doorknob, Stanton looked Becky up and down, appraising her for a couple of seconds. "And you are?"

"Your boyfriend's wife. I thought it was time that we had a little chat."

Stanton's eyes widened a bit, but she showed no other sign of surprise. "I think you must have the wrong apartment,"

"Oh, I don't think so, Cathy. Now do you want to have this discussion out here in front of your neighbors or do you want to invite me in so that we can talk about things civilly?"

The woman rested her free hand on her hip, looked Becky up and down again, and then pulled the door open the rest of the way. "Sure. Why the hell not?"

Becky walked through the door into the small entryway and Stanton closed the door behind her. The two stood there for a moment, taking each other's measure, then Stanton led Becky into the living room without offering her a seat. Becky took a few seconds to appraise Stanton's taste in décor, noting an issue of *People* magazine and a paperback romance novel on the large glass-topped coffee table. There were no other books, magazines or newspapers anywhere in sight.

"Just what is it that you think we have to discuss?" Stanton asked.

Turning her focus back to the woman, Becky said, "Nothing, actually. I just wanted to stop by and tell you in person that I'm divorcing Walter. He's all yours now."

Stanton folded her arms across her chest and nodded her approval. "And about time, you frigid bitch. He deserves a woman a helluva lot better than you."

Becky allowed Stanton a slight smile. "And you think you're that woman?"

"Damn straight. I make him a whole lot happier than you do."

"Well, I don't doubt that, at least for the time being. But how long do you think that's going to last when Walter's reduced to living with you here in this lovely apartment and can barely scrape two nickels together? How happy do you think you'll be then?"

Stanton shook her head. "You think you're so fuckin' smart. Miss High and Mighty. You think you've got Walter by the balls just because you loaned him a little money from your mama's inheritance. Well, I know a couple of pretty good lawyers and we'll see who's laughing by the time they get through with you."

"Indeed we will, Cupcake. But I didn't just loan Walter a *little* money. I loaned him a *lot* of money — more than he'll ever be able to repay and still keep all his bars. He'll be lucky to hold on even to a couple of them, and even at that he'll be in hock up to his eyeballs. And you better believe that by the time we get to court and the judge sees the pictures my detective took of you and my husband together, I'll come away with the house and virtually all of our other joint assets. Poor Walter will be lucky to get away with the clothes on his back."

Stanton laughed. "You hired a detective? Jesus. ... Well, I wouldn't be too cocky, you fuckin' bitch. Somebody's liable to take you down a notch or two."

"Maybe, honey," Becky replied, returning the laugh. "But you can bet your life that it won't be some stupid little cocktail waitress whose cunt is a hundred times more agile than her brain."

The rest of it happened in a blur.

Stanton's right hand flew out and slapped Becky hard across the face. Becky took a step back in the direction of the couch and raised her arms to cover her face as Stanton swung at her with a closed left fist. But as Stanton stepped forward, attempting to put some weight behind the blow, the heel of her right shoe got tangled up in the thick pile of the carpet. Slightly off balance, she landed a glancing blow on Becky's upraised arm.

Becky took another step back and attempted to get out of Stanton's way. But Stanton's heel remained caught in the carpet and as Becky stepped aside, Stanton fell, her left side turning to the floor.

And in the millisecond before Stanton's shoulder hit the floor, the left side of her head slammed into the corner of the heavy glass coffee table.

27

Walter Miller and Ted Ogilvie followed us back to Miller's home, trailed by Greg Chickris and Elaine Pierce, two other members of the Homicide Unit who would assist us in the search. Our warrant empowered us to look anywhere in Miller's home, his vehicles, and his various businesses for a tool that might have been used to sever his wife's head and arms from her torso, and for anything that might have been used to wrap up the body before dumping it into the canal.

The crime lab techs had already been through Becky Miller's car and had come up with nothing to indicate that the car had ever been near the site where we believed her body had been put into the canal. That certainly didn't mean that the car hadn't been there; it only meant that, if it had, someone had been clever enough — and careful enough — to leave no evidence of it. The judge now also gave us permission to have the techs go through Walter Miller's Lexus looking for dirt and gravel or other evidence to suggest that it might have been at the scene.

Ogilvie had barely been able to restrain his client when we told him what we were going to do. Miller flew into a rage, insisting that we were trying to take the easy way out by framing him for his wife's murder rather than working to find the person who actually killed her.

We attempted to explain that the inconsistencies in his own story, along with the evidence of his relationship with Cathy Stanton, left us no alternative other than to consider him a serious suspect. Again, we tried to assure him that if, in fact, he was innocent, the most sensible thing to do would be to cooperate with us so that we could eliminate him from suspicion and move the investigation in another direction. But Miller was having none of it.

Back in the car, Maggie said, "So what did you think of the lawyer's comment about the life insurance policy?"

"I don't know, Maggie. On the one hand, I guess it makes some sense. If Miller had told us immediately that his wife knew the combination to the safe, we'd at least have to consider the possibility that she could have put the policy in there and that he knew nothing about it.

"But I'd bet my paycheck for this week that the guy was genuinely shocked when we told him that we knew about the safe. And I think he was so damned anxious to keep us from getting a look at the cash he's got squirreled away in there that he blurted out the truth without considering the consequences. His immediate reaction was to insist that his wife didn't know the combination to the safe, and I believe him. And, having been so insistent about it, he really couldn't change his story once he or his lawyer realized that he would have been better off telling us that she *did* know what the combination was."

Maggie nodded. "Yeah, that's what I think too. He had to've been the one who put it in the safe, but I still can't shake the feeling that something very screwy is going on here. Again, what the hell did he have to gain by lying about the policy in the first place?"

"I don't know. Maybe he figured that the fact that they bought the policy so soon before his wife was murdered would automatically point a finger at him, and so, dumb as it sounds, he pretended not to know about it. Maybe he thought that later, when the investigation had gone cold, he could "accidentally" discover the policy when he was going through his wife's things and claim that she took it out without his knowledge."

"Maybe," she replied, not sounding entirely convinced.

"Look, Maggie," I said. "I grant you that the guy does seem genuinely befuddled and righteously angry. But he certainly did have motive to kill his wife so that he could be with his girlfriend and not get stripped to the bones in a divorce settlement.

"He also certainly had opportunity. He's got no one to vouch for him between ten o'clock that night when he left his office and three a.m. the following morning when he reported his wife missing. Say for the sake of argument that she comes home from the book club and tells him that she knows about Stanton and wants a divorce.

They fight. In the heat of the moment, he bangs her over the head or something. She winds up dead, and in a panic, he cuts her up, disposes of the head and arms, and dumps the torso in the canal. And while he's doing all of this, he's periodically calling his wife's friends, pretending to be alarmed by the fact that she isn't home yet.

"He uses the wife's car to dump the body, being careful to use a piece of plastic or something in front of the driver's seat so that he doesn't track any dirt into the car that we can match up to the bank of the canal. Then he wipes down the area around the driver's seat, but forgets to return the seat to the position that she would have used. He leaves the car at the Basha's, makes his way home somehow, waits until three o'clock, and reports her missing."

"And you think, what — he cuts off the head and arms, not realizing that we'll be able to identify the torso from DNA? He hopes that it will remain unidentified and his wife will officially be a missing person forever?"

"Damned if I know. From a logical standpoint, that makes no sense. If he wants to be free to inherit his wife's money and eventually to marry Stanton, then he needs his wife's body to be identified. But in the heat of the moment, he may not have been thinking that clearly. Maybe he was simply trying to confuse matters and point us in any direction but him."

***

Back at Miller's home, Greg and Elaine began working in the house, while Maggie and I went through the garage. Fifteen minutes after we got there, several members of the crime scene response team arrived. They would tow Miller's Lexus to the police garage for a thorough examination. They would also conduct tests looking for evidence indicating that Becky Miller's body might have been dismembered somewhere in the house or the garage.

One wall of the garage was lined with storage cabinets, and in one of the cabinets we found several thick plastic sheets that had obviously been used as drop cloths for a number of painting projects. We collected those so that the lab could check them, but saw nothing else that might have been used to roll up a body and transport it.

A pegboard on one wall of the garage held a number of tools, including two carpenter's saws and a curved pruning saw with a red handle and a row of jagged teeth. To the naked eye, the carpenter's saws appeared pristine, but Gary Barnett, the lead tech, set the saws on a piece of plastic that he spread across a workbench and sprayed the saws with luminol just to be sure. Once he'd done so, he instructed his assistant to close the garage door and turn off the lights. We waited a couple of minutes until the light in the garage door opener finally went out, plunging the garage into darkness. But neither of the saws showed any trace of blood.

The pruning saw also appeared almost perfectly clean to the naked eye, save for a tiny spot of what looked like rust at the point where the blade was joined to the handle. Again, Barnett carefully set the saw on a piece of plastic, sprayed the saw with luminol, and told his assistant to turn off the garage lights. The garage again went dark, and on the work bench the entire length of the pruning saw slowly began to glow with a bluish-green light as the iron in the hemoglobin on the saw reacted to the chemicals in the luminol.

Barnett instructed his assistant to snap the lights back on and I looked over to Maggie. She nodded her head, and together we walked over to the spot where Miller and Ogilvie were standing on the opposite side of the garage. "Mr. Miller," I said, "We're placing you under arrest."

## 28

Cathy Stanton hit the floor with a sickening thud.

She came to rest on her back between the coffee table and the couch, her head contorted toward her right shoulder at a totally impossible angle. Her blue eyes looked vacantly in the direction of the ceiling. She hadn't uttered a sound on the way down.

Frozen in place, Becky stared at the other woman in horror and in total disbelief. For a very long moment, her mind simply refused to process the signals that her eyes were transmitting to her brain. Then, as the initial shock dissipated, Becky dropped to her knees on the floor and touched her fingers to Stanton's throat, going through the motions of checking for a pulse that she knew she wasn't going to find. Her own heart racing, she sat back on her legs and willed herself to think rationally.

The obvious thing to do was the right thing. Call nine-one-one. Wait for the police, and explain to them that Stanton had swung on her. Becky had only defended herself. It was all a horrible, tragic accident.

But who would believe her?

The police would find her in the home of her husband's mistress. The mistress was lying dead on the floor, and there were no witnesses to support Becky's version of the story. She would have to admit that she had deliberately confronted the woman — why else would she be here? And once she confessed to that, would the police not jump to the logical conclusion that she had provoked Stanton; that the two had struggled, and that Becky deliberately pushed Stanton in the direction of the table?

No one could ever prove that Becky had come to Stanton's apartment intending to kill her rival. But the circumstances being what they were, Becky realized that she might very well be charged with manslaughter or some other such offence, and that she might very well be convicted of it. How could she defend herself against such a charge?

Her second option was simply to run.

Becky had conceived and set into motion a plan in which she had intended to disappear under circumstances that would lead the authorities to believe that she had been the victim of foul play. She then scattered a variety of false clues to point the police at Walter and his girlfriend.

Having completed her preparations, she'd intended to leave her car in a parking lot somewhere. She would then walk a few blocks to a pay phone, call a cab, and take the cab to the Phoenix bus station. There she would buy a ticket for cash and take a Greyhound to San Diego. Using her mother's credit cards, she would check into a residence hotel and live quietly under the radar.

After letting Walter squirm for a month or so, she would return to Phoenix, claiming total ignorance of the events she had set into motion. She would tell anyone who asked that she simply wanted to be completely alone so that she could think things through after discovering Walter's affair. For this reason, she did not disclose her intentions even to Jennifer Burke, her closest friend. She would later apologize to Jennifer and pray that, in the end, her friend would understand and forgive her.

If they asked, she would tell the authorities that she left her car, took the bus, and used her mother's identity so that Walter would not be able to trace her movements and follow her. She had no idea that Walter would bring in the police and that they would confiscate her computer and read the secret diary in which she poured out her feelings upon learning of her husband's betrayal.

As for the life insurance policy, she would insist that the whole thing *was* Walter's idea and that she opposed it. The evidence being what it was, who could ever prove otherwise?

She would insist that she spent her time away in virtual seclusion; that she had paid no attention whatsoever to the news from Phoenix, and that she had heard nothing regarding the events that transpired in her absence. She was very sorry, she would say, for any worry or inconvenience that she might have caused anyone other than her husband.

And she would say that, after thinking very carefully about her situation, she reluctantly concluded that her only option was to consult an attorney and file for divorce. She would ask for the house and for a healthy percentage of the other assets that she and Walter had jointly accumulated. Considering that her husband had so callously deceived her, she would also ask for a reasonable amount of alimony. And, of course, she would also insist that Walter immediately repay the money she loaned him.

That had been the grand scheme. But now, staring down at the lifeless body of "Cathystanton2," Becky realized that she needed another plan.

## 29

We read a stunned Walter Miller his rights, cuffed him, and stuffed him into the back seat of my Chevy for the ride to the station. Ted Ogilvie promised to follow us back downtown and warned Miller not to say a word to us outside of the lawyer's presence. We were hardly out of the drive, though, before Miller began protesting his innocence. "Please, you've got to believe me. I loved Becky. I would never have harmed her. I don't understand what's going on here."

Ideally, we would have preferred to interview the man back at the station in a formal setting, with the audio and videotapes rolling. But, of course, back at the station, his lawyer would be in the room, advising him not to answer our questions.

We'd advised Miller of his rights, including the right to remain silent, but if he was determined to talk, we were more than willing to listen. Looking at him in the rearview mirror, I said, "Trust me, sir, we'd like to believe you, but certainly you can see how the evidence is piling up against you. First there's the business with your mistress. Then there's the matter of the life insurance policy, and now we find a saw in your garage that's covered with blood. What would you have us think about all of that?"

Tears of frustration welled up in his eyes. "I don't know, Detective Richardson. I swear to God I don't fuckin' know. Cathy, yes — that was a huge mistake, and I've admitted to that. But that's all it was, just a mistake. As I tried to tell you, I would've never left Becky for her, and I swear on everything that's holy, I would've never killed Becky to be with Cathy.

"As for the insurance policy, I have absolutely no explanation. I know how bad it looks, but I'm being completely straight with you. I never heard of it until you told me about it, and I have no idea in hell how it could have gotten into my safe. There is just *no* way that could have happened."

"And the saw," I said, glancing again into the rearview mirror. "What were you using that for?"

"Nothing! Jesus Christ, I swear I haven't touched the thing in months — years maybe. I got it when we moved into the house and I used it to prune trees and shit like that. But for the last three years at least, we've been using a landscape maintenance service. I haven't done hardly a damn thing in the yard in all that time."

"Does the landscaper's crew use their own tools or do they use yours?" Maggie asked.

"They bring their own. I suppose that they might use one of mine if they forgot a tool or something, but as far as I know, they never have."

"How do you explain the blood on the saw?" I asked.

Miller shook his head. "I can't. Your test must be mistaken. How could there be blood on a goddamn pruning saw? That makes no fuckin' sense at all."

"Kind of like the insurance policy?"

"Exactly. I don't know how I can convince you of any of this. Hell, I listen to myself and it makes no goddamn sense to me either. But it's the truth. I didn't kill Becky, and the most frustrating thing about it is that the guy who did kill her is still out there somewhere. Honest to God, at this point I don't even care what happens to me. I just don't want the asshole who did this to her to get away with it."

Some fifteen seconds passed while Miller stared out the window. Then Maggie turned and laid her arm across the back of the seat. Looking at Miller, she said in a quiet voice, "Look, Mr. Miller, I'm not saying that we don't believe you. But we're about twenty minutes away from the station. Once we get there, we're going to take a formal statement from you, and wheels are going to be set into motion. Once they start rolling, it's going to be very hard to turn them in a different direction."

"What the hell is that supposed to mean?"

"It just means, sir, that if there's anything else you want to tell us, now would be the best time to do it — before we get back to the interview room and start formally putting things on tape."

"Like what?"

"I don't know, Mr. Miller. That's what I'm asking you. We all know that Mrs. Miller discovered your relationship with Ms. Stanton. We also know from her diary that the night she disappeared, she was going to confront you about your affair. Let's say, just for the sake of argument, that she came home from the book club that night and told you she wanted a divorce. Let's say, again just for the sake of argument that she insisted that you repay the money you owed her. And let's say that you argued about it. Maybe something bad happened. Something that nobody planned. An accident — something that was really nobody's fault.

"Let's say that you might have panicked — really, anybody might have. Instead of calling for help, maybe you tried to make it look like something altogether different had happened. And maybe now you regret it. It's just that if something like that *might* have happened, now would be the time to tell us, before things get entirely out of hand and you get charged with a crime way more serious than the one you might have actually committed."

From the back seat, Miller stared at Maggie and shook his head in disbelief. "Nothing like that happened, Detective. Nothing. Read my lips if it will help. I did not kill Becky — not accidentally or any other way."

"Let's look at it another way, then, Mr. Miller," I suggested. "Where do you suppose Cathy Stanton has taken off to, and why do you suppose she decided to run?"

"I swear I don't know the answer to either question, Detective. I had no idea that she had disappeared until you told me."

"Do you still believe that she could not have been involved in your wife's death?"

Miller hesitated for a moment, looking out the window at the traffic passing on the other side of the freeway. "I don't know what to think about that anymore. I told you before, I didn't for a second think that she was serious about how we'd be better off without Becky. But I can't explain why she'd take off like that. I guess something like that could've happened."

"Has Ms. Stanton ever been to your home?" Maggie asked.

"Hell no. I'm not a total idiot."

"In other words, then, she would have had no way of knowing that you even had a pruning saw, let along know how she might get at it?"

"No."

I signaled the turn for the exit that would take us back to headquarters. "Is it possible, somehow, that Ms. Stanton decided to take matters into her own hands?" I asked. "Maybe she confronted your wife? Again, maybe something happened that no one intended. In a panic, Ms. Stanton appealed to you for help, and anything you might have done to help her was completely after the fact?"

Miller waited a long moment and then looked from Maggie to me. "You two are both totally fuckin' nuts. I have nothing more to say to you."

## 30

Back at the department Walter Miller was photographed and fingerprinted. Upstairs in Homicide, we formally questioned him a second time, recording his answers as before, but we learned nothing new. He steadfastly insisted that he knew nothing about the circumstances of his wife's death. He had not killed her. To the best of his knowledge, Cathy Stanton had not killed her. And certainly, he had not assisted Stanton in disposing of the body and covering up the murder after the fact. At the conclusion of the session, Miller was booked and taken to jail, pending his arraignment.

Having completed all the relevant paperwork, I dropped onto my usual stool in the bar at Tutti Santi a little after nine o' clock. Stephanie poured me a drink and recommended the shrimp pasta special for dinner. The bar was fairly quiet and over the next hour we discussed the events of the day in and around the drink orders she was filling for the handful of diners who were still scattered through the restaurant.

At ten fifteen I paid my check and as Stephanie returned my credit card, she leaned across the bar and said, "Here's a novel idea. Why don't you give me a few minutes to finish up here and then tonight we could go over to your place for a change."

I'm not sure what she read into the panicked expression on my face, but still leaning close she smiled and whispered, "What? You didn't make your bed this morning? You left your underwear in the middle of the floor? You haven't dusted in a month? C'mon, Sean, we always go to my apartment. Even though you live just up the street, I've never even *seen* your house. Don't you think it's about time you took me home and showed me your stamp collection or something?"

"Jesus, Steph, I don't know if that's such a great idea..."

"Don't tell me. You've got another woman stashed away there that you don't want me to know about?"

"Not hardly. It's just that…"

"Good, that settles it. I'll pour you a splash of Jameson to calm your nerves, and I'll be ready to go in about fifteen minutes."

There was no way to explain to her that it was going to take a lot more than just a splash of whiskey to calm my nerves. Since the morning Julie last left the house, no other woman had ever set foot in it, especially not for the reasons Stephanie had in mind. But I knew that this moment was bound to happen sooner or later and there was no graceful way to get around it.

I told myself that I was being silly and that my relationship with Stephanie was not in any way a betrayal of Julie, even if it did involve taking another woman into the bed we had once shared together. I had honored my commitment to Julie for the last nine years and would always cherish her memory. More than that, I knew her well enough to know that she would have encouraged me to move on as I would have encouraged her, had our situations been reversed.

Sitting there sipping the whiskey, these were the things I told myself. But I really wasn't buying it.

\*\*\*

Ten minutes after leaving Tutti Santi, Stephanie pulled her car into the driveway beside mine. Leaving the car in the driveway, I sorted through my keys, looking for the one that would unlock the front door and trying to remember the last time I'd used it. We stepped into the darkened entryway and I snapped on a couple of lights. Stephanie took a few steps into the house and then stood for a moment, appraising the great room, dining area and kitchen. Finally, she turned, gave me a bright smile and said, "Very nice. And surprisingly clean and neat for a single male. What were you so nervous about?"

"Nothing." I shrugged. "Would you like a glass of wine?"

"That sounds great."

She followed me into the kitchen and I pulled a bottle of Chardonnay from the wine storage unit that was built in under the kitchen counter. I poured a couple of glasses and handed her one as she continued to appraise the house. She took a sip of the wine, nodded her approval, and I said, "It's a really nice evening. Would you like to take the wine outside?"

"Sounds good. I'd like to see the yard."

I snapped on the pool lights, opened the sliding glass door, and led her over to the small couch at the fire pit, overlooking the pool. Once there, I lit a couple of candles and we settled onto the couch. It *was* a perfect evening, at least weather-wise, with temperatures in the low eighties, a very light breeze, and a billion stars, give or take a few, shining in the clear night sky. Stephanie took a drink of the wine and sat for a moment, playing with her wineglass. Then she looked over to me and said, "Can I ask you a really personal question?"

"Sure."

"Well, I can't help noticing that this is a pretty spectacular house in a very upscale neighborhood. I'm quite sure that in this city, homicide detectives aren't paid all *that* well…"

"Believe me, they aren't. Especially not in this economic climate."

I waited a moment, toying with my own wine glass, then said, "Julie's father is extremely wealthy. When she and I got married, he gave us a very large check and told us that it was specifically for the purpose of making the down payment on a house. As a banker, he was convinced that for most people, their home is their principal investment, and he wanted to give us a good start in that department."

She nodded. "I don't mean to be snotty, but of course I don't know the man. Was he worried that you wouldn't be able to support his daughter in the style to which she'd become accustomed?"

"No, not at all. In fact, quite unlike her sister and her greedy, grasping mother, Julie was never very interested in material possessions. She could have been happy living virtually anywhere. She was her father's favorite, though, and perhaps for that reason, he wanted us to be comfortable. To some extent, he may also have been trying to make up for the fact that Julie's mother strongly opposed our marriage and refused even to attend the wedding."

"Did it bother you when he made such a grand gesture?"

"No. It was clear that the gift came from the heart and with no strings attached. In some cases, I'm sure, a guy might do something like that in an effort to demonstrate that he's still the alpha male in his little girl's life and he might try to use it as a means of exerting control over his daughter and her husband. But it wasn't like that with John. He's a real salt-of-the-earth kind of a guy who pulled himself up by the bootstraps and became a huge success. But for all of that, he's very modest and self-effacing, and he insists that a lot of his success was due to good luck as much as anything else.

"Unlike Julie's mother, he took to me right away, and it was clear when he gave Julie away that he was handing her into my care. He understood and was happy to accept the fact that I would now be first in her affections. So, no, I wasn't bothered. I accepted the gift in the spirit in which it was given."

I refilled the wine glasses and we sat for a while, saying nothing, enveloped in the silence of the night around us. I had no idea what Stephanie might be thinking, but her question had unleashed a flood of bittersweet memories for me. We passed fifteen minutes or so sitting that way, then she set down her glass, took my hand in hers and said, "I think there still must be a couple of rooms that I haven't seen yet."

I drank the last of my wine, set the glass on the table next to hers, then rose to my feet and pulled her into my arms. I spent a moment, looking into her eyes, wondering what she might be thinking. I pulled her close and kissed her, then I walked her back into the house.

I paused in the great room to kiss her again, then led her down the hall to the bedroom. The door was standing open and I flipped the switch on the wall to turn on the lamps that flanked the bed. Standing in the doorway with her arm around me, Stephanie turned her head to look into the room and saw the picture of Julie that was sitting on the nightstand. A couple of long seconds elapsed, then she loosened her grip on my waist and dropped her head into my chest. "Maybe this wasn't such a bright idea, after all," she whispered.

I put my arms around her, holding her loosely. "Maybe it wasn't. I'm sorry Steph."

"No, don't apologize. It was my idea and I could see that you were reluctant. I just really didn't understand why until now. I should have had more sense."

"But I *am* sorry. It's just…"

She pulled away a bit and put a finger to my lips. "It's all right," she said. "You don't have to explain, but I think I'd better be going."

I walked her out to her car and she insisted that she'd be fine driving home alone. Again, I slipped my arms around her and pulled her close. "I *do* care for you, Steph."

"I know you do, Sean. And I hope you know that I care for you too. Sorry about putting you in such an awkward spot tonight."

We held each other for another minute or so, then she kissed me goodnight and got into her car. I stood in the driveway, watching until her taillights disappeared into the dark. Then I shook my head, walked back into the house and went to bed, alone with my memories and regrets.

## 31

Becky Miller stood and checked her watch. It was twelve thirty-seven p.m., which meant that she had roughly five and a half hours before Walter would be home, expecting dinner to be on the table. Forcing herself to remain calm, she went into Stanton's kitchen. Under the sink, she found a pair of rubber gloves that Stanton might have worn while washing dishes. She also found a box of plastic bags in a size to fit the garbage can under the sink, as well as a number of cleaning supplies.

She put on the gloves and pulled a garbage bag from the box. Back in the living room, she again knelt next to Stanton's body. To Becky's surprise, Stanton's wound had bled very little. The blood was already clotting in the woman's hair and, fortunately, none of it had yet dripped onto the carpet. Becky steeled herself, then lifted Stanton's head from the floor and slipped the plastic bag over Stanton's head. Grateful that she no longer had to look at the woman's face, she gently laid Stanton's head back on the floor.

With a dust cloth from under the sink, Becky then carefully wiped down the few surfaces that she had touched before putting on the gloves. That done, she took twenty minutes to walk carefully through the apartment and the attached garage, taking a mental inventory of Stanton's possessions, and assessing the resources that might be available to her. Then, trying to avoid looking at Stanton's body on her way through the living room, she went back into the kitchen, sat down at the small table, and considered her options.

Her principal advantage, she decided, lay in the fact that she and Stanton were roughly the same height and weight. They also had much the same hair color and skin tone. No one looking at their faces would confuse them, of course, nor would anyone comparing their fingerprints. Stanton also appeared to be a little bustier than Becky, but Becky calculated that most likely this would not be a problem. Then it suddenly struck her that Stanton might have had implants, which definitely *would* be a problem.

And what it the woman had a tattoo somewhere?

Reluctantly, Becky got up and went back to the living room. Grabbing Stanton's body by the heels, she dragged it out into the center of the living room. Leaving the bag over Stanton's head, Becky carefully removed Stanton's shoes, blouse, skirt, and bra.

It took all the strength of will that Becky possessed to force herself to touch the body. Irrationally, she feared that the moment she did, Stanton would sit up and lock her in a death grip from which she would never escape. But thankfully, that didn't happen, and as Becky began to examine the body, it remained lifeless and inert on the floor in front of her.

Becky discovered, to her relief, that Stanton did not have implants. And once released from the support of a well-engineered bra, Stanton's breasts did not appear to be noticeably larger than her own.

Becky carefully examined the front side of the body, but found no tattoos, birthmarks, or other blemishes that might distinguish Stanton's body from hers. The thought crossed her mind that, given the circumstances, it would be more than a little sacrilegious to pray that her luck would hold, but Becky said a silent prayer anyway. Then she rolled the body over and looked at Stanton's backside.

Looking at the other woman's butt, it struck Becky for the first time that Stanton's muscle tone was not nearly as firm as her own. But she was already planning that Stanton's body — or at least the bulk of it — would be discovered under conditions where this would not be apparent. Thankfully, Stanton did not have any distinguishing marks on her backside either.

Becky sat for a moment, mentally taking stock of her own body and comparing the image with that of the one that lay before her on the floor. The she pulled her left knee to her chest, reached down, and removed the silver ring from the second toe of her left foot. Picking up Stanton's left foot, she slipped the ring onto the second toe and then laid Stanton's foot back on the floor.

## 32

On Friday morning, the crime lab technicians reported that the blood on the pruning saw from Walter Miller's garage matched that of the torso that we had pulled from the canal. Regrettably, the techs did not find Miller's fingerprints on the saw, nor did they find anyone else's. Whoever had attempted to wipe the blood from the blade of the instrument had also carefully wiped down the handle.

Technically, there was no way we could actually tie that particular saw to Miller, save for the fact that it had been found in his garage. In the car with Maggie and me, and later in the formal interview at the station, Miller had not denied owning the saw — or at least one exactly like it, but we knew that his attorney would almost certainly raise the issue once we got to trial.

The crime scene techs spent the next couple of days going through Miller's home, garage, and car, looking for any particle of evidence to suggest that he had murdered his wife in the house or garage, that he had dismembered her body somewhere in his home, and that he had then transported the torso to the canal in his Lexus. But in the end, they came up empty.

Maggie and I spent that time interviewing the employees at all of Miller's bars, particularly with reference to the night his wife had disappeared. None of them offered any useful information, and we found nothing to suggest that Miller might have committed the crimes in one of his bars rather than at his house.

Miller was arraigned the morning after his arrest and, given the gory circumstances of his wife's death, plus the added angle of Cathy Stanton's disappearance, the arraignment attracted national attention. The vultures from the various cable news networks as well as from all of the local channels set up shop outside of the courthouse and several of them covered the arraignment live from the steps of the building.

The case against Miller was strong, but certainly not airtight: He had a mistress, and the computer techs uncovered the e-mails in which he expressed his love for the woman and his regret at the fact that they could not be together always. By his own admission, a divorce would have been financially ruinous, while the death of his wife would provide him with a financial windfall.

Only weeks before her death, Miller made arrangements to take out a life insurance policy on his wife, with a provision for double indemnity in case of an accidental death. He denied any knowledge of the policy, but the policy was found in his home safe. And by his own repeated admission, he was the only one who had access to the safe.

Miller had no alibi for the night of his wife's disappearance and murder, and the saw used to dismember her body was found hanging in his garage. Again, by his own admission, he owned the saw, or at least one exactly like it.

Ultimately, then, Miller had the means, motive and opportunity to have committed the crime. We still did not know, however, whether he might have conspired with his mistress to do so. Stanton suggested that they would both be better off if Becky Miller were no longer in the picture. But did she actually assist Miller in removing his wife from the picture? Although he continued to deny it, Maggie and I still wondered if perhaps Cathy Stanton might have actually committed the murder and that Miller came to her rescue, dismembering the body, and dumping the torso into the canal.

Immediately following Miller's arrest, we issued a nation-wide bulletin, looking for Stanton as a person of interest in the case. Given the publicity that the story had attracted, the "Missing Mistress" became a prominent fixture on the cable news channels.

Tracking Stanton's credit card receipts, we learned that two days after Becky Miller was reported missing, Stanton drove her Buick to Amarillo, Texas. Using her credit cards, she'd purchased gas in Flagstaff, Arizona, and again in Albuquerque, New Mexico. Using her Visa card, Stanton checked into a Holiday Inn Express in Amarillo and stayed one night. From the hotel, she reserved a seat for the following afternoon on a United Airlines flight from

Amarillo to Boise, Idaho. But she did not appear for the flight, nor did she attempt to cancel the reservation.

And from there the trail went completely cold. Both Stanton and her Buick had disappeared, and there had been no activity on any of Stanton's credit cards since she paid for her room at the Holiday Inn.

Given that Stanton's face was now constantly in the public eye 24/7 — on one cable network, even with its own theme music — reported sightings of the woman flooded in from all over the country and from at least three foreign countries as well. But none of the reports panned out and it was beginning to look as though the woman had simply dropped off the face of the earth.

Then, four days after we arrested Walter Miller, the phone on my desk rang. Looking at the caller ID, I saw the name and number of Andy Sheldahl in the crime lab. I picked up the phone and wished him a good morning.

On the other end of the line, Sheldahl sighed heavily and said, "Houston, we have a problem."

## 33

Still wearing the yellow rubber gloves, Becky Miller retrieved Cathy Stanton's purse from the kitchen counter. She opened the purse and spread the contents out across the counter. In the purse, Stanton carried a wallet, her keys, a cell phone, a small address book, and the usual assortment of cosmetics — lipstick, eyeliner, a fingernail file, and the like. There were also two lubricated condoms, and Becky wondered if Stanton intended to use the condoms with Walter or if there were other men in Stanton's life in addition to Becky's husband.

In the wallet, Becky found Stanton's driver's license. The photo was two years old and, like most drivers' license photos, it was not particularly flattering. But looking at it, Becky decided that, unless someone looked closely at the photo, she might be able to pass off the license as her own.

The wallet also contained three credit cards — a Visa, a MasterCard, and a Discover card. Becky wondered what the limit on each card might be and how close to the limits Stanton might have been running.

Behind the credit cards were two photos. The first was of an older woman who bore a slight resemblance to Stanton, and Becky speculated that it was probably Stanton's mother. The second was a snapshot that had obviously been trimmed to fit the plastic holder in the wallet. It showed a smiling Stanton kneeling on a lawn somewhere, with each of her arms around a small girl. The two girls were also smiling. One of them was looking at the camera, the other at Stanton. Her nieces, perhaps?

Becky shook her head and closed her eyes for a moment. Then she closed the wallet and returned everything but the keys to the purse. There were five keys on the ring, one of them obviously a car key. Becky went out into the garage, got into Stanton's Buick, put the key into the ignition, and turned the key to the first position.

The radio came to life in the middle of "Missing," by Everything But the Girl, and Becky realized immediately that Stanton must have been a KYOT Loyal Listener. In the glow of the instrument panel, she saw that Stanton left her a half a tank of gas. In the trunk, Becky found the spare tire, which appeared to be fully inflated, along with the usual tools. Otherwise, the trunk was empty.

In addition to the Buick, the garage contained a number of boxes. The boxes were all sealed with packing tape, and Becky assumed that they contained things that Stanton was storing, rather than things that she might be using on a regular basis. It did not appear that Stanton had any tools in the garage, and Becky figured that she didn't have time to sort through the boxes, checking to see if Stanton might have stored some tools in one of them. Leaving the garage, Becky tried two keys in the door leading from the garage to the house before finding Stanton's house key.

Back in the kitchen, she found a box of one-gallon freezer bags in a drawer next to the refrigerator. She pulled a bag from the box and went upstairs to the bathroom off the master bedroom.

On her earlier pass through the apartment, she had seen Stanton's red toothbrush in a holder near the sink, and a hairbrush lying on the vanity. She put both items into the freezer bag, then zipped the bag shut. She walked back down the stairs and set the freezer bag near the front door. Then she looked again at her watch: two fourteen p.m.

34

I pushed through the door of the computer lab and found Andy
Sheldahl waiting for me at his desk. Taking the chair in front of the
desk, I said, "What the hell is our problem?"

Sheldahl shook his head and said, "It's the Miller woman's
diary."

"How so?"

"Well, we pulled the diary off the computer and printed it out for
you. Then, when you brought in the husband's computer, we set
hers aside and went to work on his. Once we found the e-mails you
were looking for, Bill went back to the wife's machine and began
going through it more carefully.

"Without making this any more complicated than it has to be,
whenever you create or modify a Microsoft Word document, like
this diary, the software not only records and saves the information
that you type into the document, it also records a significant amount
of data about the document itself. This metadata, as it's called, isn't
readily visible to the user, and most people don't even know that the
program does this. But the information is sitting there on the
machine, and any competent computer forensics tech can get at it.
That's what Bill did. And checking the metadata, he discovered that
the dates that Miller recorded in the diary don't match up with the
metadata that the software recorded."

"What sort of discrepancies are we talking about here?"

"Major."

He turned and snagged a folder from the cluttered worktable
behind him. Turning back, he opened the file and set it on the desk
facing me. Picking up a pencil, he pointed to the date that Becky
Miller had made her first entry in the diary.

"You notice," he said, "that she dated the first entry in the diary
as April sixth." Moving the pencil down the page, he said, "The
second entry is dated April eighth."

"And now you're telling me that the entries weren't made on those dates?"

"Nope. They were not made until May twenty-fourth — seven weeks later. In fact, the first seven entries were all made on that date, not on the dates that Miller indicated in the diary. A number of other entries were made on May twenty-fifth, and all but the last entry were made on May twenty-seventh. The last one was made on June second, the day before her husband reported her missing. That's the only entry when the date given in the diary conforms to the date that she actually made it."

"So, the goddamn thing is a fake?"

Nodding, he said, "Almost certainly. I gather that there's no question about the fact that Miller was having an affair and that the wife hired a P.I.?"

"No, none."

"So, the content of the diary may be fairly legitimate?"

"It sure as hell looked like it to us."

"Well, I don't know what to tell you here, Sean. All I know is that the damned thing was written over the space of four days, and not eight weeks as the dates in the diary itself would indicate."

"No chance of a mistake — a computer glitch of some sort."

"None."

"So, the next logical question is, who wrote the damned thing? Was it Miller herself, or is someone else trying to jerk us around here?"

Sheldahl just shook his head. "Thankfully, Sean, that's your department, not mine."

*\*\**

Back on the third floor, I found Maggie in her office and relayed the news.

"What the fuck?" she said.

"My sentiments exactly. There are, obviously, three possibilities: Either Becky Miller wrote the damned thing, or her husband wrote it, or some third party did it. The question is whether even the husband, let alone a mysterious third party, would have had access to the computer on the three dates that the diary was written."

156

"What were the dates?"

"May twenty-fourth, twenty-fifth and twenty-seventh — a Monday, a Tuesday and a Thursday."

Maggie thought for a moment, then said, "You'd assume that the husband would likely have been at work on those days. Where was she?"

"Give me a second, and I'll look."

I went back across the hall to my own office and retrieved the printout of Becky Miller's calendar. I checked the dates as I walked back to Maggie's office. Shaking my head, I said, "Nowhere. At least she had nothing scheduled on her calendar for the Monday and Tuesday. Wednesday, she worked at the bookstore, and on the Thursday, she had a one o'clock lunch with Jennifer Burke. Nothing before or after the lunch."

"So, she could have been at home pounding out the diary. And if she wasn't, she probably would have been at home and would have known if someone else was using her computer all that time."

"That's what I'd assume. And having read both the diary and the e-mails that the husband sent to Cathy Stanton, I'd say that the diary doesn't sound like something he would have written."

Maggie shrugged, exasperated. "Well, we sure as hell can't ask Becky Miller about the damned thing."

"No, but maybe there's somebody that we can ask."

## 35

Unfortunately, there was only one bathtub in Cathy Stanton's apartment, and it was upstairs in the master bath.

With a little under four hours before Walter would expect dinner on the table, Becky returned to Stanton's living room and stood looking down at the body lying on the carpet in the middle of the room. Sighing heavily, she reluctantly bent down, slipped her own arms under Stanton's, and began dragging the body in the direction of the stairs.

For the first time in her life, Becky understood the concept of "dead weight." Although her husband's lover was probably not more than a hundred and thirty-five pounds, it felt like her lifeless body weighed a couple of hundred pounds. Becky strained at the task, tugging the body some fifteen feet to the foot of the stairs. Then she stopped to take a break. After a minute or so, she looked up the stairs, shook her head, and again hooked her own arms under Stanton's.

Bracing herself on the first step, Becky jerked the body back another couple of feet. Then she moved her right foot up to the second step and tugged again. After a couple of minutes of effort, she was standing on the fourth step, and Stanton's body was sitting at an awkward angle on the second.

The apartment's thermostat was set somewhere in the middle seventies, but what with her overloaded nervous system and the strain of the weight she was attempting to move, Becky found herself perspiring heavily. It took her ten long minutes to work the body a third of the way up the stairs. She took a break, then glanced at her watch and returned to the task at hand. Ten minutes later, she'd pulled Stanton a little over halfway up the stairs. Again, she allowed herself a short break.

Breathing heavily, Becky sat down on the stairs above the body. Stanton's head rested on the second step below Becky, and the body, naked save for panties and the white plastic bag tied over its head, lay splayed out down the stairs. After a couple of minutes had passed, Becky used her arm to wipe the sweat from her brow and returned to work. Fifteen minutes later, she braced herself and jerked Stanton's upper body across the top step.

Relieved to have the obstacle of the stairs behind her, Becky found a renewed strength and tugged the body through the master bedroom and into the bathroom.

The lip of the large white tub was about thirty inches off the floor. Becky dragged the body parallel to the tub, then sat on the stool for a moment pondering the situation. After a minute or so, she rose and grabbed Stanton by the ankles. Pulling at the ankles, Becky rotated the body ninety degrees, raised Stanton's legs, and set them over the edge of the tub.

The body was now resting at a right angle to the tub, with its knees hooked over the edge of the tub and the lower half of its legs dangling into the tub. Again, Becky positioned herself behind Stanton's head and slipped her arms under Stanton's. Straining, she lifted the woman's body about four inches off the floor, but as she did, Stanton's legs fell back out of the tub onto the floor. Cursing, Becky looked again at her watch: Three hours and ten minutes to dinner.

Again, she maneuvered Stanton's legs into the tub and resumed her position behind the body. Again, she took a grip through Stanton's arms, this time lacing her fingers and locking her hands together below the other woman's breasts. Taking two deep breaths, Becky flexed her knees. And then, summoning every fiber of strength she could muster, she rose, lifting Stanton with her, while pushing forward at the same time.

For a moment, Stanton sat awkwardly on the lip of the tub, leaning out and threatening to fall back against Becky. Straining to hold her position, Becky braced her legs, leaned her shoulder into Stanton's naked back, and took one more quick breath. Then she rolled the body forward into the tub.

\*\*\*

In the closet in Stanton's guest bedroom, Becky found a large suitcase and an overnight bag. She left the suitcase in the master bedroom and took the smaller bag into the bathroom. Attempting to avoid looking at the body that was now lying awkwardly in the tub, she scooped most of Stanton's cosmetics and other personal items out of the vanity drawers and into the overnight bag.

She found a few more things in the medicine cabinet above the sink and added them to the bag. In the medicine cabinet, she also found a prescription bottle half full of Valium. She was about to drop the Valium into the bag with the rest of the items, but hesitated, thinking about it for a moment. Then she set the Valium off to the side on the vanity.

Becky zipped the small bag shut then stepped out of the bathroom and closed the door behind her. In the bedroom, she pulled open the closet doors, revealing the bulk of Stanton's wardrobe. Then she forced herself to sit down on the bed for a few minutes and think carefully through the situation. She would only have one chance to get this right; she couldn't afford to make a careless mistake at this point.

Ten minutes later, she looked at her watch and rose from the bed. For the moment, at least, she'd done all she could here, and she'd need at least a couple of hours back at her own home.

## 36

Jennifer Burke answered her door, apparently dressed for work in a black blouse and skirt and the same heels she'd been wearing the first time I'd interviewed her. She was also wearing a perfume I hadn't noticed before, and again, I was struck by the fact that she was an exceptionally attractive woman. She led me up the stairs into her living room. Declining a cup of coffee, I said, "I understand that you're doubtless busy, Ms. Burke, and so I'll try to be brief and get out of your way."

She waved her hand in a gesture of dismissal. "Please don't worry about that at all, Detective Richardson. If there's anything I can do to help, I'm more than happy to do so, no matter how much of my time it might take."

"I appreciate that, and I'll get right to the point. When we talked earlier, I asked you if Ms. Miller kept a diary. You said that you didn't know for sure, but that you didn't think so."

Burke nodded, and I continued. "Well, in the course of the investigation, we picked up Ms. Miller's computer, and on the computer, we found a diary. Apparently, she'd begun the diary when she began to suspect that her husband was cheating on her. It looks like she was using the diary as a sounding board — someplace where she could privately work through her thoughts about her situation. The diary covers a period of about six weeks, and ends just before she disappeared."

Burke shifted in the chair and pushed a stray hair back into place. "Well, if so, it's news to me. As I said before, she did tell me that she suspected that Walter was cheating on her. But she was reluctant to talk about the situation in any detail, and she said nothing to me about starting a diary.

"Still, I'm not surprised by the fact that she did. Becky was a very methodical person — a very organized and disciplined thinker. It would be very much in character for her to create a diary and use it as a device for sorting out her feelings and considering her options."

I pulled a sheaf of papers from an envelope. "Would you mind taking a few minutes to look at the diary?" I asked.

Burke knotted her brow. "I take it you have a good reason for asking?"

"Yes, I do. But to be honest, I'd prefer not to explain the reason until you've looked at it."

She nodded. "It's just that Becky was my best friend. If she chose to confide her thoughts to a diary, as opposed to sharing them with me, I'd hate the thought of violating her privacy, even under these circumstances."

"I understand that, Ms. Burke, and I wouldn't ask you to do it if it weren't important."

"Okay," she said, extending her hand.

Burke took the pages, leaned back in her chair, and began reading. When she was about halfway through the document, tears glistened in her eyes and began slowly trickling down her cheeks. Saying nothing, I handed her my handkerchief. She set the pages down in her lap, took the handkerchief and wiped at her eyes.

"I'm sorry," she said in a breaking voice. "It's just that reading her words on these pages — it's almost like she was sitting here in the room talking to me. I miss her so much ..."

"I understand. And I'm sorry to put you through it. But that gets right to the heart of the matter. Does this diary sound to you like something that Ms. Miller might have written?"

Again, a look of confusion rose in her face. "Absolutely. The phrases that she uses, the voice ... As I said, it's almost as if I can hear her speaking the words. Why do you ask — is there some doubt about the fact that this is Becky's diary?"

"Not really. It purports to be her diary and we found it on her computer in her bedroom. We just wanted to make sure that she actually wrote it."

"I see," she said, the expression on her face clearly suggesting that she didn't understand at all.

We sat quietly for a minute and Burke looked at me expectantly as if waiting for a further explanation. When I offered none, she leaned forward in her chair, closing the distance between us. Again, I found myself acutely aware of the scent she was wearing. Raising her eyes to mine, she said in a soft voice, "Is your case against Walter a good one?"

I hesitated a moment, then said, "I'll tell you in confidence that we believe it is. At this point, all of the evidence points in his direction, and there was certainly enough of it to charge him with the crime. Naturally, we're still investigating the case and searching for all of the evidence we can find. And, of course, you can never predict what's going to happen at a trial, but that said, the case against him does look very strong."

She nodded almost absent-mindedly. Then maintaining her position on the edge of the chair, she focused on me again. "So why are you worried about the diary?"

Again, I hesitated. Under normal circumstances of course, I would never discuss a key piece of evidence with a potential witness unless it was absolutely necessary. However, this appeared to be one of those situations. If anyone were likely to be able to explain why Becky Miller had forged her diary, that person was most likely to be Miller's best friend. I leaned forward in my own seat and said, "We have a problem with the diary."

Saying nothing, Burke arched her eyebrows and waited for me to continue.

Although there was no one else to hear, I lowered my voice and said, "I'll ask you to please keep this in strictest confidence, Ms. Burke. We can't afford to have this leaking out until we can determine what it actually means. But the problem is that Ms. Miller seems to have manufactured the diary for some purpose and we're not sure what her motive might have been for doing so."

Burke shook her head. "How do you mean?"

Pointing at the papers in her lap, I said, "You will have noticed that Ms. Miller apparently began the diary about seven weeks before she was reported missing. She then apparently made an entry in the diary every two or three days, explaining what she had discovered and describing her reactions to those discoveries."

"Okay … I saw that. … Sure."

"Well, our problem is that she didn't actually make the entries on the dates indicated in the diary. Save for the last entry, which she wrote on the date that she disappeared, she wrote the entire document over the space of four days about a week and a half before the night she went missing."

I explained how the computer techs discovered the inconsistencies in the diary and asked Burke if she could think of any reason why Miller might have manufactured the document. She leaned back in the chair and ran a hand through her hair. After thinking about it for a moment, she said, "To be completely honest, Detective Richardson, I don't know why she would have created the diary like that. I want to believe that there was a logical reason — a good reason — why she would have done it, and consequently I may be grasping at straws here."

"Please do. I'd really appreciate knowing your thoughts on the matter."

Moving forward in the chair again, Burke rested her elbows on her knees and tented her hands together under her chin. "You say that she actually began the diary on May twenty-fourth?"

"Yes."

"Which was a couple of days after she apparently got the report from the detective she hired, confirming her suspicions about Walter?"

"Yes."

"Well, as I said before, Becky was a very methodical person. Once she knew for certain that Walter was having an affair, she would definitely want to think through her options very carefully before taking any action — that's simply the kind of person she was."

"Okay."

"So, knowing Becky, I would say it's very possible that, once the detective confirmed her suspicions, she might have wanted to create a chronological record of the way the events had unfolded. She might very well have sat down with a calendar and, over the space of a few days, created a record of what she had known or suspected and when she had first known or suspected it — just as a means of helping her sort out her own thoughts.

"In fact, she may not have intended to deceive anyone. This was a private record that she created for her own use. I notice that in the pages you gave me, there is no reference to this record as a diary. In fact, it appears to have no title at all. Is it possible that your technicians found this document and simply assumed that it was a diary when Becky had intended it to serve an entirely different purpose?"

"Now that you explain it in that light, I suppose it's a possibility. You're absolutely right, of course, Ms. Miller never actually described the document as a diary, although it certainly looks like one at first glance."

"Well, I'm sorry, Detective, but that's the best explanation I can come up with at the moment. And I'm being perfectly honest when I say that, knowing Becky as I did, the other explanation makes more sense to me. I can't imagine why she would have deliberately fabricated a phony diary. What would she have to gain by doing so?"

"Nothing that I can think of."

*\*\**

Burke walked me to the door and I thanked her for her help. She insisted that it was no trouble whatsoever and that she was happy to do whatever she could to bring her friend's killer to justice. Standing in the entryway, she said, "I miss her so much, Detective. I still find myself automatically reaching for the phone because I've thought of something I wanted to talk to her about. And every time I do, it catches me up short."

"I understand," I said. "And again, I'm sorry for your loss."

## 37

Becky Miller made a quick trip to the bank, opened her new safe deposit box, and retrieved the coins that she purchased over the last several weeks. Twenty minutes later, she pulled her car into the garage and breathed a huge sigh of relief when she saw that Walter had not decided to come home early for some reason.

She pushed the button to close the garage door behind her, then flipped on the garage lights. Walter had installed a pegboard along one long wall of the garage, and his tools were carefully arranged, hanging on hooks from the pegboard. Becky stood for a moment, looking over the tools, then took the pruning saw off of its hook. She popped the trunk on her Audi and set the saw into the trunk next to the bags that she'd packed earlier.

A row of cabinets lined the other long wall of the garage. Becky opened one of the cabinet doors and found a number of plastic drop cloths that she and Walter used for painting and for other such projects. A thick, heavy-duty plastic cloth, nine-by-twelve, was stacked on top of the pile. Becky picked up the cloth and dropped that into the trunk as well, along with a roll of duct tape.

Thankfully, the gym bags were not jammed full. She opened one of the bags and carefully repacked it, arranging her coin collection in and around a couple of sweaters and some underwear. Then she put the saw, the plastic cloth and the duct tape into the second bag and zipped both bags shut.

Becky closed the trunk, reached into the car, and scooped up her purse along with the plastic bag containing Cathy Stanton's toothbrush and hairbrush. Then she switched off the garage lights and let herself into the house. Upstairs in her bathroom, she ran some hot water on the corner of a washcloth, then took Stanton's toothbrush and hairbrush out of the bag.

Using the wet end of the washcloth, Becky wiped the handles down carefully, then dried them with the other end of the cloth. She spent thirty seconds or so handling the two instruments in an effort to leave as many of her own fingerprints on them as possible and then put the toothbrush in the holder on the vanity and laid the hairbrush in the place normally occupied by her own. She dropped her own tooth and hair brushes into a fresh plastic bag from under the vanity and carried the bag into her closet.

When she'd been packing to leave for only a month, Becky had deliberately taken nothing that anyone might possibly notice missing. Now that she was packing to leave forever, she opened the jewelry box that sat on the dresser in the closet and began sifting through the pieces.

The things that she most hated to leave were those that had belonged to her mother. Sorting through them, she selected a pair of plain gold earrings that were among her mother's favorites. She slipped the earrings into the pocket of her jeans, certain that neither Walter nor anyone else would ever notice that they were gone. She spent a few precious moments handling a few of the other pieces, remembering the way they had looked on her mother. Then, reluctantly, she closed the jewelry box and went downstairs.

From a shelf in the living room, she picked up a framed picture of her mother and another of her parents together that had been taken on their honeymoon at the St. Francis Hotel in San Francisco. Her mother always insisted that Becky was conceived at the St. Francis, and the photo was one of Becky's favorites.

Upstairs at her computer, she removed the photos from their frames and scanned them into a file. She spent another thirty minutes scanning a variety of documents from the files in her desk and then again copied all of her computer files to the flash drive she'd used earlier in the day.

At five fifty-five, Becky shut down the computer and put the flash drive back in her pocket. She returned the photos to their proper places in the living room and put the bag with her toothbrush and hairbrush into the trunk of her car. At six o'clock, she pulled a container of marinara sauce from the freezer, put it in the microwave, set the dial to "Defrost," and punched "Start." And at ten minutes after six, Walter walked through the door and asked if she could use a drink before dinner.

***

Dinner consisted of the marinara sauce tossed with some pasta, and a salad that Becky threw together at the last minute. Mentally reviewing the things that she still had left to do, she nursed a glass of Shiraz and absent-mindedly picked at her dinner while Walter went on at length about some problem he was having with the company that supplied paper goods for his bars. Halfway through dinner, Walter interrupted his monologue and asked Becky if everything was okay. "You seem a little distant and distracted," he said.

Becky insisted that she was fine and apologized for seeming preoccupied. She told Walter she'd simply been thinking about the book that her group was going to be discussing tonight. Walter nodded, wrapped up his story about paper towels and napkins, and then announced that he was going up to the study for a little bit before going back to the office.

Becky remained sitting at the table for a couple of minutes after Walter left the room. Then she got up, put the dishes in the dishwasher, and stood for a moment in the middle of her kitchen, thinking about all of the time and effort she put into its renovation. It was the perfect kitchen, and as she stood there alone for the last time in her life, the events of the day overwhelmed her.

Tears flooding down her cheeks, she wondered how she could have possibly found herself in such a position.

Why couldn't she have simply thrown Walter out and filed for divorce like any normal, intelligent woman would have done? Why did she have to get so goddamned cute about it all? Why did she have to confront Cathy Stanton, and why in the hell had she provoked her like that?

How in the name of God could things have spun so completely out of control?

How could everything have gone so terribly wrong?

## 38

"What do you mean, it's not really a diary at all?"

I sat in the guest chair in Maggie's office, drinking a Coke and recounting my conversation with Jennifer Burke. Maggie peeled and sectioned an orange and was eating it for her afternoon snack.

"I didn't say that it *wasn't* really a diary, Maggs. I'm simply telling you that Burke suggested it might not be."

She swallowed a bite of the orange. "What do *you* think?"

"I don't know what to think. I suppose the idea makes some sense, especially if Miller was the methodical, organized person that Burke describes. On the other hand, it sure as hell looks like a diary to me."

"Me too. So, what do we do now, Sherlock?"

"Let's assume for a moment that the document is not simply Miller's effort to organize her thoughts. Let's assume that she really did intend that someone would find it and regard it as her diary. Who did she expect would find it — who was she writing it for?"

Maggie leaned back in her chair and thought about it for a couple of seconds. Leaning forward again, she said, "Two possibilities come to mind. Maybe she writes it for the husband. Maybe she imagines some dramatic scene where she tells him that she knows he's been screwing another woman. She tells him that she's suspected it for some time and that she's heartbroken about it. And maybe she really is. Maybe she plans to hand him a copy of the diary as proof of how his cheating has devastated her."

"And the other alternative?"

"Maybe it's for her lawyer. Maybe she's decided to divorce the cheating bastard and she's forging 'evidence' to prove how she's been emotionally destroyed by what he's done. Maybe she's planning to ask a judge for a big whopping settlement."

"Actually, I like your second idea better. It fits more logically with the Becky Miller that Burke has described for me. But I still don't like the fact that she did it."

Maggie narrowed her eyes. "You're not beginning to have doubts about our pal, Walter, are you?"

I shook my head. "No, not really. There's just too much evidence pointing in his direction, and he's told us too damned many stories that don't add up. But I don't like this diary business and I can't figure out why his girlfriend went on the lam. And I especially don't like the fact that we can't find the damned woman."

Maggie swallowed the last bite of the orange and wiped her lips with a paper napkin. "'His girlfriend went on the lam?' Jesus Christ, Richardson, you've been reading way too many hundred-year-old detective novels."

## 39

Stephanie had a rare Friday night off and earlier in the week I'd made a reservation for dinner in the lounge at Vocé. I arrived at her apartment a little after eight o'clock and she greeted me at the door wearing heels and a simple black cocktail dress. I gave her a quick kiss and then, still holding her hand, stepped back for another appraisal. "You look spectacular," I said.

Smiling, she said, "Thanks. You so rarely see me in anything other than the clothes I wear for work that I wanted to look especially nice tonight."

"And so you do," I said, kissing her again.

Traffic was fairly light and on the way to the club we talked very generally about our respective days. Neither of us broached the subject of her visit to my house. I found a reasonably decent parking place and as we walked toward the door, Stephanie took my hand and said, "I'm really looking forward to this."

Once inside, we waited briefly while the hostess seated another party, then she led us to a table near the stage. The lights had been dimmed; candles flickered on each of the tables, and smooth jazz played softly through the excellent sound system. As usual by this time on a Friday night, the small, intimate room was already packed with people enjoying dinner and drinks while they waited for the band to begin the first set.

We each ordered a cocktail and while we waited for the drinks we took a look at the menu. As was the case in nearly all of my favorite restaurants, the menu was largely superfluous. In each instance, I'd narrowed the choices down to two or three personal favorites and inevitably chose one of them unless the chef had come up with a special that sounded irresistible. In the end, we each ordered a salad; Stephanie chose a chicken dish, and I opted for the Veal Saltimbocca. We agreed on a Rex Hill Pinot Noir to drink with the entrees and settled in with our cocktails while we waited for the salads.

At about five minutes before nine, Mel Brown made his way through the tables with his bass in a case strapped on his back, which was the signal for the drummer and the keyboard player to join him on stage. They greeted each other and spent some time tuning up. Then a few minutes after the hour, they launched into their opening number. The crowd responded warmly and at the end of the song, the drummer, Mike Florio, who was also one of the club's proprietors, introduced the vocalist, Khani Cole, and the evening was officially under way.

The first set lasted just under an hour, during which Stephanie and I ate our dinners and made a significant dent in the bottle of wine. The band closed the set with a cover of Amos Lee's "Seen It All Before," and I led Stephanie to the small, crowded dance floor. She came into my arms, put her head on my shoulder, and for the next several minutes, the universe narrowed down tightly to only the two of us and Cole's great, heartrending version of the song.

Cole left the stage to a huge round of applause as the band slowly wound down through the last bars of the song. When it ended, I followed Stephanie back to the table and poured each of us a little more of the Pinot Noir. I set the bottle back on the table, reached over to take her hand and said, "For the last two hours, we've both studiously avoided talking about what happened last night. I feel like I should try to explain…."

She shook her head. "You don't have too, Sean. I was insensitive and should have had brains enough to realize why you hadn't invited me to your house. I'm sorry I put you in a bind like that."

"No, it's not your fault, Steph. We've known each other for six months now; we've been intimate for several weeks and it was a perfectly logical request. You know that you're the first woman I've been involved with since Julie died and so, obviously, you're the first woman I've ever taken to the house since then. I've been telling myself for the last couple of weeks that it was time to invite you over and while I was working my way in that direction, I guess I just hadn't quite gotten there yet."

"I understand. But it really didn't hit me until we were standing in the bedroom doorway and I saw her picture. Then I realized that I was invading her space and that you were probably not very happy about it."

I shook my head. "I wasn't unhappy about it, and I certainly wasn't upset with you. Naturally, I still feel Julie's presence in the house and I will for as long as I live there. But until recently, I've had no reason not to continue doing so. I've been slow getting to the point of selling the house just as I was slow to allow for the possibility that I might finally come to care for someone else.

"But, obviously, that *has* happened. For the first time since Julie, I *am* beginning to develop those kinds of feelings. I have no idea what the future might hold for us, but in the last few weeks I've been thinking that it's time to sell the house and move on."

She squeezed my hand. "I'm not asking you to forget her."

"I understand that, and of course I never will. She'll always have a place in my heart, but that doesn't exclude the possibility that I might ultimately love someone else who would be just as special to me. And it certainly doesn't mean that I'm going to spend the rest of my life comparing other women to some idealized version of Julie.

"Regardless of what might happen between you and me, I know that it's time for me to be through mourning her and to be fully engaged in living again. And I also know that's what she would have wanted as well."

"She was a very lucky woman and I know that you'll always treasure your memories of her. If you were the sort of man who could just turn your back on that, I'd have no interest in you at all. I don't know what's going to happen between us either. But you've somehow broken through all the defenses I thought I was throwing up around myself, and I guess I'm feeling a bit vulnerable. I don't expect you to ever forget Julie, let alone forget her overnight just because you met me. But it's becoming increasingly important to me to know that there might be a place in your life and in your heart for me as well.'

"You can be sure of that," I said, squeezing her hand.

She nodded and for a minute or so, neither of us said anything. Then she squeezed my hand again and said, "I know how much you love this band, but would you mind if we slipped out before the next set begins? I'd really like to go back to my apartment and spend some time alone with you."

"So would I. Let me get the check."

39

Just before seven thirty, Becky steeled herself and walked into Walter's study. After breaking down in the kitchen, she'd splashed cold water in her face and repaired her makeup. She hoped he wouldn't look closely enough to notice that she'd been crying.

As usual, Walter was sitting at the desk, doing something on his computer. Becky wondered if he might be checking his e-mail, looking for a message from "Cathystanton2." He looked up from his screen as Becky walked into the room and said, "Time for you to go?"

Becky nodded and walked around behind the desk. "I just wanted to stop in and say goodbye on my way out."

Walter swiveled around in his chair to face her, and Becky noticed an Excel spreadsheet on the computer monitor. "Will you be home at the usual time?"

"I should be."

"Well, I'm going to go back to the office for a couple of hours, but I should be home ahead of you. I'll see you then."

"Okay."

"Becky leaned forward, put her arms around his neck and held him for a moment. Then before she started crying again, she gave him a quick kiss on the top of the head, and said, "Bye, Walter."

"G'bye, Beck. See you later."

By the time she reached the door of the study, he'd already returned to his computer screen.

***

Becky made her way down the stairs and through the kitchen to the door that led to the garage. She stood at the door for a moment, taking one last look, then pulled the door closed behind her, got into her Audi, and drove away.

Ten minutes later, she began shaking almost uncontrollably. She pulled over to the side of the road, and sat for a minute, trying to regain control, willing herself not to dissolve into another sobbing fit. She had no idea how she would get through the book club meeting, let alone carry on so that Jen would not realize that something was terribly wrong.

She took several deep breaths, then picked up her cell phone, speed-dialed Jennifer, and explained that she was held up at home and that she might be a few minutes late — that the other women should go ahead and start the discussion without her and that she'd get there as quickly as she could. Jennifer asked if she was all right, and Becky lied to her friend for the first time ever. She told Jennifer not to worry, and that she'd try to be no more than a few minutes late.

Becky sat in the car for a few more minutes, breathing deeply and trying to focus. When the dashboard clock read seven fifty-five, she pulled away from the curb, hoping that by the time she arrived at Jennifer's, the discussion would have already started.

She pulled into Jennifer's condominium complex at eight ten and punched in the code that Jennifer had gave her to open the security gates. She found a parking place in front of the building and rang the bell. Jennifer answered the door, gave Becky a quick hug and told her that the discussion had just started. Then she turned and led Becky up the stairs. Fortunately, the lights at the bottom of the stairs were relatively dim.

The book for that evening was a fairly lame romance novel that one of the newer members picked. Becky skimmed much of the book and, under normal circumstances, would have been highly critical of it. But these were not normal circumstances, and so she largely sat out of the discussion. The woman who had recommended the book strongly defended it, while most of the others suggested that they really hadn't enjoyed it and would not want to read another book by the author.

The meeting finally wound down a little after ten o'clock and three of the women said goodnight and left immediately. Becky and one other woman, whose name was Sarah, stayed long enough to get the coffee cups and dessert plates into the dishwasher. Then

Sarah left and Jennifer asked Becky if she'd like to stay long enough for a glass of wine.

There was nothing in the world that Becky would have loved more. But standing there in the living room alone with Jennifer, she knew that she'd be lucky to last five minutes without breaking down and pouring out her heart to her best friend.

"I'd love to Jen, but it's been a very long day. I need to get home and get to bed, especially if we're going to do the Art Walk tomorrow night."

Jennifer nodded. "Are you feeling okay? You were awfully quiet tonight."

Becky waved off the concern. "No, Hon, I'm just a little tired and irritable. I was afraid that if I opened my mouth I would have cut Mindy to shreds for recommending such a dopey book, and the two of us would have wound up bitch-slapping each other in the middle of your living room."

The two women turned and started down the stairs together. "Believe me, I understand," Jennifer laughed. "I felt the same way myself. That's the last time we let Molly suggest a new addition to the club."

At the bottom of the stairs, Becky opened the door. As her tears started to rise, she turned and gave Jennifer a quick hug. "Love you, Jen," she said.

"Love you too, Becky. See you tomorrow night."

Becky squeezed her friend tightly for a long moment then turned and walked quickly to her car. As she backed out of the parking place, Jennifer was standing in the door, watching her safely away. They gave each other a small wave, and as Becky drove through the gate, she burst into tears.

## 40

I got into the office early the next morning and spent an hour or so moving paper between my "In" basket and my "Out" basket. At eight thirty, Maggie walked into the office and dropped into the guest chair next to my desk. Before we could even wish each other a good morning, the phone on my desk rang. I picked up to find Andy Sheldahl at the other end of the line. "Things are getting curiouser and curiouser," he said.

I shot Maggie a look and said, "What the hell is wrong now, Andy?"

"Well, the good news is that we've now been through Becky Miller's computer six ways from Sunday. You won't be getting any more surprises there."

"And the bad news?"

"Well, after we discovered the business with the diary on her machine, we went back over the husband's computer with a fine toothcomb. And we discovered that someone installed a spyware program on it."

"What the hell?"

"Yeah, my sentiments exactly. This is a desktop machine, and I would assume that he used it only at home, especially since he had one just like it on his desk at work. The spyware is a very sophisticated program, and only someone who really knows what he's doing would ever find it. But Bill did find it. The program was installed on the computer on May third. Once he found it, Bill checked the computer from Miller's office. That one was clean."

"How would someone have bugged the computer? Would they have had to be at the computer itself, or could they have done it remotely?"

"In this case, they had to have access to the computer itself. The spyware is installed from a CD."

"Well, shit, Andy. What the hell is going on here?"

"Hey, I'm just a simple administrator, remember? I only report this crap. You're the one who gets paid the big bucks to make sense out of it. But I do think it's safe to say that we won't be getting any more out of either computer. You've got it all now."

"Jesus, I hope so, Andy. I don't need to be getting any more calls like this."

"Don't worry, you won't be — not on this case anyhow."

I hung up the phone and relayed the conversation to Maggie. She said, "Somebody bugs Miller's home computer a month before his wife disappears? Who in the hell would do that? And why?"

Rising from my chair, I said, "I don't have the slightest idea on either score, Maggie. But I think we'd better go over to the jail and have another chat with Mr. Miller."

\*\*\*

While awaiting trial, Walter Miller was a guest of the Maricopa County Jail and although he'd only been in residence for a couple of days, the toll was already evident. A guard brought him into the interview room and he dropped listlessly into a chair across the table from Maggie and me. His face was ashen and he looked for all the world like a man who'd completely abandoned hope. Once seated, he simply looked from Maggie to me, saying nothing, and expressing no curiosity whatsoever about why we might want to see him.

"Mr. Miller," I said, "we've got a couple of questions for you."

A small spark of life flashed in his eyes and he said, "Like I give a shit about your questions. Fuck the both of you."

Nodding, I said, "I understand that we're doubtless not your favorite people on the planet at the moment, Mr. Miller. However, whether you believe it or not, we are anxious to get to the truth of the matter here."

He gave a small, disparaging laugh. "Well, I hate to disappoint you, but so far, you're doing a lousy fuckin' job."

"We have a question about the computer from your home office."

The question caught him off guard, and for a moment at least, the hostility in his face gave way to a look of genuine confusion. "My computer?"

I nodded. "How long have you had the computer, Mr. Miller?"

He shook his head. "I dunno. About eighteen months, I guess."

"Since you bought the computer, have you had any problems with it? Have you ever had to take it in to be repaired?"

Miller looked even more puzzled. "Once, about six weeks after I bought it. The network adaptor card failed and I couldn't access the Internet through the cable modem. I had to send it back to Dell to be repaired."

"Otherwise the computer has always been in your home office? You've never taken it to the office or used it someplace other than in your home?"

"No. ... I mean, Yes. It's always been at home. I have a computer in my office. Why would I need to take my home computer there?"

Maggie said, "So since Dell sent it back to you well over a year ago, the computer has never been out of the house?"

Miller shook his head.

"Besides yourself, who's had access to the computer in your house?"

"Nobody. I'm the only one who ever used it."

"Mrs. Miller never used your computer?"

"No, she had her own. You know that."

"But she did have access to the machine, didn't she?" I asked. "I mean, obviously she was often home when you were not there. I take it that you didn't lock the door to your study when you weren't at home?"

"No, of course not."

"Was the computer password protected?" Maggie asked.

Again, Miller just shook his head.

"So theoretically, at least, if her computer wasn't working or something, Mrs. Miller could have gone into the study and used yours?"

"Well, yeah, she could have, But I'm sure she never did."

"Who else might have had access to the machine?" I asked. "I assume that you had a cleaning service, for example. Who else would have been in the house and had the opportunity to get into your study?"

He shook his head. "No one. Lisa, the cleaning lady, came in once a week and of course she cleaned my study along with the rest of the house. But certainly, she wouldn't have ever used my computer."

"How long have you been using this cleaning lady?" Maggie asked.

Miller shrugged. "Shit, I don't know. Three or four years anyhow."

Maggie nodded. "And you've never had any problem with her?"

"No. She was great. Becky loved the woman."

"Have you had any servicemen to the house in the last couple of months?" I asked. "Plumbers, cable repair men, anybody like that?"

"Not that I know of. That would have been Becky's department, but certainly she would have mentioned it."

"What about guests who might have been in the house during that period?" Maggie asked. Would any of them have had occasion to go upstairs?"

"No. In the last couple of months, we had friends in for dinner two or three times, but none of them were upstairs."

"What about friends of Mrs. Miller?" I asked. "Members of her book club, for example, or other friends she might have entertained while you were not at home?"

Miller shrugged and threw up his hands. "It's possible. Becky did have friends over at the house from time to time. Jennifer Burke was there on a fairly regular basis. But none of them would've had any reason to be upstairs in my study, let alone to use my computer."

I looked him in the eye. "And Cathy Stanton was never in your home."

He shot me a look of contempt. "Never."

"And you still have no idea where she might have gone?"

"None."

"Okay then, Mr. Miller. Thanks for your time."

I signaled the guard that we were through and Miller said, "But what the hell is all this about? Why are you so concerned about my damned computer?"

"We're just wrapping up loose ends, Mr. Miller," Maggie answered. "Thanks again."

\*\*\*

The guard led Miller back to his cell, and Maggie and I walked out into the blazing heat of another summer day in the northern Sonoran desert. She'd been uncharacteristically quiet most of the morning and as we sat in traffic, I looked over to see her staring out the window to her right, apparently oblivious to everything that was going on around her. "Earth to McClinton," I said.

She snapped out of her reverie and turned to face me. "Sorry. What did you say?"

"Nothing. You're just awfully subdued today. Everything okay?"

She turned to look back out the window, hesitated for a couple of seconds, and then said, "I had dinner with my mom last night. I told her that Patrick and I were done."

"How'd she take it?"

"About like you'd expect. She put up a good front and told me that it was my life and that I had to live it the way that seemed right for me. But I know she was disappointed. Remember that she's the one who threw Patrick and me together in the first place. She likes him a lot and I know that she was really warming up to the idea of being an instant grandmother. So, in the end, I disappointed her as well as Patrick, Yolanda and Claire, and I'm feeling pretty low about it."

"I understand, Maggs. But there's really no reason for that. Patrick's at least as much responsible as you are for the fact that things didn't work out, and I know your mom well enough to know that she really *does* want what's best for you. As much as she might have become attached to Patrick and his girls, she'd never want you stick with the guy just because it would make her happy."

"I know that, Sean. It's just that she's made so many sacrifices for me through the years, and she had such a great relationship with

182

my dad. She wants me to be as happy as she was, and I know she worries that I'm going to miss my chance by being too inflexible and too attached to this job. I don't know how to make her understand that I *am* happy, maybe not in the same way that she was, but in my own way. I can't help feeling like I've failed her and I'm just not very happy with myself at the moment."

41

Becky Miller realized that she didn't dare drive her own car back into Cathy Stanton's apartment complex. Only belatedly did it occur to her that there might be video surveillance of the complex and that her visit earlier in the day might already be recorded somewhere. There was nothing she could do about that now, but she knew that she couldn't risk being seen in the complex a second time, either by a camera or by a curious neighbor.

Three blocks away from Jennifer Burke's condo, Becky pulled into the parking lot of a small strip mall. The stores in the mall were all closed for the night, and only three other vehicles remained in the parking lot. Alone in her car, Becky finally surrendered to the storm of emotions swirling within her. For ten minutes, she sat, sobbing uncontrollably. Then, feeling thoroughly spent, she wiped her face with a couple of tissues and forced herself to focus again on the tasks at hand.

It was nearly eleven p.m. Becky figured that Walter would not begin to worry for another thirty minutes or so, and that he probably wouldn't take any action for perhaps another hour after that. She assumed that when she did not return home within an hour or so of when Walter expected her, he would first call her cell phone. When she didn't answer, he would probably then call Jennifer and perhaps a couple of her other friends.

What would he do next? Would he call the police and report her missing? Would he get in his car and start checking the roads between their home and Jennifer's? Would he do both?

Becky figured that she probably had another hour at the most when she could safely use her own car. And, obviously, she could no longer use her own cell phone. She reached into her purse and turned off the phone so that she wouldn't answer it automatically and without thinking in the event that it did ring. Then she popped the trunk of the car, took a shop rag from the tool kit in the trunk, and closed the trunk again.

***

The Basha's supermarket anchored a shopping center on Scottsdale Road, about a mile or so north of Cathy Stanton's apartment. At eleven thirty at night, the market and all of the surrounding stores were closed, save for the gas station/convenience store at the front of the shopping center. Becky parked her Audi in the darkened lot, well away from the convenience store.

Using the shop rag, she reached down and pressed the button to move the driver's seat well back from its usual position. She then used the rag to wipe down the steering wheel, the gearshift lever, and the area around the driver's seat. She hoped her actions would suggest to the police that someone significantly taller than she had last driven the car and had then attempted to eliminate any fingerprints that they might have left in it.

She sat for a moment, trying to think of anything else that she might need from the car. Then she got out and used the shop rag to wipe down the interior and exterior handles of the driver's side door. She popped open the trunk, then stuffed her keys into her purse. She hoisted a gym bag over each shoulder and closed the trunk again.

Careful to avoid the lights of the convenience store, she walked north for fifty yards or so, then turned west and made her way out of the parking lot. The traffic on Scottsdale Road was fairly light at this time of night, and Becky waited for a solitary northbound car to pass. Then she crossed to the west side of the street and headed south, moving in the direction of the traffic in the lanes closest to her.

Her heart racing, she walked as fast as she could, trying to cover the distance to Stanton's apartment as quickly as possible without attracting attention to herself. She hated not being able to see the traffic coming up behind her, but she felt that she didn't dare risk walking against the traffic for fear that someone might pick up her face in their headlights and recognize her or later remember having seen her.

As a woman walking the street alone at this time of night, Becky would have been nervous enough under normal circumstances. But tonight, potential muggers and rapists were only two of the things that frightened her practically to death. What if a police officer should spot her and ask if she needed assistance? What if the cop demanded to see her ID? What would she tell him or her? What explanation could she possibly offer for her actions?

Although Scottsdale Road was a major artery, there were no sidewalks along this stretch of the street. Vacant desert lots alternated with ones that had been developed by car dealerships, small strip malls, a car wash, and other such businesses. Moving down the street, Becky tried to stay well to the right of the roadway, hoping to remain as inconspicuous as possible.

She was about halfway from the Basha's to Cathy Stanton's apartment when the van passed her. Coming up behind her, the driver had probably been going about fifty, five miles an hour over the posted limit. But as the vehicle came abreast of Becky, the driver touched his brakes and slowed.

The brake lights glowed for three or four seconds, and then the van continued down the street at a deliberate speed. At an intersection fifty yards ahead, the brake lights glowed again and the van turned right without signaling. After making the turn, the van picked up speed and disappeared from Becky's view.

Becky knew instinctively that the van was circling around the block and would be coming up behind her again, perhaps in less than a minute. She was now in front of a small group of stores that were set about forty yards off of the street. Her heart pounding, she raced in the direction of the buildings and ducked around the corner of a pet supply shop. She dropped the two gym bags and crouched down to the ground, exposing nothing more than the top of her head as she peered around the corner of the building, watching Scottsdale Road. Thirty seconds later, the van rolled slowly down the street.

A small alley ran behind the stores, and as the van disappeared from her view, Becky grabbed the two gym bags and ran down the alley. At the south end of the pet supply store, she chanced another look out into the street. The van was moving very slowly now, and was approaching the intersection again.

Perhaps ten yards separated the pet store from its immediate neighbor to the south. Becky was wearing jeans and a navy-blue shirt; the two gym bags were both black. As the van turned right to circle around the block again, Becky took a deep breath and moved quickly across the open space, praying that in the darkness she wouldn't be seen.

Two large dumpsters sat a foot or so apart from each other behind the next building, and about twenty-four inches of space separated the dumpsters from the building itself. Becky shoved the gym bags behind the first dumpster, one on top of the other. Then she squeezed herself behind the second dumpster and worked her way to a spot where she was almost at the middle of the point where the two dumpsters were practically joined together.

Her purse was hanging off her right shoulder. Becky opened the purse, took out her cell phone and turned it on again. If she had no other option, she would dial nine-one-one and take her chances with the police rather than with the asshole(s) who might be in the van.

Forty seconds later, headlights illuminated the space between the two stores and Becky heard the sound of an engine pulling into the small parking area in front of the buildings. The vehicle came to a stop and Becky listened to the engine idling on the other side of the building, twenty or twenty-five yards away from her position.

The van sat there for another minute or so and then began moving again, now heading south, away from her. The sound of the vehicle's engine had almost faded away when its headlights flashed around the corner, illuminating the alley.

Becky's heart jumped into her throat. Afraid even to breathe for fear of giving away her position, she carefully opened her cell phone and punched in the numbers nine-one-one. She poised her finger over the "Send" button and watched as the van began rolling very slowly down the alley. The driver had turned on his brights, and in her panic, Becky feared, irrationally, that the lights were strong enough to penetrate right through the two dumpsters, exposing her position.

The van crawled down the alley and pulled even with the spot where Becky was hiding. Again, she held her breath. Time seemed literally to stand still as the van inched slowly past her position. At long last, it crept past the second of the two dumpsters and Becky found herself looking at the van's bright red taillights.

And then her cell phone rang.

## 42

When I got into the office on Monday morning, I found a note asking me to call Walter Miller's attorney, Ted Ogilvie. I dialed the number and the secretary buzzed his extension. Ogilvie came on the line and thanked me for getting back to him so quickly. I leaned back in my chair, propped my feet on the desk and said, "What can I do for you, Mr. Ogilvie?"

"I'm not sure, Detective, but I discovered something very odd this morning."

"How so?"

"Well, with Walter in jail, his assistant manager has been handling his personal mail, seeing that the bills get paid and things like that."

"Okay."

"Anyhow, this morning, Marsha — she's the assistant manager — got a statement from Mrs. Miller's broker. It appears that during the last few weeks before her death, Mrs. Miller liquidated virtually all of her stock holdings and converted them to cash."

I thought about that for a minute, then said, "How much money are we talking about here, Mr. Ogilvie?"

"In round numbers, about two hundred and fifty thousand dollars. And that's just in this account. I have no idea what she might have been doing with her other accounts."

"And what happened to the money?"

"I have no idea about that either, Detective Richardson."

"Have you spoken to Mr. Miller about this?"

"Not yet, but I'm sure that it'll be news to him as well."

\*\*\*

Ogilvie gave me the name of Becky Miller's broker, David Spencer. I called Spencer to make sure that he was in his office, and thirty minutes later, he offered me a seat in front of his desk. A heavy-set man in his early fifties, he had a look about him that invited trust and somehow suggested that you could do very well by placing your financial future in his hands. I explained the reason for my visit, and he shook his head.

"Believe me, Detective, I was very surprised by her decision. Mrs. Miller was not an active trader. Her approach was to do careful research and then to buy stocks that she thought were undervalued and that had potential for long-term growth. And once she bought a stock she held onto it. It was a conservative approach, of course, but over the long term, it paid off for her."

"So why did she cash in?"

"She came in about six weeks ago and told me that she intended to cash out most of her holdings. She explained that she was going to invest the money in her husband's business."

"And what did you say to that?"

He shrugged. "As I said, Mrs. Miller was a woman who largely did her own research and who certainly had her own opinions on these matters. Occasionally she asked my advice, and when she did, I gave it. Otherwise, I simply executed her decisions."

"And in this case?"

"In this case, I asked her if she was sure that this was the most prudent approach. I suggested that she might borrow the money instead, perhaps using the stock as collateral, which would allow her to preserve the positions that she had taken. But she said that she'd considered that, and that this was the approach she wanted to take."

"So, you cashed her out?"

He threw up his hands. "I had no choice. She was the client. It was her money and it was certainly her decision to make. Over the next few weeks, I executed the "Sell" orders as she phoned them in to me, and by the end of last month she had liquidated virtually all of her holdings."

"And this amounted to about a quarter of a million dollars?"

Spencer nodded.

"What about her other finances? Did she have accounts with other brokers?"

He shook his head. "No, at least not as far as I know. And I'm sure I would have known. Mrs. Miller had a checking account, of course. And naturally, she had other money readily available in a savings account and in a money market account at her bank. But I'm sure that all her other investments were through this office."

"No real estate investments, or anything like that?"

"No, at least not to my knowledge."

"And as Mrs. Miller liquidated her account with you, how did she take the money?"

"We sold the stocks and as we did, we transferred the proceeds to her checking account. I have no way of knowing what she did with the money once it reached her bank. Based on what she told me, I assumed that she simply passed it on to her husband so that he could invest it in his business."

***

I thanked Spencer for his time and went back to the office, propped my feet up on the desk, and tried to figure out what in the hell was going on in this goddamned case.

Two months before her death, Becky Miller had apparently first begun to suspect that her husband was cheating on her. And four weeks after that, she began converting her stocks to cash so that she could invest a quarter of a million dollars in her husband's business? That simply made no damned sense at all.

I could readily believe that Miller might have invented the story as a cover because she didn't want to explain to her broker what she actually intended to do with the money. But what had she intended to do with it? And, more to the point, where in the hell did the money actually go?

And where in the world was Cathy Stanton? Thanks principally to the cable "news" shows, the woman's face and physical description had been plastered all over the country. But her trail had gone completely cold after she left the hotel in Amarillo.

Why had she booked a ticket to Boise and then not taken the flight? Why had there been no additional activity on her credit cards? Why had no one spotted her car?

As I'd told Jennifer Burke, I still believed that the case against Walter Miller was a strong one. Nonetheless, I was beginning to get a decidedly bad feeling about the whole goddamn mess.

## 43

Becky Miller was not the sort of woman who would download some stupid song to signal that she had an incoming call on her cell phone. She used a simple, straightforward ring tone, with the volume set on medium. But when it went off in the alley, it seemed loud enough to have been heard all the way down in Tucson.

Becky jammed her thumb onto the cell phone's "Off" button and held it there. A second later, the phone went dark and silent, and Becky looked up to see the brake lights flash on the van, no more than ten feet from her position.

There were no windows in the back of the van. She'd only had a brief look, but she thought that the window in the door on the passenger's side of the van was closed. She hadn't seen the driver's side of the vehicle; was that window closed or open?

Although it seemed like an eternity, the phone had probably not rung for more than a couple of seconds before Becky had been able to silence it. Could the driver have really heard it?

The van sat there, its taillights glowing as the driver continued to apply the brakes. The engine idled smoothly and quietly, but no other sounds escaped the vehicle.

The next thirty seconds seemed to last an hour, but finally the taillights dimmed a bit and the van began rolling slowly forward again. It reached the north end of the alley and turned right, back into the parking lot in front of the shops. Once clear of the shops the van picked up speed, and perhaps twenty seconds later the sound of its engine faded into the night, heading south down Scottsdale Road.

Becky held her position for another ten minutes, terrified to move. Finally, she reluctantly squeezed her way out from behind the dumpsters and into the alley again. Hugging the building and moving very cautiously, she made her way to the end of the building and peeked around the corner. The parking area in front of the buildings was deserted. A pickup truck sped north up Scottsdale Road, but she could see no other vehicles.

She hated to expose herself again, but she had no other choice. She retrieved the two gym bags and hurried south, attempting to stay in the shadows and trying to keep as much distance as possible between herself and the street.

A few blocks south of the pet supply store, she passed in front of another gas station/convenience store. A police car was parked in front of the store, and the officer was nowhere in sight. Becky stood in the dark and debated the idea of circling around the block behind the store. But as she did, a policeman emerged from the store, carrying a paper bag and a cup of coffee. He got into his patrol car, backed out of the parking spot, and headed south down the street.

Wasting no more time, Becky hurried past the bright lights of the convenience store. Two and a half blocks later, she breathed a huge sigh of relief as she walked through the gates of Cathy Stanton's apartment complex.

***

Becky's reprieve lasted only for the minute or two that it took her to reach the door of Stanton's unit. She knew that Stanton was dead. Certainly, there was no doubt of that, not in the rational world anyway. But standing in front of the woman's door, Becky imagined Stanton come back to life, still naked, still wearing the white plastic bag over her head, and waiting to jump out at Becky the instant she walked through the door.

Becky desperately wanted to do nothing more than simply run away, but that was no longer an option. Her hand trembling, it took her several seconds to fit the key into the lock and open the door. She set the two gym bags on the floor ahead of her, then walked into the darkened apartment and closed the door behind her.

Cursing herself for not having been smart enough to leave at least one light on, Becky fumbled in the dark for a few seconds until her fingers found a switch and an overhead light illuminated the small entryway. Thankfully, Cathy Stanton was not waiting to pounce on her — at least not downstairs.

Becky locked the door and engaged the deadbolt. Then she double-checked to make sure that all the drapes and blinds were closed downstairs and turned on a few more lights. It was now thirty minutes after midnight, and Becky needed nothing so much as a good, stiff drink — or maybe two or three, considering the task that lay immediately ahead of her.

In the kitchen, she found a couple bottles of cheap red wine, a bottle of vodka and another of Jack Daniels. She opened a couple of cupboard doors before discovering Stanton's glassware and grabbed a large water glass. She poured an inch of the whiskey into the glass, then sank into a chair in the living room and took a large first sip.

Five minutes later, she remembered the cell phone. She dug it out of her purse, turned it on again, and scrolled through the menu to "Missed Calls." At eleven fifteen p.m., eleven thirty-five p.m., and again at eleven fifty-five p.m., she had missed calls from Walter's cell phone. She had three messages waiting, all of them presumably from Walter.

The last thing she needed at this point was to hear Walter's voice. She knew that that he would be genuinely concerned about what might have happened to her, but she reasoned that these were the sort of things he should have thought about before taking up with the woman who now lay dead in the bathtub upstairs. She also knew that at some point the police would doubtless check her cell phone records and that they would probably be able to determine when the phone was last used. She shut off the cell phone and as a precaution, removed the battery and the SIM card. Then she put the components back in her purse, and drained the last of the whiskey.

*** 

Becky sat there for another five minutes or so, savoring the warmth of the liquor. She could have easily stayed there for hours, she thought, but she still had a great deal of work to do before the night was over. Cathy Stanton had been dead for nearly eleven hours. Becky knew that the body would already be decomposing, and that the longer she waited, the more unpleasant her task would be.

Reluctantly, she set down the glass, walked into the kitchen and put on the yellow rubber gloves that she'd left on the counter.

Becky couldn't imagine why a woman who worked as a waitress and who probably ate most of her meals at work, would have an oversized side-by-side refrigerator/freezer — especially in an apartment kitchen. She wondered if Stanton might have inherited the thing from a previous tenant.

The interior of the freezer side was little over five feet high, about three feet deep, and perhaps two and a half feet wide. It was only about a third full, and most of the food in it consisted of frozen dinners, a couple of California Pizza Kitchen pizzas, and three bags of frozen mixed vegetables. The contents further reinforced Becky's assumption that Stanton had not had the refrigerator installed herself.

Becky opened the refrigerator door and transferred all of the food from the freezer into the refrigerator. The food would doubtless thaw over the course of the next couple of days, but Becky had no intention of eating any of it, and Stanton certainly wouldn't be needing it.

Becky closed the refrigerator door and removed the shelves from the freezer. Fortunately, the automatic icemaker was relatively small and located near the top of the unit. She pulled out the drawer from under the icemaker and poured the ice cubes into the sink.

She stood for a moment, staring into the now-empty cavity, then closed the freezer door. Back in the entryway, she opened the larger of the two gym bags and pulled out the plastic tarp, the duct tape and the pruning saw that she'd brought from home. Then she took a deep breath, turned, and headed up the stairs.

## 44

Becky Miller's bank records showed four deposits from her brokerage account into her checking account. Curiously, she had not entered these deposits into her checkbook, nor had she left the statements reflecting this activity in the bank file folder in her desk. We found the deposits only by getting a court order that compelled the bank to show us their records of her accounts.

Once deposited by the brokerage firm, the money remained in the checking account only briefly. Within a few days of each deposit, Miller came into the bank and took out the exact amount that the brokerage firm deposited in the form of cash.

On the day before she disappeared, Miller withdrew twenty-five thousand dollars from her money market account. Again, she took the money in cash. None of it had been deposited to any of her husband's accounts, at least not to any account that we could find, and Walter Miller appeared to be genuinely flabbergasted by his wife's actions. Both Miller and his attorney insisted that something very odd was going on and that we should be rethinking our case against Miller.

Certainly, something very odd *was* going on, but Becky Miller's puzzling behavior with respect to her finances did not alter the fact that she was dead. Nor did it change the fact that there was a significant amount of evidence suggesting that her husband was involved in her murder and in the subsequent dismemberment of her body.

I checked my notebook, picked up the phone, and dialed Jennifer Burke's number. She answered on the second ring, and I imagined her sitting in the club chair in her living room, dressed as she'd been when I had last interviewed her. The recollection triggered a memory of the perfume she'd been wearing and I took a deep breath and tried to focus on the matter at hand.

I described Becky Miller's financial transactions and asked Burke if she had any idea what her friend might have been doing. There was a long silence at the other end of the phone, and then Burke said in a very quiet voice, "I have absolutely no idea, Detective Richardson.

"Becky and I talked frequently about our investments and we sometimes shared the research that we were doing. We invested in some of the same stocks, although my portfolio wasn't nearly as large as hers. But she said nothing at all to me about liquidating her stocks, and I can't imagine what she might have done with the money. None of it has turned up anywhere?"

"No, none of it. Of course, we just found out about this business today, and we really haven't had a chance to look for it. But we certainly haven't stumbled across anything like two hundred and seventy-five thousand dollars in cash."

\*\*\*

Burke promised to give the matter some additional thought and to call me if she had any ideas. I thanked her again for her help and hung up the phone.

As much as I didn't want to, I honestly believed that Walter Miller knew nothing about his wife's financial transactions. And, given the circumstances of their marriage, I couldn't really believe that she converted her assets to cash so that she could make an additional investment in his business.

Given the facts, a child of five would have suggested that Miller might have converted her investments to ready cash because she was preparing to disappear. But why would she have been planning to do that?

I was no longer prepared to take her "diary" — or whatever it was — at face value, but she'd made no mention there of any plans to leave. In the document, she sounded like a wronged woman who was alternately hurt and angered by her husband's betrayal.

But the woman who wrote the "diary," and the Becky Miller that her best friend described, did not sound like a woman who would have run, shattered and humiliated, away from the situation. She impressed me, rather, as a woman who would have held her ground and who would have ultimately confronted her husband. This was a woman who would have made Walter Miller pay for his sins, and who would have fought him for everything she believed to be rightfully hers.

But perhaps Becky Miller *had* been planning to disappear — not permanently, but rather as a strategic move in a larger campaign that she was planning to wage against her husband. Perhaps she'd come home from the book club meeting and told him that she was going to leave and that she was also planning to file for divorce. Perhaps they'd fought, and Miller killed her just as we thought, without even realizing what she had done with her money.

But if that were the case, where was the money?

Then there was the question of who bugged Walter Miller's computer? And why?

And, if all of that weren't enough, where in the hell was Cathy Stanton?

I spent another twenty minutes turning the problem around in my mind, coming at it from every angle I could think of. Then I picked up the phone and called Gary Barnett in the new crime lab building across the street. Obviously seeing my name and number in his caller ID, he picked up the phone and said, "What's up, Sean?"

"Becky Miller."

"What about her?"

"Well, Gary, I'd certainly never doubt the quality of your work or that of anybody else in that new palace that the taxpayers have built you over there. But it occurs to me that we've got a torso in the vault with no head and no fingers — one that we've identified on the basis of a toe ring and DNA samples from a hairbrush and a toothbrush."

"And?"

"And I want you to get a crew over to Walter Miller's house. I want you to go through the place from top to bottom, looking for whatever other physical evidence you can find to confirm the fact that the body we've got is, in fact, Becky Miller."

## 45

At two fifteen a.m., Becky leaned over the bathroom sink and washed the rubber gloves in hot, soapy water. Then she rinsed off the gloves and pulled them off of her hands. She'd cut holes for her head and arms in a large plastic garbage bag and was wearing the garbage bag over her bra and jeans. Now she reached inside the hole that she'd cut for her neck and slowly tore the bag down the middle. The outside of the bag was spattered with blood, and Becky carefully slipped her arms out of the bag, then folded it up and put it inside a second, clean garbage bag.

She took a fresh washcloth from a drawer in the vanity and turned the hot water on in the sink again. She soaked the cloth in hot water and pumped a generous amount of liquid soap onto the cloth. She scrubbed her arms, neck and face, then rinsed them thoroughly and dried them. She dropped the washcloth and the towel into the garbage bag and tied the bag closed.

Becky put her blouse on again, and then the rubber gloves. In the master bedroom, she randomly pulled some of Cathy Stanton's clothes from the closet and dropped them into the bottom of a fresh garbage bag. She grabbed another handful of clothes, threw them over her arm and took the clothes and the garbage bag into the bathroom.

She dropped the bag containing the washcloth and towel on top of the clothes in the bag that she'd brought from the bedroom. Then she picked up another sealed bag, which held Cathy Stanton's head and arms, and put that into the bag as well. Becky filled the bag nearly to the top by adding a few of Stanton's blouses and sweaters. Then she tied the bag shut and set it out in the hall.

Stanton's body, absent its head and arms, was now securely wrapped in the thick plastic sheet that Becky had brought from home, and was lying in the middle of the bathroom floor. Once finished working with the pruning saw, Becky had draped the plastic sheet over the edge of the tub and had wrestled Stanton's remains out of the tub and onto the sheet. In the confines of the small bathroom, she had then turned the torso over several times until it was rolled up in the middle of the sheet. Using several long strips of duct tape, she'd sealed the package so that it would not come undone.

Getting Stanton's body back down the steps was a far easier task than getting it up the stairs had been. Becky positioned the package at the top of the stairs, then stepped over the package and stood on the third step down from the top. Taking the steps slowly, one at a time, she eased the body down the stairs and then dragged it across the living room carpet and into the kitchen.

Becky was now thoroughly spent, physically and emotionally. She dropped onto a kitchen chair and rested for a moment, trying to summon up enough strength to carry on for another forty-five minutes or so. Finally, she got up from the chair and pulled open the freezer door. As the cold air began leaking out into the room, Becky stooped over, took a grip on the package, and set Stanton's shoulders into the bottom of the freezer compartment.

It was going to be a tight fit, and Becky panicked briefly, afraid that the freezer was not big enough to accommodate the torso. She stepped away for a moment and took a few deep breaths to calm herself. She looked again at the freezer and at the package lying before her, calculating the size of the body and the capacity of the freezer. The package *would* fit. It *had* to fit.

She steeled herself, then bent down again and lifted Stanton's body by the ankles. Straining as she rose to a standing position, she pressed forward, swiveled the package a quarter turn, and by sheer force of will, muscled it into the freezer and closed the door.

\*\*\*

Becky walked back up the stairs, retrieved the garbage bag that she'd left in the hall, then turned off the upstairs lights. She set the bag next to the front door, and then, working her way from the kitchen back to the entryway, she turned off all of the lights downstairs.

Looking out through the peephole in the front door, she could see nothing moving outside of the apartment building. In the guest coat closet, she found an Arizona Diamondbacks baseball cap. She put the cap on, tugged it low over her eyes, and cautiously opened the door.

The apartment complex was weakly illuminated by a number of lights attached to each of the buildings. Fortunately, though, most of the light was directed back on the buildings themselves and the area between the buildings remained mostly in the shadows.

Becky had earlier noticed a garbage dumpster between Stanton's building and the next building north. Carrying the plastic bag, she stepped out the door, pulled the door closed behind her, and stepped away from the building into the shadows.

It took her only a few seconds to reach the dumpster. With her left hand, she lifted the lid of the dumpster, praying that the hinges wouldn't squeak and alert the entire complex to the fact that some idiot was taking out the garbage in the middle of the night.

Thankfully, the hinges made no noise, and in the dim light, the dumpster appeared to be about half full. She pitched the bag into the dumpster, then gently set the lid down and hurried back into Stanton's apartment.

***

Becky was now thoroughly drained and desperate to get some sleep. But she knew that she didn't dare wait until tomorrow to finish cleaning the bathroom. She found a can of Comet, a roll of paper towels and a sponge under the kitchen sink and took them upstairs.

The pruning saw was still lying in the bottom of the tub. Becky unrolled a long sheet from the roll of paper towels and then picked up the saw. Wearing the rubber gloves again, she turned the saw over in her hands a few times, wiping the handle clean of fingerprints.

She used the paper towels to wipe down the blade of the saw, then tore the bloody sheets into small fragments and flushed them down the toilet. She unrolled another long sheet of paper towels and wrapped the saw up in it. Then she attacked the tub with steaming hot water, the Comet, and the sponge.

Thirty minutes later, the bathroom looked perfectly clean. Becky had read enough crime novels to understand that no trained professional would ever be fooled. But the casual observer, looking at the room with a naked eye, would never guess the horror that had unfolded there during the night.

She ripped the dirty sponge into pieces and flushed the pieces down the toilet and finally hit the wall for tonight.

*\*\*\**

Becky was not at all enamored about the idea of sleeping on Cathy Stanton's couch, only a couple of feet away from the spot where the woman had died. But there was no way she could bring herself to sleep in Stanton's bed, and the couch was the only other alternative.

She found a fresh sheet and a blanket in the linen closet upstairs and laid them out on the couch. She dug her toothbrush and a tube of toothpaste out of one of the gym bags and brushed her teeth in the guest bathroom downstairs. Earlier, she'd set the bottle of Valium aside, worried that she might not be able to sleep tonight, but that was no longer a concern. In the living room, she stripped off her jeans, took off her blouse and bra, and dropped the clothes over a chair.

She switched off the table lamp next to the couch, plunging the apartment into darkness. Then she lay down on the couch, pulled a throw pillow under her head, and wrapped herself up in the blanket and sheet that she'd laid out earlier.

Lying there alone in the dark, the events of the day began roiling through her mind. It was as though she were watching some sort of perverted highlight reel in which a woman walked out of her home intending to spring a well-deserved trap for her unfaithful husband, only to wind up sawing a woman to pieces in the middle of the night.

Becky could hardly recognize herself in the images. Surely this nightmare could not be hers.

## 46

While Maggie was out interviewing witnesses on another case, I went over to the Miller house alone. The crime scene techs had not yet arrived, and so I let myself in, walked up the stairs to the bedroom and sat down at Becky Miller's desk.

I opened the file drawer where she kept her financial records and found folders for a Discover card and for two different Visa cards. Miller had routinely filed her monthly statements, and behind the statements in each of the files, she had paper clipped together in chronological order the receipts for the charges that she had made on each of the cards since the last statement. Apparently, her practice was to check the receipts against the statements as they came in and then discard the receipts.

It looked as though she used the Discover card and one of the Visa cards for her own personal expenses. On those accounts she'd charged clothing, jewelry, spa visits, books, her auto expenses, and other such things. I looked back through four months of statements as well as the current receipts that she had saved, but found nothing that triggered any questions.

Miller apparently used the second Visa card for routine household expenses, and there I found charges for groceries, gardening supplies, cookware, and the like. She also had the phone bill, the cable bill, and a couple of other household expenses automatically charged to the card.

Miller received the last statement on the card she used for household expenses a week before she disappeared. All of the charges on the statement were similar to those that appeared on the earlier statements. But in the middle of the statement was a charge from PC NoSecrets in the amount of $59.95. And according to Andy Sheldahl, PC NoSecrets was the company that manufactured the spyware program that his techs found on Walter Miller's computer.

The date of the purchase was listed as May third, four weeks before Miller disappeared and about the time she had allegedly begun to suspect that her husband was having an affair. The logical conclusion was that, in addition to hiring Jerry Calhoun, the private detective, Miller bugged her husband's computer in another effort to monitor his behavior.

But what did she discover? The CSB staff found Walter Miller's e-mail correspondence with Cathy Stanton. Did Becky Miller find it too? If she had, it would certainly have confirmed her suspicions. But why didn't she told Jennifer Burke of her discovery? And why didn't she mentioned it in her "diary"?

As Sheldahl had noted, things were getting curiouser and curiouser.

***

I spent another hour going very carefully through all the other records in Becky Miller's desk, but found nothing else that raised any red flags. Finally, I closed the file drawer, got up from the desk, and walked into her closet.

The closet was perhaps ten feet square with a door on the far wall that opened into the master bath. The contractor, or perhaps the Millers themselves, had installed what looked like a very expensive closet "system" in the room. Shelves of dark cherry wood, or a very good imitation thereof, lined the walls on two sides of the room, and held neatly folded sweaters, tee-shirts, and a few polo shirts. Below that, several racks contained a fairly large collection of shoes ranging from athletic shoes to some fairly wicked-looking high heels.

Two sets of drawers were built into the shelves and I opened them to find neatly folded lingerie, athletic socks, and a few pairs of running shorts. On the other two walls, clothes hung from chrome rods. Again, the clothes were neatly organized by category from athletic wear, to casual wear, to dresses, skirts, and several blouses that Miller chose to hang up rather than to fold and put on a shelf.

To all appearances, the closet appeared to be comfortably full. There were no half-empty drawers, no obviously vacant shelves or empty spaces on the hanging rods. I had no way of knowing if anything might have been missing from the closet, but standing there, it looked like a closet that would belong to a well-organized, logical woman like Becky Miller. Certainly, it did not look like a closet where someone might have packed up even a few of her clothes in preparation for going somewhere.

The same was true in the bathroom beyond the closet. Toiletries and cosmetics were carefully arranged on the top of the vanity and in the drawers below. Miller's toothbrush and hairbrush were missing, of course, but otherwise it was hard to imagine that anyone might have gone into the bathroom and picked out even a few things to take on a trip.

I spent another twenty minutes or so, wandering through the house, trying to get a feel for Becky Miller, and looking for anything that seemed jarringly out of place — either by its presence or by its absence. Again, I had no way of knowing what might have been missing from the home in the wake of the woman's disappearance, but if her husband were to be believed, he didn't notice anything missing.

I saw nothing that struck me either, and after spending nearly two hours in the home, the only new evidence I developed was the credit card charge, suggesting that almost certainly, Becky Miller was the one who bugged her husband's computer.

Just as I was leaving, Gary Barnett and two members of his team rolled into the driveway. We spent a couple of minutes comparing notes and I told him, not that he needed to be told, that he should find a wealth of material in Becky Miller's closet and bathroom that he could check against the torso the lab had identified as Miller. He promised to get to work and to let me know the instant he had any additional news.

47

Becky woke with a start out of a dream in which two beefy, tattooed men in a white van were chasing her down a dark alley. It took a couple of moments for her pulse to stop racing. Then she remembered where she was and realized that, sadly, her real life was now infinitely scarier than any nightmare.

A bright sun filtered into the room around the closed blinds, and Becky guessed that it must be somewhere in the middle of the morning. She glanced at her watch, which read ten seventeen.

She got up from the couch, stretched her arms over her head, and then went down the hall to the guest bathroom. She brushed her teeth, stripped off her panties, and stepped into the shower. Twenty minutes later, dressed in clean underwear, her jeans, and a fresh tee shirt, she reluctantly walked into the kitchen.

While moving things from the freezer to the refrigerator, Becky noticed a loaf of wheat bread on one of the refrigerator shelves. Trying to avoid even looking at the freezer door, she opened the refrigerator, took out the bread, and popped a slice into the toaster. A quart of orange juice was sitting on a shelf in the refrigerator door. Becky drank half a glass of the juice and then ate the toast dry.

On her first trip through the apartment, Becky had noticed a laptop computer on the desk in Stanton's second bedroom. Breakfast over, she walked up the stairs and sat down at the desk in front of the computer.

The computer was connected to a cable modem, and Becky thought about putting on the rubber gloves again before attempting to use it. She realized, though, that even if she hadn't left a single fingerprint in the apartment up to now, she'd certainly been in the place long enough to have left evidence of her presence that no trained forensic scientist would ever miss. Besides, she'd be taking the computer with her anyway.

Sighing, she turned on the computer. The machine came to life and Becky clicked on the Internet Explorer icon. The screen refreshed and took her to Stanton's MSN homepage. A message at the top of the page welcomed "Cathystanton2" to the Microsoft Network.

Becky clicked on the "Hotmail" link and opened Stanton's mail account. Again, the screen refreshed, showing that Stanton had thirty-seven new messages, about half of which were enticements for breast augmentation devices, penis enlargement pills, and stock tips that the recipient dare not ignore.

There were no new messages from Walter. However, there was a folder named "Walter," and in it Becky found virtually all of the messages between Stanton and Walter that she earlier found on Walter's computer. It appeared that Stanton last wrote Walter two nights ago and that Walter had not responded to the message.

Becker also noticed a folder labeled "work." Curious, Becky opened the folder and found several messages between Stanton and the man who was apparently her boss. The messages dealt mostly with Stanton's work schedule.

Becky leaned back in the chair for a couple of minutes, thinking through the situation and mentally listing the things she had to do yet today. Then she leaned forward again, clicked on one of the messages to Stanton from her boss, and clicked "Reply."

The reply window opened, and Becky erased both the subject line and the body of the message in which the restaurant manager told Stanton that it would be fine if she came in to work forty minutes late because of her dental appointment.

Becky left the subject line blank, and in the message box, she wrote, "Dear Steve: Im having some personel problems that I cant really talk about in a message like this. I apologise, but I am going to have to quit work at least for a while. Sorry not to give you more notice. Will you please mail my last check to my apartment? Thanx, Cat. PS Im really sorry."

Becky read through the message again and hit the "Send" button. She then opened the window to compose a new message and typed in the address that Walter used to correspond with Stanton. In the body of the message, she explained that she was tired of waiting around for Walter to "leave that bitch so that we can get on with our lifes." She concluded by telling him not to call, write or see her again until he was ready to make a commitment to her. She signed the message, "Love, your Cathy," and sent it off to Walter's mailbox.

Leaving Hotmail, Becky went to Yahoo.com and opened a new e-mail account in her mother's name. She then went to the home page of the bank that issued her mother's Visa card. She entered the screen name and password that she'd created for the account and opened the link to "Manage My Account." There she instructed the bank to send electronic statements on the account to the Yahoo address that she'd created. She checked the box indicating that the bank should no longer mail paper statements for the account. She went through the same procedure for her mother's American Express card and then leaned back in the chair and spent a couple of minutes mulling over the most critical task that still confronted her.

While doing her other chores last evening, Becky spent a fair amount of time trying to determine how she would dispose of the remainder of Cathy Stanton's body. Her objective was to leave the torso in a place where it would not be discovered for at least a few days and where it would continue to decompose to a point where it would be virtually impossible to identify except by DNA testing.

Becky also hoped to dispose of the body in a way that would eliminate as much as possible any trace evidence of the fact that she had had any contact with it, and while walking back to Stanton's apartment the previous evening, she hit upon the idea of putting the body into the CAP canal. The first critical obstacle in the way of such a plan was finding a spot where she could get the body into the canal unobserved. The second would involve getting the body out of the car, through the fence that guarded the canal, and then into the canal itself.

After again considering the problem, Becky returned to Stanton's computer and brought up Google Earth. Once the program loaded, she typed the address of Stanton's apartment into the search box. The globe on the screen in front of her revolved around to the southwestern United States and then zoomed in to show a view from above the apartment complex with Scottsdale Road running north and south alongside it.

Using the dragging tool, Becky slowly pulled the scene down, looking farther north until she found the canal. She then began following the path of the waterway to the north and west. Initially, she saw nothing other than the city pressing hard up against the banks of the canal, but then the housing and industrial complexes began to thin out and large patches of vacant land now appeared on the screen. Becky zoomed in a bit closer and carefully examined a couple of sites where roads crossed the canal, but neither seemed to provide the prospective cover she was seeking.

On her fourth try, Becky zoomed in to a spot where a two-lane road crossed the canal in what appeared to be a fairly remote area. She noted that a gravel road left the paved road and ran parallel to the fence that guarded the canal for at least a short distance; it was impossible to tell exactly how far.

After looking at the site for a minute or so, Becky zoomed back out a bit and traced the path of the paved road back to the west. After something like a mile and a half or so, the road widened first into a street with two lanes running each way and then three, and the map indicated that she was crossing the intersection of Happy Valley Road and 23rd Avenue. Suddenly realizing where she was, Becky pulled the map a little more to the west until she was looking at the traffic circle where Happy Valley Road intersected I-17. Nodding in satisfaction at the discovery, she exited Google Earth and shut down the computer.

\*\*\*

It was now a little after noon and unfortunately Becky had things that she needed to do out in the light of day. In Stanton's bedroom closet, Becky had seen a straw cowboy hat with a wide purple band and a turquoise stone of some sort set in the front of the band. She retrieved the hat and put it on in the guest bathroom downstairs, piling as much of her hair under the hat as she could. Then she put on a pair of oversized sunglasses that she'd found on Stanton's kitchen counter and studied the image staring back at her in the bathroom mirror.

In truth, she probably wouldn't pass for Cathy Stanton, but she really didn't look like Becky Miller, either. Unless she encountered someone who recognized Stanton's car, she probably wouldn't get challenged on either score. In the garage, Becky hit the button to open the garage door, and fired up Stanton's Buick.

Becky realized that the most critical period would be the time it took her to drive from the garage through the gates of the complex. If a neighbor hailed her, expecting to chat for a moment with Cathy Stanton, things would get very dicey. But there was nothing she could do except to hope that her luck would hold. Becky dropped the car into gear, backed out of the garage, pressed the remote to close the garage door and then drove through the complex and out of the gates without incident.

Once out of the complex, Becky drove north on Scottsdale Road and then turned west on the 101. Traffic was relatively light and a few minutes later, she took the northbound exit for I-17. Happy Valley Road was the third exit off of 17 and she drove slowly through the commercial development that paralleled both sides of Happy Valley Road at that point. Shortly, though, just as Google Earth promised, the development thinned out to virtually empty desert and the road slimmed down to two narrow lanes. Only a few minutes after leaving the Interstate, Becky crossed the canal and turned down the gravel road that ran alongside it.

The canal was protected by a chain link fence that was about five feet high at this point and topped by three strands of barbed wire. Perhaps ten yards of desert gravel lay between the fence and the canal itself. Now looking at the scene live, Becky estimated that the road paralleled the canal for about eighty or ninety yards.

The land surrounding the scene was rough desert, populated by a few cacti and a variety of scrub plants. A small sign on Becky's right indicated that the vacant land south of the canal was part of the state land trust. A few low hills guarded the area and on the other side of Happy Valley Road, what appeared to be a small industrial or commercial site looked to be pretty quiet even in the middle of the day.

As Becky stood there surveying the scene, the occasional car or truck passed by on the roadway, but she assumed that late at night the place would be nearly pitch dark and traffic would be even lighter. She figured that she could back the Buick down the access road as far as possible, park tight up against the fence, then get out and do her business as fast as she could. If any vehicles should pass by, she assumed that it would be difficult if not impossible for the drivers to notice the dark blue car parked down by the fence.

She concluded that the only real danger would be if a roving canal security patrol happened along just as she was dragging the torso from the car to canal. But she calculated that, all things considered, the odds of successfully executing the plan were probably better here than they would be anywhere else. Sighing heavily, Becky turned a full 360 degrees, looking over the scene; it wasn't perfect, but it was the best she could hope for.

***

At a hardware store on Thunderbird Road, Becky paid cash for a heavy-duty bolt cutter, a box cutter, and a small roll of thin silver wire. Reluctant to go anywhere near Cathy Stanton's refrigerator/freezer unless she absolutely had to, she chanced going through the drive-through lane at a McDonald's and bought a salad and a medium Diet Coke to go. She managed to make it back into Stanton's garage without incident and gratefully watched the garage door close behind her.

She ate her lunch in the living room and then went back upstairs. In the master closet, she picked out two blouses and set them on the bed. Then she dumped more of Stanton's clothes into the large suitcase that she'd set out yesterday, leaving the closet about half full.

Stanton apparently did not own a carrying case for her laptop computer, so Becky unplugged the cables leading to the cable modem and the printer, then wrapped up the power cord and put it and the computer itself into a small plastic garbage bag and wrapped the bag tightly around the machine. Back downstairs, Becky took the suitcase, the computer, and her gym bags out to the garage and put them into the trunk of Stanton's car.

From the hardware store bag in the back seat, Becky retrieved the spool of wire and the bolt cutter. She unrolled about three feet of the wire and used the bolt cutter to snip off several pieces, each about five inches in length. She returned the tools and the wire to the bag and set the bag back in the car. At a little after three o'clock, she slipped out of her jeans and lay down on the couch, hoping that she could get some sleep. For the moment, there was nothing more that she could do but wait.

## 48

I got back to the office a little after one and found Maggie in her office. I brought her up to date on my morning's activities and told her that I'd left Gary Barnett's crew at Miller's house. She set down the report she was reading and said, "You're not seriously thinking that our victim is not the Miller woman?"

"Not really. But I will feel a lot better about things when the lab tells us that the victim's DNA was all over the Miller house and not just on the toothbrush and hairbrush. I'd certainly feel a lot better if we could have a little chat with Cathy Stanton, and I'd also feel a lot more comfortable if I could figure out why Becky Miller behaved the way she did in the few weeks before she disappeared."

"But, you can certainly understand why she bugged his computer and why she hired the P.I. She suspected that her husband was screwing another woman and she wanted to get the goods on him.

"Once she had solid evidence, she decided to divorce the bastard. She manufactured the diary to use as a weapon of some sort. She probably suspected that ol' Walter would fight dirty, so she converted her stocks to cash and hid the money where he couldn't get his hands on it and where she could use it to fight him.

"Then, when she confronted him, he flew into a rage and killed her. He cut up the body, reported his wife missing, and pretended to be devastated when she popped up in the canal. We caught him in a whole bunch of lies; we found the saw in his garage, and we busted his sorry ass. Case closed. The good guys win again."

"But why does he cut up the body, Maggie? Why doesn't he just bury it out in the desert somewhere?"

"Well, she can't just go missing forever or it will be years before he can have her declared dead and inherit her money. The body has to be found and identified. He probably cut her apart and buried her head and arms someplace because he wanted us to think that there was some truly sick fuck out there who grabbed his wife on the way home from her book club and did unspeakable things to her."

"Maybe, but where the hell is Stanton in all of this? I mean, maybe she did just take off to think things through or some damned thing. And maybe it was just a coincidence that she took off the day after Becky Miller disappeared, even though you have to admit that would be one helluva coincidence. But the media's been all over this case like white on rice. Stanton has to know we're looking for her. Why hasn't she surfaced?"

Maggie shook her head. "I don't know. The logical answer would be because she and Walter were in it together. Don't forget that she was the one who apparently first suggested that the two of them would be a lot better off if Miller's wife were out of the picture. But maybe once they actually did the deed she panicked and decided to get the hell out of Dodge for a while."

"Maybe, but we should have found her by now."

***

Back in my own office, I found a note on my desk asking me to call Detective Bud Porter in the Amarillo P.D. Thinking that maybe there was something to be said for the power of suggestion, I dialed the number. At the other end of the line somebody picked up the phone and said, "Grand Theft. Porter."

The voice sounded like it belonged to a large, hail-fellow-well-met sort of a guy. I identified myself and told him I was returning his call. "Right," he said. "You guys're lookin' for a three-year-old navy-blue Buick Regal?"

He read off the VIN number, and I said, "Well, actually, Detective Porter, what I'm really looking for is the woman who goes with the Buick."

"Well, I'm sorry to say that I have no idea where the woman is, but we do have the car. A patrolman pulled it over at three in the a.m. this morning. A bunch of kids were in it and when our guy ran the plate number, the plate came up stolen. The driver, who had no license, said that he borrowed the car from his brother. I don't 'spose you'll be surprised to hear that the kid knew nothin' at all about any stolen plates.

"Anyway, we hauled the brother out of bed and had a talk with him. He's seventeen and has one juvie prior for joy riding in a borrowed car. He says he found this one about two weeks ago in the parking lot of a Seven Eleven store."

"Were the keys in it?"

"Yup. So, he and a pal decided that the car was begging to be stolen and that if they didn't do it, somebody else more than likely would. They drove it off, then stole a set of plates and replaced the AZ plate. It took them this long before they did something stupid enough to get pulled over and found out."

"Did you discover anything interesting in the car?"

"Nada. The trunk was empty and there was nothing in the passenger compartment save for the kids and a coupla bottles of liquor that they were way too young to be drinkin' legally."

"Were there any keys on the ring other than the car key?"

"If there were, they're long gone. Our joy rider, whose name is Darius Clinton, put the key on a chain with his lucky rabbit's foot, which turned out not to be all that lucky, I guess. That was the only key we found."

I thought about that for a couple of seconds, then said, "Have you had any unidentified female bodies turn up there in the last week? The woman we're looking for is blonde, late thirties, fairly good build."

"Not that I know of. But then that's really not my department. I will check upstairs, though, and if Homicide's come up with anything along those lines, I'll get back to you."

I thanked Porter and told him that we'd be making arrangements to ship Stanton's Buick back to Phoenix. I assumed that if a bunch of kids had been riding around in the car for a week or so, our chances of getting any useful evidence out of it were somewhere between slim and none. But at this point we couldn't afford to overlook anything, no matter how remote, that might help clear up the confusion surrounding this case.

49

Becky tossed fitfully on the couch for a couple of hours, too wired to fall asleep. Finally, she gave it up and turned on Stanton's television set. She spent the rest of the afternoon and evening pacing back and forth in the living room and mindlessly flipping through the channels.

More to occupy her time than because she thought it would really do any good, she went through the apartment with a cloth, carefully wiping down any surface that she might have touched when she wasn't wearing the rubber gloves. She forced herself to wait until a little after midnight and finally could wait no longer. She walked into the kitchen, pulled on the rubber gloves again, and opened the freezer door.

The torso appeared to be frozen nearly solid. Becky took hold of the ankles and wrenched the body out of the freezer and onto the kitchen floor. Condensation had formed on the plastic sheeting and had then frozen, making the plastic slippery to the touch. Becky slid the package across the linoleum floor and out of the kitchen, then dragged it across the living room carpet and into the entryway. There she opened the door to the garage and pulled open the back door of Stanton's car.

Ideally, Becky would have preferred to conceal the package in the trunk, but she wasn't sure that she was strong enough to lift it up and into the trunk. Even more important, she was not at all confident that she'd be able to lift the package back up over the lip of the trunk and out when she got to the canal. There, time would be of the essence. She could ill afford to be caught trying to wrestle the remains of a woman's body out of the trunk of a stolen car.

Using concrete blocks and a few pieces of three-quarter-inch plywood, Stanton — or someone — had cobbled together some shelves in the front of the garage, and a number of boxes were stacked on the shelves. Earlier in the afternoon, Becky had set three of the boxes on the floor, freeing up one piece of plywood, perhaps twenty-four inches wide and sixty inches long.

Becky now positioned the plywood so that one end was resting on the threshold of the door leading from the entryway out to the garage. The other end rested on the back seat of the Buick. Becky positioned the package at the lower end of the plywood, then positioned herself behind the package with her legs straddling the board.

The package slid up the ramp and into the car with less difficulty than Becky had expected. She took the dark blue blanket she'd been using on the couch and tucked the blanket around the package. Then she picked up the plywood, set it back on the concrete blocks, and put the boxes back on the shelf.

In the kitchen, she put the shelves back into the freezer compartment and returned the ice cube drawer and the no-longer frozen food to the freezer. Then she snapped off the lights in the kitchen, living room and entryway. Careful to lock the door to the garage behind her, she got into the Buick and drove out of the apartment complex.

***

At one o'clock in the morning, there was very little traffic either on Scottsdale Road or on the 101. Terrified of attracting the attention of a police officer by driving either too fast or too slowly, Becky drove exactly at the speed limit and carefully signaled every turn.

With Stanton's body lying on the seat behind her, it felt like it took three times longer to make the journey out to the canal than it had earlier in the afternoon. But she made it without incident and when she reached the canal, there was no traffic moving in either direction on Happy Valley Road. She carefully backed the Buick down the gravel road that ran alongside the canal, stopping about seventy-five yards away from Happy Valley Road. Earlier in the evening, she had switched off the dome light, and as she opened the driver's door, the car remained dark. From the floor behind the driver's seat, she retrieved the sack with her tools.

A pale half-moon hung in the clear night sky, only weakly illuminating the scene; otherwise, it was pitch dark out. The temperature was somewhere in the high sixties or low seventies and the night was eerily quiet. Adrenaline pumping through her system, Becky raced around the back of the car and crouched down near the fence.

She was dressed again in her jeans and a dark blue tee shirt. Huddled down in the darkness, she prayed that both she and the Buick would be virtually invisible to anyone who was more than thirty yards away. Shivering in spite of the warm temperature, Becky reached into the sack and pulled out the bolt cutter.

The tool was more than a match for the chain link, and Becky methodically cut the fence in a straight line from the ground up about three feet. Then she crab-walked four feet to her right and cut another line up the fence parallel to the first. Laying the bolt cutter aside, she pushed the cut section of the fence inward toward the canal. She dug the box cutter out of the hardware store bag and stuck it into the back pocket of her jeans. Then she rose to her feet, opened the back door of the Buick, and tugged Stanton's body out of the car.

The package hit the ground with a heavy thud. Becky pulled it to one side and closed the car door as quietly as possible. At each end of the package, the plastic sheet had been folded over several times and then taped. Becky took a firm hold on the excess material at one end of the package and tugged the package toward the hole she'd cut in the fence. Once there, she lined the package up in front of the hole and pushed it through the fence. Just as she did, the lights of a vehicle moving south down Happy Valley Road illuminated the roadway to her left.

Becky dropped to the ground and froze in place holding her breath, mostly because she was frightened to death and not just because it seemed like the strategic thing to do. A truck sped past down the road and faded into the distance, gone as quickly as it had appeared. Her heart pounding, Becky took a couple of deep breaths and then followed the package though the fence. As she did, the section Becky had cut snapped back toward its original position, raking down her back. Two of the wire strands ripped her tee shirt and cut into her skin.

Becky cursed softly, but continued to push the package forward toward the canal. She stopped a couple of yards from the edge of the canal and pulled the box cutter out of her pocket. Moving around to the other end of the package, she cut through the tape, releasing the folded-up plastic sheeting. She slashed through several more pieces of tape, then returned to the other end of the package.

Gripping the excess plastic at the head of the package, Becky cautiously shoved the package right to the edge of the canal. Then she dug her heels into the ground and strained to lift the end of the package.

As the weight of the body tipped over the edge of the bank, the entire package began slipping inexorably down toward the water, threatening to take Becky with it. She leaned back, clinging to the plastic sheeting, and desperately digging her heels into the ground. Then, at the last possible moment, when it appeared that she would be unable to prevent the entire package from falling into the canal, Stanton's body finally slipped free and splashed into the water, six feet below.

Becky crawled quickly back through the fence, pulling the plastic sheeting behind her. She crumpled the plastic into a large ball and then dug into the hardware store sack and retrieved the small pieces of wire that she'd cut earlier. She pulled the section of fence back into place and, working as quickly as she could, she secured it at several points with the wire. Then she stood and took a couple of steps back. In the darkness, at least, she thought the repair job looked pretty good.

She gathered up her tools, the blanket from the back seat, and the balled-up plastic sheet, and threw them into the trunk. Then she slammed the trunk lid down, jumped into the car, drove slowly back out to Happy Valley Road, and turned right.

Thirty minutes later, she drove slowly past the front of her own home. All the lights were out, and Walter was apparently fast asleep. She parked on a darkened side street a block away, then retrieved the house key from her purse and the pruning saw, still wrapped in the paper toweling, from the trunk of the car. Moving deliberately, she walked back up the street, carrying the saw down close to her right leg.

She assumed that the police would ultimately discover the saw and that chemical tests would confirm that the saw had been used to dismember Stanton's body. She also assumed that this would leave Walter in deep shit, at least for a while. But she also assumed that he would not be there forever.

She reasoned that ultimately the police were bound to discover that the victim was really Stanton. They would also discover that Becky had liquidated all of her assets and had disappeared. They would doubtless find forensic evidence confirming the fact that Becky had spent a considerable amount of time in Stanton's apartment. And in the end, they would certainly realize that Becky and not Walter was most likely the person who had killed Stanton.

If they did not come to the realization themselves, Becky would ultimately lead them there. As much as Walter had disappointed her, she would not allow him to be convicted of a crime that she had committed. In the meantime, though, she needed him to serve as a distraction, while she tried to effectively disappear forever from the picture.

At the side door of the garage, she held her breath for a moment and then inserted her key into the lock. The door opened quietly and Becky slipped into the garage and closed the door behind her. She waited for a moment, allowing her eyes to adjust to the darkness, then felt her way along the wall to the spot where the saw belonged on the pegboard.

She unrolled the paper toweling, hung the saw in its proper place, and quietly let herself out of the garage again. Then she walked quickly back up the street to the car, pitched the paper toweling into the back seat, and pointed the Buick in the direction of the state line.

***

A little after four in the morning, Becky pulled into a small truck stop just outside of Flagstaff. She was bone tired, and she would've given anything to be able to check into a motel and sleep for the next ten hours. But her luck had held this far, and she didn't want to test it now. She put on the cowboy hat, pulled it low over her face, then got out of the car and filled the tank with gas, paying at the pump with Stanton's credit card. In the truck stop café, she bought a donut and a large cup of coffee from a middle-aged waitress who looked as tired as Becky felt.

Becky ate the donut in the car and took a couple of sips of the hot coffee, then she cranked the ignition again. As she backed out of the parking spot, her headlights picked up the shape of a dumpster sitting off the darkened corner at the back of the building. The dumpster was positioned so that it couldn't be seen through the windows of the café.

Half a mile away, traffic sped past on I-40, but there was no one at the truck stop gas pumps and Becky could see no activity anywhere around the outside of the café. Through the window, she could see the waitress and the cashier huddled in conversation and paying no attention to anything that might be happening outside.

Becky killed the headlights and pulled up next to the dumpster. It took her less than forty-five seconds to drop the tools, the blanket and the balled-up plastic sheeting into the nearly empty dumpster, and then she was back on the road again, headed east.

Two hours and a hundred and fifty miles later, she could barely keep her eyes open. A sign flashed by, advertising a rest stop two miles ahead. Reluctantly, Becky decided that she had to take advantage of the opportunity to get off of the road and take a short nap.

A long string of semis lined the exit ramp leading off the interstate, and a number of vehicles were scattered around the rest stop parking lot. Becky found a spot directly in front of the main building and parked the Buick. Careful to lock the car behind her, she went inside and used the rest room. Once outside again, she popped the trunk and pulled a Jacket out of one of her gym bags.

She laid the driver's seat back as far as it would go, then rolled up the jacket, leaned back, and laid her head on the makeshift pillow. The sun was just beginning to crawl up the eastern horizon as Becky closed her eyes and fell immediately into sleep.

## 50

We had a suspect in custody and the case against him was strong. But there were too damned many parts of the picture that remained out of focus, and I continued to feel uneasy and frustrated.

In large part, the frustration grew out of the fact that there wasn't a helluva lot I could do at this point. It would take the techs a few days to confirm that our victim was Becky Miller, or — god forbid — to tell us that it probably wasn't. We had bulletins out nation-wide for Cathy Stanton, and had alerted her credit card companies to notify us the instant that any charges were made on her accounts. But until someone spotted her, or until we got a hit on one of the credit cards, there was nothing more I could do in that direction.

I didn't know whether to be encouraged or discouraged about the credit cards. Obviously, Stanton had not left her purse — or at least her credit cards — in the car at the convenience store in Amarillo. If she had, certainly the kids who boosted the car would have sold the cards or attempted to use them themselves, and we would have seen activity on the accounts.

Bud Porter had called back to tell me that the Amarillo P.D. had no unidentified bodies matching Stanton's description. He also told me, though, that the convenience store where the car was stolen was located in a fairly rough neighborhood.

I wondered what Stanton might have been doing in that neighborhood. I also wondered why she had stopped using the credit cards when she had used them so freely on the trip from Phoenix to Texas and then to book the flight to Boise.

It was possible that she was making an effort to mislead anyone who might be attempting to trace her movements. But it was also possible that she drove to Amarillo for some specific reason and booked the flight to Boise with every expectation of taking it. Then, before she could do so, she could have been the victim of foul play in Texas, totally unrelated to the case unfolding in Arizona.

I phoned Stanton's former boss, Steve Abernathy, and her friend, Jennifer Johnson, to make sure that they had heard nothing from Stanton. I then spent a couple of hours calling all of the hospitals I could find listed in Amarillo, checking to see if Stanton, or an unidentified woman matching her description, had been admitted. When I had no luck there, I dug through the public records and found Stanton's maiden name, which was Kramer. On the off chance that she might have been going to Boise to visit relatives, I then worked my way through all of the Stantons and Kramers in the Boise phone book. But none of the people I managed to reach had ever heard of a Cathy Stanton or a Cathy Kramer who lived in Phoenix.

What the hell was in Boise? And even if it was an attempt at misdirection, why had Stanton chosen that particular city? By the end of the day, I was no closer to answering either question — or any of the others that were nagging at me — than I had been at the day's beginning. And so, thoroughly frustrated, I finally decided to give it up for the day and hope that in the absence of any new information, the following day might at least bring some new inspiration.

51

Just before noon on Friday, Becky pulled into a gas station on the west side of Albuquerque, New Mexico. She assumed that, like so many others, the station probably had video cameras watching customers at the pumps as a means of deterring drive-offs.

Before leaving the rest area, she'd used the bathroom again and put on one of the blouses she'd saved from Cathy Stanton's closet. Now, before pulling up to the pumps, she piled up her hair and put on the cowboy had she'd found in Stanton's closet. To complete the outfit, she slipped on Stanton's large sunglasses.

At the pump, Becky swiped Stanton's Visa card and filled the tank. That done, she found a Subway Sandwich shop in a small strip mall and ate a Turkey sandwich for lunch.

Two doors down from the Subway was a Hair Express franchise. Becky walked into the shop and asked if they could take her without an appointment. The receptionist, who looked to be about nineteen and who sported a closely cropped head of pink hair, assured Becky that they could squeeze her in, "No prob." Ten minutes later, Becky sat down in a chair and described for the stylist the relatively short, layered haircut that Cathy Stanton had worn.

Like every other woman who'd blinked back tears while watching her long tresses fall to the salon floor, Becky saw her old life slipping away. Only in her case, of course, the illusion was literally true. Thirty minutes later, the stylist put away her blow dryer, fussed over a couple of final touches, and asked what Becky thought.

Looking in the mirror, what Becky thought was that you get what you pay for.

The style was all wrong for her, and she felt like some alien being was staring back at her from the mirror. But she was now a whole lot closer to passing for the woman in the picture on Cathy Stanton's driver's license, and that, after all, was the whole point.

She could worry about repairing the damage somewhere down the road.

***

Becky paid the woman, made her way back to I-40, and headed east again. She made one more stop to use a restroom and, four and a half hours after leaving Albuquerque, she pulled under the canopy of a Holiday Inn Express in Amarillo. She checked into the hotel, this time using Stanton's MasterCard, and thought about walking over to the restaurant next door to the hotel for dinner. The alternative was to go straight to bed and, tired as she was, the choice was no contest.

Following the desk clerk's directions, she drove around to the side of the hotel and parked. She lugged the two gym bags and the suitcase into her room, hung the "Do Not Disturb" sign outside the door and shot the deadbolt home. She used the phone in the room to call United Airlines and book a flight to Boise at two thirty-seven the next afternoon. Then she stripped off her clothes, took a brief hot shower, and gratefully crawled into bed.

She slept straight through for twelve hours. At mid-morning she got up, showered again, and put on fresh clothes, including the second blouse that she'd taken from Cathy Stanton's closet. She ate a large, late breakfast in a restaurant next door to the motel and then, back in the room, she scribbled an approximation of the signature on Stanton's credit cards onto the express check-out form. She left the form on the desk in the room and carried the two gym bags out to Stanton's car.

She abandoned the suitcase with Stanton's clothes next to a dumpster behind the hotel, got into the Buick, and began driving south into the city. As she drove further south away from the Interstate, the neighborhoods steadily deteriorated, and after driving for ten minutes or so, she found a convenience store at the corner of what appeared to be a major intersection.

A pay phone hung off the wall of the store and Becky parked in front of the phone, hoping that it was still in working order. She stepped out of the car wearing Stanton's cowboy hat and sunglasses. As she did, a man stumbled through the door of the store carrying a

226

bottle of malt liquor, and nearly tripped over the concrete parking barrier immediately in front of the door. He righted himself at the last possible moment and lurched off down the street, heading away from the spot where Becky was standing.

She hurried to the phone and dug some change out of her jeans, along with the number of the cab company that she'd copied down from the phone book in her hotel room. The dispatcher promised to have a cab at Becky's location within twenty minutes. She thanked the woman, hung up the phone, went back to the car and locked all the doors.

Fifteen minutes later, the cab pulled up in front of the store. Becky pushed the button to unlock the trunk and got out of the car, leaving the keys in the ignition. She retrieved the two bags from the trunk, got into the cab, and told the driver to take her to the airport.

In front of the terminal, she paid the cab, walked through the doors, and headed toward the nearest women's restroom. She ditched the hat and sunglasses in a garbage can, found an empty stall, and changed out of Stanton's blouse and into one of her own, grateful for the simple pleasure of wearing her own clothes again, if not her own hairstyle. Outside the terminal, she found a shuttle to the bus station, and there she bought a ticket to Portland.

52

After tossing fitfully through most of the night and getting very little sleep, I was back at my desk a little after seven the next morning. I was cleaning up some paperwork a little after nine when Gary Barnett walked through the door and dropped into my guest chair. "Let me guess," I said. "You didn't walk all the way across the street and up two flights of stairs to bring me good news."

"No, I didn't. I'm afraid that your Miller case is totally fucked up."

Given the doubts that had been nagging at me for the last couple of days, I really wasn't all that surprised. Shaking my head, I said, "How so?"

"Well, the DNA from the toothbrush and hairbrush that you gave us definitely matches up to the victim that was pulled from the canal. And the blood that was on the pruning saw also came from the victim. The problem is, that we can't find anything else in the Miller house that does. We went through the place with the proverbial fine toothcomb, Sean. We found all kinds of trace evidence, but none of it came from your victim."

"So, you're telling me that, as a practical matter, there's no way that the woman we found in the canal could have been living in that house?"

"Almost certainly not. There's just no way she could've done so without leaving evidence of her presence all over the damned place."

"Okay, Gary, I'm guessing then, that our vic is probably a woman named Cathy Stanton. She lives — or lived — in an apartment on Scottsdale Road. Let's get a warrant, take a team over there and see what we can come up with."

\*\*\*

I found Maggie coming out of the women's john. Reading the look on my face, she said, "Oh, shit. What's the hell's the matter?"

228

On the way down the hall to the sergeant's office I described my conversation with Barnett. Maggie was still cursing and shaking her head when we got to the Sergeant's door. We waited outside for a couple of minutes while he finished a phone conversation, then he waved us in and we took the two seats in front of his desk. Martin made a quick note, then put down his pen, dropped his reading glasses on the desk, and said, "What's up?"

"I hate to have to tell you this," I said, "but it looks like the torso we pulled out of the canal is not Becky Miller after all."

A look of disbelief registered on his face. "And how the hell is that possible? I thought you had a positive ID?"

"So did we. DNA samples from the toothbrush and hairbrush we took from Becky Miller's bathroom definitely match up to the torso, no question about it. And, of course, the victim was also wearing a toe ring exactly like Miller's. But the lab's now telling us that there's no other evidence apart from the toothbrush and hairbrush to suggest that the victim was ever in Miller's house."

"So, who the hell is the victim?"

"I'm guessing that it's most likely the husband's girlfriend, Cathy Stanton. She disappeared at virtually the same time the Miller woman did, and nobody's seen or heard from her since. We're taking a team over now to go through her apartment."

"But I thought that you'd tracked the Stanton woman to Texas long after the M.E. says that the victim was dead."

"Well, actually," Maggie said, "We tracked somebody using Stanton's credit cards to Texas. We don't know for sure that it really was Stanton."

"And if your victim is Stanton, then who in the hell killed her?"

"We don't know yet," I said. "But there's still an excellent chance that it was Walter Miller. He was involved with the woman, and she was pressuring him to leave his wife. Maybe she threatened to expose the affair and he killed her to keep her quiet. Even if we initially misidentified the victim, the saw that was used to dismember the body was still found in Miller's garage. DNA from the saw matches up to the victim — that hasn't changed."

Martin shot us a skeptical look. "Then where the hell is Miller's wife?"

"We don't know that, either," Maggie said. "We know she discovered that her husband was cheating on her and that she was apparently planning to divorce him because of it. It's possible that he killed Stanton to keep the affair quiet, not knowing that his wife already knew about it."

"Then, when the wife confronted him anyhow, he killed her because a divorce would have ruined him financially. He dismembered Stanton, dumped the torso into the canal, and buried his wife out in the desert someplace with Stanton's head and arms. Then he started playing games with the evidence, hoping to confuse things to the point that he'd get away with both killings."

Martin shot her a look of disbelief and in the silence that followed, I said, "Of course it's also possible that Becky Miller is our killer and that she's the one who's playing games with the evidence. Maybe Stanton confronted her or she confronted Stanton and Stanton somehow wound up dead. Maybe Becky Miller put her own toe ring on Stanton's foot, dumped the torso into the canal, and swapped Stanton's tooth and hairbrushes for her own, hoping that we'd identify Stanton as the victim."

"And she set her husband up to take the fall?" the Sergeant asked?

I shrugged. "Well, he was cheating on her. And *somebody* used Stanton's credit cards to go to Texas."

He shook his head and pinched the bridge of his nose. "Good Christ. Given all the attention this case has attracted, do you realize the shit storm that's gonna rain down on us when we have to tell the fuckin' media that the case has blown up?"

"I know," Maggie said. "But we did it by the book, Loo. We had a part of a corpse. We had a woman reported missing, and we found DNA evidence in the missing woman's bathroom that matched the vic. It was S.O.P., straight down the line. We had no way of knowing that some asshole was jerking us around."

"I understand that, Maggie, and I'm not blaming you guys. I'm just not looking forward to explaining it to the Assistant Chief. And he's damned well not going to look forward to answering questions from the media about it."

"Well, I hope he won't be answering questions about it," I said. "At least not for the time being. We don't even know for certain yet that Stanton is the victim. I know that you're going to have to brief the A.C., but let's at least get a better idea of what the hell is going on here before anybody starts holding press conferences."

"We will. In the meantime, you two get out there and figure out what in the hell is really going on in this goddamned case."

*\*\**

When the manager opened the door for us, Stanton's apartment looked exactly like it had a week earlier. Outside the temperature was in the high nineties, but someone had set the apartment's thermostat to the low seventies, and the air conditioner was hard at work. Still, the place had a stale air about it, as if it had been closed up tight since Maggie and I last visited.

We took a quick walk through the apartment, then Maggie and I got out of the way so that Gary Barnett and his team could get to work. I asked Gary to start in the second bedroom upstairs. Once they were through with the room, Maggie and I began a detailed search through Stanton's desk and through several boxes that she had stored at the bottom of the closet in the room.

Stanton was obviously the polar opposite of Becky Miller in terms of her organizational skills. She'd simply pitched her bills and bank statements into one of the desk drawers, apparently in the order that they'd come in the mail. Sorting through the material, I noted that she rarely bothered to reconcile her bank statements with her checkbook and that she usually paid only the minimum amount due on her credit cards. She'd "filed" her copy of the lease agreement on her apartment in a box in the closet under her tax return from two years earlier. We'd been working in the room for about thirty minutes when Gary Barnett poked his head into the room and said, "You might want to come take a look at this."

We followed him down the hall to the bathroom. The fixtures had been treated with chemicals, and one of the techs had taken the bathtub drain apart. Pointing at the tub, Gary said, "I can't tell you who it was yet, but somebody got butchered in that bathtub.

"Whoever did it scrubbed the tub down pretty well, but either they didn't think to clean out the drain or they didn't have the time or the tools to do it with. Whichever the case, they left more than enough evidence behind them. DNA will take a while, of course, but once we get back to the lab, we'll be able to tell you pretty quickly if the blood type matches your victim."

\*\*\*

I was pretty certain that the blood type would match our victim, and I was also increasingly certain of the fact that the victim would turn out to be Cathy Stanton and not Becky Miller. I was also pretty sure that if the victim was Stanton, we weren't going to find anything in her apartment that would tell us where Becky Miller might be.

We left Barnett and his team to finish up in the apartment, and back in the office I dug out the records of Stanton's most recent credit card purchases. Since the night Walter Miller had reported his wife missing, someone had used Stanton's Visa card at a gas station in Flagstaff, and at another in Albuquerque. Someone had used the woman's MasterCard to check into a Holiday Inn in Amarillo, and had then used the Visa card again to charge an airline ticket to Boise.

I called the gas station in Flagstaff and the manager told me that they had signs on their gas pumps warning customers that their pictures had been recorded and that drive-offs would be prosecuted. "But we don't really do it. The signs cost us next to nothing, but putting in the video equipment would cost more than what we actually lose to thieves."

The station manager in Albuquerque told me that they digitally recorded transactions at the pump and that the images were stored in a computer file for two weeks. I told him that we were looking for someone who had bought $43.25 worth of gas a little after noon on June fourth. I told him that most likely the customer was driving a blue Buick Regal. The guy promised that he'd look at the file for that date and e-mail it to me within the hour.

232

The manager at the Holiday Inn was not nearly as accommodating. He told me that they did record video of the registration desk and that they would still have the files for the date in question. But he refused to send me a copy of the file without making me jump through a lot of hoops. I called Bud Porter in the Amarillo P.D. and asked him if he could go over to the hotel and give the manager a swift kick in the ass. He said that he'd be happy to do so and would get back to me as quickly as he could.

I spent the next forty minutes pacing up and down the hall, and checking my e-mail every five minutes. Just after three o'clock, the message from Albuquerque hit my computer and I clicked open the attachment. In it were three photos showing a woman in a cowboy hat and oversized sunglasses pumping fuel into a dark blue Buick sedan. I printed out the photos and then, too keyed up to wait to hear back from Bud Porter, I called Jennifer Burke and asked if I could run out to see her.

Burke told me that she was working at home and that I could come over anytime. She asked me why I wanted to see her, but I deflected the question and told her I'd get there as quickly as I could. Forty minutes later, she led me up the stairs and into her living room. I declined her offer of something to drink and she asked again why I wanted to see her. I pulled an envelope with the three photos out of my suit coat pocket. "If you wouldn't mind," I said, "I'd like you to look at some pictures."

A look of concern flashed across her face. "Don't worry," I assured her. "These aren't crime scene photos or anything like that. They're just regular pictures."

"Okay," she said, obviously relieved.

I pulled the pictures out of the envelope and passed them to her, one at a time. She took a good long time with each of the photos, and a look of confusion spread across her face. Shaking her head, she looked up at me and said, "I don't understand."

"Do you recognize the woman in the photos?"

Burke shrugged her shoulders, looking even more confused. "It's Becky. But that's not her car."

"You're sure that's Becky Miller?"

She nodded. "Yes, of course. I've never seen her in those sunglasses and I can't for the life of me imagine why she'd be wearing a hat like that, but it's her."

She handed the pictures back to me. "What's going on here, Detective Richardson?"

"I wish I knew, Ms. Burke. I need to ask you to keep this in strictest confidence, but these pictures were taken in New Mexico two days after Walter Miller reported his wife missing."

Burke's hands flew to her face. "What are you telling me? Are you saying that Becky is not dead?"

"I honestly don't know. But if the woman in these pictures is in fact Becky Miller, then the body that we found in the canal cannot be hers."

Tears sprung to Burke's eyes and began rolling down her cheeks. Making no effort to wipe them away, she said, "But I thought you were certain."

"We were. And I apologize for springing this on you like this. But as you know, we had to make the identification through a DNA match, and the DNA of our victim clearly did match the DNA that we found in Ms. Miller's bathroom. It looks like someone's playing games with us, trying to confuse the identification."

Crying harder, Burke said, "But why? Who would do that?"

I shook my head. "Again, I'm sorry, but I don't know the answer to that either. Obviously, we need to find out."

Burke finally snatched a tissue from a box on the table next to her club chair, sank down into the chair and wiped at her tears. In a soft voice, she asked, "If the body you found is not Becky's, then whose is it?"

"We're not sure. We're trying to determine that as well."

Burke shook her head. "I'm sorry, Detective, but I just don't believe it. Becky was my best friend. She wouldn't have just left and gone off to New Mexico or some damn place without saying anything to me. Even if something terrible had happened, she would have told me. As much as I don't want it to be true, she must be dead."

"And, of course, she may be. Unfortunately, just because hers wasn't the body we found in the canal doesn't automatically mean that Ms. Miller is still alive somewhere."

Burke swiped at her tears again and I said, "You told me that Ms. Miller was the principal crime fiction fan in your book club. Did she read a lot of crime novels and police procedurals?"

She nodded. "Why do you ask?"

"To be honest, I'm simply curious to know how much she knew about the subject."

She flared. "Wait a minute. You're not suggesting that you think Becky is the one who's manipulating evidence?"

"No, Ms. Burke, I'm not. At this point I have no idea who's doing it, but it's obviously someone who has a pretty good idea of how the police would work in a case like this. Whoever it is, he or she has been running us around in circles so far."

"Well, it couldn't be Becky. To be honest, I'll admit that I think she's smart enough and that she probably has read enough books to be able to do it. But she's not the kind of person who would do something like that. And besides, why would she?"

\*\*\*

I wasn't about to suggest to Jennifer Burke that her friend might be doing something like that because she'd killed her husband's girlfriend, then chopped up the body and planted evidence to suggest that she herself had been the victim. But I was sure as hell beginning to suspect that was indeed the case.

I couldn't buy into Maggie's suggestion that Walter Miller might have killed both women, especially not if his wife was alive and well and seven hundred and fifty miles away from Phoenix two days after he reported her missing. Certainly, though, our killer was someone who had access to the Miller's house. He, or she, had planted Stanton's toothbrush and hairbrush in Becky Miller's bathroom. He or she had also apparently killed Stanton, dismembered the body in Stanton's bathtub, and then, for whatever reason, returned the pruning saw to the pegboard in the Millers' garage.

If Walter Stanton had killed and dismembered his mistress, then why in the world would his wife have assumed Stanton's identity and left a trail for us to follow to Amarillo? That made no sense to me, and I couldn't imagine a scenario in which the Millers together had conspired to kill Stanton for some reason. By process of elimination, then, that left Becky Miller.

Perhaps she had decided to fight for her man after all. Or perhaps she wanted to punish both her husband and his lover by killing the woman, leading us to believe that she herself was the victim, and putting her husband in the frame for the crime. Whatever the case, I was increasingly certain of the fact that we had the wrong person in custody.

## 53

In Portland, Becky checked into a Hyatt Hotel downtown, using her mother's name and credit card. She told the clerk that she'd be there for two or three nights, depending upon how her business in the city went.

Once in her room, she put away the few clothes she brought with her. From the bottom of one of the gym bags, she retrieved the envelope containing her cash. She counted out ten of the hundred-dollar bills and put them into her purse. Then she returned the balance of the cash to the envelope and put the envelope back in bottom of the gym bag. She piled her dirty laundry on top of the cash, coins and clothing, zipped the bag closed and tossed the bag into the back of the closet, saying a silent prayer that no one would get into the room and into the bag.

Leaving the television on, she hung the "Do Not Disturb" sign on the door and spent the rest of the afternoon shopping for clothes. She bought a number of basic items that would hold her for at least a while, and paid cash for all of her purchases. In Nordstrom, she bought a skirt and a couple of blouses. Becky told the attractive saleswoman that she was new in town and wondered if the woman would mind telling her who did her hair.

The woman said that she didn't mind at all, and wrote the stylist's name and number on Becky's sales receipt. Back at the Hyatt, Becky put away her purchases and then called the salon. The stylist had an opening at ten fifteen the next morning and Becky took the appointment.

In the "Nightlife" section of the complimentary hotel magazine, she found a club that advertised live jazz nightly. Becky showered, then dressed in a black skirt that showed her off her legs, and a blouse that complemented her dark brown eyes. She ate a light dinner in the hotel dining room and at eight thirty she took a cab to the nightclub.

The place seemed to be doing a reasonably good business for a Monday night. Most of the seats around the horseshoe-shaped bar were taken, and about half of the tables in the room were occupied. The stage was a step up from the small dance floor, and on the stage a group advertised as the Foster Oden Trio was doing a version of the Joe Henderson classic, "Lush Life."

The audience consisted of several couples, a few groups of women and men who were apparently out for a night with the girls and boys respectively, and a handful of singles. The customers appeared to range in age from the mid-thirties to the mid-fifties, and most were dressed casually but expensively.

Becky stood for a moment, surveying the situation, before spotting an attractive woman who appeared to be about her own age, sitting at the bar on the side opposite the dance floor. Becky walked over, took the vacant stool next to the woman, and hung her purse on a hook under the bar in front of her. The woman next to Becky was apparently out on a date with her husband. A petite, attractive brunette, she was wearing a major-league diamond set on the second finger of her left hand and she turned and gave Becky a smile as Becky sat down.

The husband looked to be a good ten years older than his wife and was making a largely unsuccessful effort at holding back the years. His black silk shirt was open to the third button, exposing a tuft of matted gray chest hair, and his designer jeans, though doubtless expensive, did nothing to flatter either his butt or his protruding stomach. Becky thought that the guy would have been much more appealing if he'd just been smart enough to dress and act his age. But doubtless he was making a game if misdirected effort to keep up with a younger second wife.

The bartender was a good-looking guy in his late twenties. He dropped a couple of napkins on the bar in front of Becky and she ordered a glass of Pinot Grigio. The guy gave her a smile and promised to be right back. Good to his word, less than a minute later he returned with a glass and a small carafe of wine. He poured about half of the wine into the glass and set the carafe on the napkin next to it. He gave Becky another smile, said "Enjoy," and smoothly turned to the next customer.

Becky took a sip of the wine and relaxed back into her stool. The band was now covering Tony Bennett's, "I left My Heart in San Francisco," and again doing a very nice job. Three couples were out on the floor dancing, and the hum of the conversations around the room lay just under the sound of the music. Becky concluded that it was a very comfortable club — somewhere that, under different circumstances, she would enjoy spending time. But she hadn't come here tonight looking to relax and enjoy herself.

Ten minutes later the bartender was back. Leaning over to Becky, he said, "The gentleman down the bar would like to buy you another glass of wine."

She looked down the bar to see a guy in a light blue sweater looking back at her. He appeared to be alone, mid-forties, maybe, and not a bad-looking guy, with a confident air about him. Becky turned back to the bartender. "Please tell the gentleman that I said thanks for the offer, but I'm expecting my husband at any minute, and I'm probably only going to have the one drink anyway."

The bartender nodded, moved back down the bar, and relayed the message. The guy in the sweater turned back, raised his glass to Becky, smiled, and gave her a little shrug as if to say, "You can't blame a guy for trying."

A few minutes later the band segued into a slow bluesy version of "Misty." The couple next to Becky got up and moved out to the dance floor, and the woman left her purse hanging on a hook under the bar next to Becky's. Becky watched as the couple wrapped their arms around each other and began slow-dancing to the song, then she looked casually around the bar.

No one was now sitting within four stools on either side of her. The bartender was at the head of the bar, pouring a couple of drinks. Mr. Blue Sweater was now locked in conversation with a busty blonde on the other side of the bar, and no one looked to be paying any attention to Becky whatsoever. Moving casually, she reached under the bar, lifted the brunette's purse off of the hook and set it in her lap.

She unlatched the purse and opened it to find the usual assortment of things, including cosmetics, a cell phone, and a billfold. She set the billfold in her lap, closed the purse again, and returned it to the hook in front of the stool next to her. Looking up, she saw that the couple was still locked together on the dance floor, moving with the music, and paying no attention to anything but each other.

Becky opened the billfold and saw the woman's driver's license, a couple of photos, a fistful of credit cards and a social security card. As the song ended, Becky retrieved her own purse, opened it, and dropped the wallet into it. She pulled a twenty-dollar bill from her purse and snapped the purse closed. The brunette settled back onto the stool next to Becky and again gave her a little smile. Becky returned the smile and finished the last few drops of the Pinot Grigio. Then she slipped the twenty under the foot of the glass and walked out of the bar.

Safely back in her room, Becky opened the wallet and made a more detailed examination of the contents. The brunette's name was Rachel Turner, and if one could believe the date on her Oregon driver's license, she was eighteen months older than Becky. Becky was relieved to see that the license would not expire for another three years.

Becky put her thumb over the photo on the license, covering the woman's hair. Fortunately, like Becky, Turner had dark eyes. Unfortunately, though, Becky realized that no one who took a good hard look at the photo would ever think that she was Turner. Still, realistically, she probably could not have done better. She now had a valid driver's license as well as a Social Security card, and if she was careful about the way in which she used them, they should suffice, at least for the time being.

Becky went carefully through the wallet, but found nothing else that looked like it might be of any use. She wiped down the wallet with a damp washcloth, eliminating any fingerprints that she might have left, and dropped the wallet into a plastic shopping bag. Then she undressed and slipped into bed, rolling her new name around in her mind, getting used to the sound of it.

\*\*\*

The salon was a far cry from the Hair Express in Albuquerque, and so was the clientele. The shop was decorated in an edgy, high-tech motif, with lots of chrome and black vinyl. The patrons all looked to be fairly well-tended, and the stylist obviously knew what she was doing.

Becky told the woman that she was ready for something different and that she was thinking about being a brunette for a change. The stylist took a moment to think about it, assessing Becky's coloring. Then she nodded. "I think you'd do fine as a brunette," she said. "And I also think that we can come up with a style that will be much more flattering."

Two hours later, Becky left the salon, not really looking like Rachel Turner, but not looking much like Becky Miller or Cathy Stanton either. She checked out of the hotel and took a cab to the bus station. There she dropped the bag containing Turner's wallet into a trash bin and bought a ticket to Seattle. And then, ninety-seven hours after pushing Cathy Stanton's torso into the CAP canal, Becky stepped off of the bus into a light Seattle rain and a new life.

## 54

I was not at all surprised when Gary Barnett called on Wednesday morning to tell me that the blood in Cathy Stanton's tub was a near-positive match with that of the torso that had been pulled from the canal. DNA evidence would confirm the obvious a few days later, but Barnett said that the techs had also collected what he described as "a ton" of trace evidence indicating that the victim had spent a great deal of time in Cathy Stanton's apartment.

Later in the day, Bud Porter sent me photos that he had somehow cajoled out of the Holiday Inn in Amarillo, showing the woman that Jennifer Burke had identified as Becky Miller checking into the hotel forty hours after Walter Miller reported his wife missing. Clearly, we misidentified our victim and, almost certainly, we also arrested and charged the wrong suspect.

At two thirty that afternoon, Maggie and I drove over to the jail and waited while a guard brought Walter Miller into an interview room. He took a chair on the opposite side of the table from us and I asked him how he was doing.

"How the hell do you think I'm doing? And why the fuck do you care?"

"Look, Mr. Miller," I said, "I know that you're going through hell here, and all I can say again, is that we're simply doing our job the best that we can. That said, we do have some news for you."

He shifted in the chair, looked from Maggie to me, and said, "What news?"

"There isn't any easy way to say this, so I'll just tell you straight out. It looks like the body that we pulled out of the canal is not your wife after all."

If I'd had any lingering doubts about the fact that Miller was an innocent victim who'd been framed for a crime that he didn't commit, the expression on his face effectively dispelled them. The man was genuinely shocked and momentarily dumbfounded. For several long seconds he struggled to process the information and then tears flooded into his eyes. In a soft voice that begged us to reassure him that we were not playing some horrible, cruel game with him, he said, "You're telling me that Becky is alive?"

"We believe so," Maggie nodded. "As Detective Richardson says, we now know that the victim we found is not Mrs. Miller. Additionally, we have surveillance photos of Mrs. Miller that were taken in New Mexico and in Texas up to two days after you reported her missing. However, we have not been able to trace her movements since that time, and if she is in fact still alive, we have no idea where she might be."

Miller collapsed back into the chair, shaking his head and weeping quietly. After a couple of minutes passed, he wiped at his tears and said, "I don't understand."

"Unfortunately, Mr. Miller, neither do we," I replied. "We're still doing some tests and waiting for the final results, but it now appears that the body we pulled from the canal was really that of Cathy Stanton."

His eyes widened and he stared at us in total disbelief. "Cathy? … How in God's name could it possibly be Cathy?"

"Well, sir, the evidence suggests that someone killed Ms. Stanton and dismembered the body in the bathtub of her apartment, using the pruning saw that we found in your garage. It would also appear that the killer put your wife's toe ring on Ms. Stanton's foot. The killer also substituted Ms. Stanton's toothbrush and hairbrush for Mrs. Miller's, leading us to misidentify the victim.

"The killer dumped Ms. Stanton's torso into the canal, and your wife then drove Ms. Stanton's Buick to Texas, using Ms. Stanton's credit cards along the way. She abandoned the car in Amarillo and stopped using the credit cards at that point. As Detective McClinton says, we have no idea where she went from there or where she might be now."

With that, Miller finally came to life again. Leaning forward in the chair, he said, "Wait just a goddamn minute. Now you're telling me you think Becky killed Cathy? No fucking way!"

"Well," Maggie said, "Look what we're up against here, Mr. Miller. Whoever killed Ms. Stanton had access to the saw in your garage. Whoever killed her also had access to Mrs. Miller's bathroom and to her toe ring. And there's no question about the fact that Mrs. Miller drove Stanton's car to Texas and checked into a hotel there using Cathy Stanton's name. We have pictures of her doing it."

Miller shook his head vigorously. "No. There's got to be some mistake. Christ, for the last eight days, you guys have been insisting that Becky was dead and that I killed her. Now you waltz in here and tell me that Becky is still alive and that she killed Cathy. What the hell makes you so sure you know what you're talking about now?"

I leaned forward, resting my elbows on the table, and waited until I had his attention. "There is another possibility, of course, Mr. Miller."

"Which would be what, exactly?"

"Which would be that for some reason you and Mrs. Miller conspired together to kill Ms. Stanton, making it appear that the victim was really your wife, and that once you did so, Mrs. Miller drove Stanton's car to Texas and then went into hiding somewhere."

"That's fucking crazy. Why would we do that?"

"I have no idea, sir, but how would you otherwise explain the evidence?"

Miller shook his head. "That's not my job, it's yours. And if you don't mind my saying so, you've fucked it up pretty good so far."

"There's something else to consider here, Mr. Miller," Maggie said softly.

He turned to look at her and Maggie continued, "Not only does it appear that your wife was involved at least to some degree in Ms. Stanton's death, but it's also obvious that she worked pretty hard to set you up to take the blame. I mean, she went to great pains to make us think that she was the victim. Then instead of throwing the saw away, she put it back in *your* garage. She had to know that we'd find it and that we'd be coming after you once we did."

A look of doubt registered in Miller's eyes, but he said, "Bullshit. That doesn't prove anything. Half the time we forget to lock the damned garage. Anybody could have done that."

"That's a possibility. It would not, however, explain the life insurance policy. I suppose you could go ahead and argue that this mysterious 'anybody' could have somehow put the policy into your safe, but certainly there's no doubt about the fact that Mrs. Miller is the one who arranged for the policy in the first place."

Miller leaned back in the chair and focused his eyes on the center of the table between us. For a long moment, no one said a word, then Miller slowly raised his eyes to meet mine. "I might have been mistaken about that. Now that I think about it, it occurs to me that we *did* decide to take out the insurance policy and then I put it into my safe and forgot that I'd done so."

55

After saying that he really had known about the insurance policy, Miller clammed up and refused to talk to us any further. Although neither Maggie nor I really believed it, there was still the remote possibility that for some unfathomable reason, the Millers conspired to murder Stanton, so we sent him back to his cell although we were both pretty sure that we wouldn't be holding him there for very long.

"Suppose we got it backwards," Maggie said on the way back to the department. "Suppose that Stanton confronts Becky Miller or the Miller woman confronts her. And it's Stanton, not Becky Miller who winds up dead, either on purpose or maybe accidentally. Then, instead of ol' Walter helping Stanton to cover up his wife's murder, he helps his wife cover up Stanton's murder."

"It makes no sense. What do they gain by trying to confuse the victim's identity? And why would they hang the goddamned saw back in their own garage? And what's the point of the life insurance policy — or the diary for that matter? And don't forget that Miller was liquidating her investments weeks before Stanton was killed. Shit, there's no conspiracy here. She did it and she set him up to take the fall just the way you laid it out. And now Miller's going to try to make amends for screwing around on her by muddying the water to try to help her get away with it."

\*\*\*

Two days later, the lab confirmed that the murdered woman was in fact Cathy Stanton and not Becky Miller. With that, the County Attorney's office agreed that there was no longer sufficient evidence to hold Walter Miller, and the charges against him were dropped. Miller returned to the home he had shared with his wife and steadfastly refused all interview requests. After a week or so, the media finally gave up, abandoned the case, and moved on to the next national sensation, leaving Miller free to return quietly to work.

The department issued a bulletin, launching a nation-wide search for Becky Miller, but since she had no known family or friends outside of the Phoenix area, we hadn't a clue as to where to even begin looking for her. We would continue to monitor the activity on her credit cards and on Cathy Stanton's as well, but I didn't believe for a moment that Miller would be stupid enough to use one of them.

As a practical matter, then, we were left to hope that someone might recognize Miller from one of the photos we'd circulated, or that she might be arrested somewhere for a traffic violation or some such thing and be tripped up in that way. Otherwise, as a practical matter, there was nothing much we could do.

And, of course, ignoring the fact that we had not yet solved the Stanton homicide, inconsiderate Phoenicians continued to commit acts of mayhem against each other on a fairly regular basis. As they did, Maggie and I and the other members of the Homicide Unit moved on to other more pressing business, and the Stanton case receded into the background, joining other regrettably unsolved cases.

In the interim, I put my house on the market and began looking for a new home. The second place the realtor showed me was a patio home in a development that was only a couple of miles away. It had a large garage with lots of storage space, enough room for my music and books, a den that would serve nicely as a study and a second bedroom that I could use as a home gym. The place was airy, comfortable, and close to all of my familiar haunts, so I made an offer and after a minimal amount of negotiation, agreed on a price with the seller.

Two weeks after that, I got an offer on the house and sold it for very close to my asking price in spite of the fact that the market was fairly soft. I sold a few pieces of furniture that really wouldn't work in the new house, including the master bedroom suite. Then, two days before closing, the movers arrived and took everything else away. On the night before the closing, I went over to the house, opened a bottle of Julie's favorite wine and walked slowly through the house, saying my last goodbyes. At the new house the next day, I unpacked the picture of her standing on the deck at the lake and placed it carefully on a shelf facing the desk in my new study.

During that time, we had several dozen false sightings of Becky Miller. We investigated all of them of course, but none of them panned out. It was as if the woman literally dropped off the face of the earth after abandoning Cathy Stanton's Buick in Amarillo. I was beginning to wonder if, in some ironic twist of fate, she might have become a homicide victim herself, and then one Wednesday afternoon, Jennifer Burke called and asked if I could come over to see her.

***

Burke met me at her front door, dressed casually in shorts and a tee shirt. I followed her upstairs to the living room and took a seat on the couch. Burke settled into her club chair and thanked me for coming.

"Not a problem. What can I do for you, Ms. Burke?"

She gave me a rueful smile and looked down at the carpet. "I've been debating calling you for the last few days, but I finally decided that I should."

She looked back up to meet my eyes and I said, "About what?

She looked away again and sat for a long moment, slowly kneading her hands in her lap. Then, in a distinctly softer voice, she said, "I have something to show you."

She opened the small drawer in the table next to her chair and pulled an envelope from the drawer. Saying nothing more, she handed me the envelope. It was a regular, white, number ten envelope that one might buy at any office supply store, and it was addressed to Burke. There was no return address, but the envelope was stamped with Canadian stamps and had been postmarked in Vancouver a week and a half earlier.

I opened the envelope and found two pages written in a distinctly feminine hand. I glanced at the signature on the second page and then looked up to Burke who had begun crying softly. I handed her my handkerchief and waited for a few moments as she wiped at her tears and folded her hands in her lap again. Then I turned back to the letter.

Dear Jen,

I've started this letter a dozen times and I still don't know how to even begin. How can I ever explain to you how very sorry I am for having been such a terrible excuse for a friend? And how can I begin to apologize for having doubtless caused you so much pain?

As weak an excuse as it certainly is, I feel like I've been living in a hellish nightmare for the last three months. During that time, I've been struggling simply to survive, trying not to make some stupid mistake that would make a bad situation even worse. But I could not go any longer without trying to tell you how sorry I am and without making some effort to explain how I wound up in such a horrible mess.

I discovered that Walter was having an affair quite by accident one night when I saw an e-mail from his mistress on his computer. Afterwards, I stooped to reading his e-mail in an effort to gauge how serious the relationship was. I had pretty much made up my mind to leave him and then I saw a message in which Walter's girlfriend told him that they would both be a lot better off if I were completely out of the picture — in other words, not just divorced but dead — so that Walter would not be forced to pay alimony or to repay all the money I loaned him.

Of course I never thought for a moment that Walter could ever do something like that, but he made such a tepid response to her suggestion that I let my emotions run away with me and decided to teach both of them a lesson. Instead of simply divorcing Walter and making him pay through the nose like any reasonably intelligent woman would have done, I decided to disappear for a few weeks under circumstances that would point the finger of suspicion at Walter.

I intended to let him sweat it out for a while, then come home and take him to the cleaners in a divorce. But, stupidly, I couldn't resist the temptation to confront his girlfriend. I went to her apartment and told her that she was welcome to him — or to what would be left of him when I got finished with him. We had words, and she took a swing at me. I tried to get out of her way, but when I did, she tripped and fell, hitting her head on the edge of the coffee table.

It all happened so fast, Jen. One moment the woman was calling me a bitch and taking a swing at me, and in the next instant she was lying dead on the floor in front of me.

I've never been so scared in my life. I knew it was an accident and that I should call the police. But I was so afraid — I was sure that the police would never believe me and that they would arrest me and charge me at least with manslaughter, if not with murder, and I panicked.

I was already packed and ready to disappear, and so instead of calling the police, I decided to try to confuse things and to make it seem like I was the victim. Because of the steps I had already taken, I thought that the police would hassle Walter for a while, giving me a chance to get away and safely hide myself somewhere. I have not sunk so low that I would have allowed Walter to go to trial for the crime, much less be convicted of it — I would have surrendered myself before that. But I figured that using him as a distraction while I got away would even the score for his cheating on me and setting this whole mess into motion in the first place.

I know that he has now been released and I hope that I am now in a place where I can live quietly and safely, at least for a while. But I also now understand that I made a terrible mistake by not calling the police immediately and taking my medicine.

If I had, and even if I would have gone to prison as a result, at least there ultimately would have been an end to the punishment for my actions. But I now know that in choosing this course instead, there will never be an end to it. For the rest of my life, I will forever live in fear of being discovered and arrested in spite of my best efforts to hide myself. And for the rest of my life, I will live with the memories of the horrible, unspeakable things that I did in the wake of the accident.

Worst of all, Jen, I will live the rest of my life without the comfort of my best friend. And that, by far, is the hardest burden to bear. I think of you so often, and there are so many things that I want to share with you — especially just the little things that we used to talk about all the time — and my heart is breaking because I will never be able to do so again.

You were the best of friends, Jen, and I will never forgive myself for not confiding in you, and for behaving in a way that caused us both to lose the special relationship that we had. I can only beg you to try to forgive me and to believe that I never would have done so deliberately. You will always be in my thoughts and in my heart.

Love,
Becky

I read the letter through a second time and then handed it back to Burke. She wiped at her eyes again and said, "Was she right, Detective? If she had called the police when the accident happened, would she have been arrested?"

"I'm sorry, Ms. Burke, but the honest answer is probably yes. Certainly, she would have been held for questioning, but beyond that I don't know what would have happened. It would have depended to a large extent on what the investigating officers found at the scene. If the physical evidence supported Ms. Miller's story, the county attorney would have had to decide whether or not to charge her and if so with what crime. But once Ms. Miller moved the body and started tampering with the evidence, she almost certainly put herself in a position where she would have been charged with a fairly serious crime."

"And what about now?"

"You mean, what would happen if she now surrendered herself?" Burke simply nodded.

"Well, again, that would be up to the county attorney's office. The problem, frankly, is that even if Ms. Stanton's death was an accident, and even if Ms. Miller was simply trying to defend herself as she says in this letter, Ms. Miller has now committed a number of fairly serious offenses in an effort to cover up what happened. Almost certainly she would wind up serving some time in prison, if not for the original incident, then certainly for the crimes she committed after it."

251

"You're sure?"

"As sure as I can be. The county attorney would doubtless throw the book at her and then offer her the opportunity to plead to lesser charges in exchange for a reduced sentence. But I can't imagine any circumstances in which he would not insist that she spend some time in prison. That said, you never know what might happen if Ms. Miller were to refuse such an offer and insist on a trial. A very good defense attorney might be able to win an acquittal and Ms. Miller would go free. But I'd say that the chances of that happening are very small."

Burke nodded and looked away. I gave her a couple of moments, then said, "I'm sorry, Ms. Burke, but I have to ask. Do you know where she is?"

She shook her head and began tearing up again.

"There wasn't a second letter, or maybe another page with this one?"

Again, she shook her head.

"And Ms. Miller has not attempted to contact you at all, save for this letter? She hasn't phoned or sent you an e-mail message?"

'No."

Again I waited, then said softly, "Look, Ms. Burke, I understand that this is very hard for you. And I appreciate very much the fact that you called and showed me the letter. But if Ms. Miller should contact you again, and if you have the opportunity to respond, you should do everything in your power to convince her to surrender. I'm being perfectly honest with you here, when I say that it would be very much in her best interest to do so.

"She's managed to avoid being caught thus far, and if she's very careful, she may be able to avoid it for some time. But the longer she's out there, the greater the odds are that she *will* get tripped up somehow. Someone will recognize her or she'll get stopped for a minor traffic violation and her driver's license or auto registration will come up bad when the officer punches it into the system.

"And if that happens — if she's arrested rather than surrendering herself — things will go much harder on her, believe me. I know that you care about her. Please, if you get the chance, *be* her friend. Convince her to surrender."

***

Burke walked me to the door and I thanked her again for allowing me to read the letter. Back at the station, I found Maggie and the two of us went down the hall to the Sergeant's office. I described the contents of the letter and my conversation with Burke, and the Sergeant said, "What's your impression? Does the Burke woman know where Miller is?"

"I don't think so. I suppose it's possible that the two of them concocted a plan whereby Miller writes a letter claiming that Stanton's death was an accident and asks Burke to show it to me and then feel me out with regard to the charges that Miller might face if she did surrender. But my sense is that Burke called me on her own initiative after she got the letter, hoping I'd tell her that Miller would face only minor charges. Then, if she subsequently found a way to communicate with Miller, Burke could relay the message and try to convince Miller to come in.

"And if Burke does know where Miller is hiding, I don't know how we'd ever persuade her to tell us. I think our best bet there is to hope that if she does know or if she should find out at some point, she'll try to convince Miller that it's in her own best interest to surrender."

"And in the meantime?"

I shook my head. "We've got her picture and her description out there everywhere. We have to keep hoping that someone will recognize her and contact us or that Miller will somehow trip herself up. I suppose we could try to monitor Burke's phone calls and e-mail messages, but I can't imagine that any judge would let us do it. And more to the point, we're talking about two very intelligent women here. If they were going to open a line of communication, it wouldn't be something that simple."

"The problem," Maggie added, "is that the woman went on the run with a quarter of a million dollars in cash. With that kind of money, she can change her looks and hide herself pretty deep. And as Sean said, she's already proved that she's no dummy. We're going to have to be very lucky to get her."

***

I walked back down the hall to my own office, thinking that Maggie was probably right. Becky Miller was a *lot* smarter than most of the nut jobs that the Homicide Unit usually encountered. She also had a lot more money. And although I'd never admit it to Jennifer Burke, my gut reaction was to think that unless Miller decided to turn herself in, she might well be among the ones that got away.

But she would not be among the ones that haunted my dreams. Her letter to Burke struck me as genuine, and given all I'd learned about the woman over the last four months, she didn't strike me as the sort of person who would have murdered her husband's lover, even in a fit of rage. I believed that Cathy Stanton's death almost certainly occurred as Miller described it — that it was a tragic accident, but an accident nonetheless. And I also believed that in going on the run, Miller almost certainly sentenced herself to a fate more severe than any court would likely have meted out to her.

I sat at my desk for a few minutes, leafing through the casebook, wondering where Becky Miller might be and if she might ever surface again. I'd be keeping the file open at least for a while, but without much hope of ever closing it.

I turned and put the casebook next to several others on the "Open and Unsolved" shelf behind my desk. As I turned back to the desk, Maggie stepped through the door with a slip of paper in her hand. "We've got a male gunshot victim lying dead in an alley off of Cactus," she said. "We're up to bat again."